THE SECRETS OF WINTERHOUSE

THE SECRETS OF WINTERHOUSE

BEN GUTERSON

With illustrations by CHLOE BRISTOL

Christy Ottaviano Books

Henry Holt and Company
NEW YORK

Henry Holt and Company, *Publishers since 1866*
Henry Holt® is a registered trademark of Macmillan Publishing Group, LLC
175 Fifth Avenue, New York, NY 10010
mackids.com

Library of Congress Cataloging-in-Publication Data is available.
ISBN 978-1-250-12390-9

Our books may be purchased in bulk for promotional, educational, or business use.
Please contact your local bookseller or the Macmillan Corporate and
Premium Sales Department at (800) 221-7945 ext. 5442 or by email at
MacmillanSpecialMarkets@macmillan.com.

First edition, 2018 / Designed by April Ward
Printed in the United States of America by LSC Communications,
Crawfordsville, Indiana

1 3 5 7 9 10 8 6 4 2

For Rosalind, Jacob, Olivia, and Natalie

WILFRED QUARLES: The rumor has persisted that there is a hidden corridor leading into the shrine. Apparently, Gustav Placídes mentioned it in the journal attributed to him.

GENERAL THRALE: I'd be surprised to learn that's true. Though I'd be more surprised to learn it's not true. The implausibility of the passageway's existence makes it all the more real to me.

—From *The Secret Mirror* by Herbert Quain

PART ONE

A RETURN TO THE NORTH—
AND THE SEARCH MUST START

CHARM

CHAPTER 1

AN INCIDENT ON THE BUS

NOTE

Elizabeth Somers hopped from the bus's stairs into ankle-high snow and was halfway to the door of the tiny, brick station when a shock of certainty made her stop: *Someone is looking for me.*

"Elizabeth Somers?" came a voice through the chill morning air. "Is there an Elizabeth Somers here?"

She looked back to the bus. These things happened with such regularity—a premonition, a sense, a *feeling* that something was about to occur—they no longer surprised her. A young man, wearing the same blue uniform as her driver, stood beside the doorway of the bus surveying the riders who'd stepped off to stretch their legs. He held an envelope.

"Anyone named Elizabeth Somers?" the man said as he looked around.

Elizabeth raised her hand. "Right here."

"Ah," said the man as he strode to her. "Then this is for you."

He handed her the small envelope—the sort you might receive from your grandmother to thank you for a gift—and said, "This was waiting for you here at the station." And as Elizabeth stood examining the envelope, wondering just who might have left it for her on her journey north to the Winterhouse Hotel and who might have made sure it reached her on this ten-minute rest stop, she realized she hadn't thanked the man. When she looked up, he was gone.

This is strange, she thought. About the only people who knew she was making this trip were her aunt Purdy and uncle Burlap, with whom she'd lived for eight unhappy years in the dull town of Drere. She was so glad to escape from them this Christmas season—just as she had escaped one year before on her first trip to Winterhouse—she feared the envelope might contain some last-minute notice instructing her to return to their shabby house. Aside from them and her good friend Freddy Knox, the only other person who knew she was on her way was Norbridge Falls. Norbridge was Winterhouse's proprietor and, as Elizabeth had learned at Winterhouse 353 days before (she kept careful track of these things), he was also her grandfather. No one else, she was sure, could have known she would be on this particular bus at this particular time.

Elizabeth tore open the envelope and slid out a note card on which was written the following:

Dear Elizabeth—We are all very excited to see you at Winterhouse once again! Please do me the favor of disembarking at the town of Havenworth, the stop just before Winterhouse, and meet me at the Silver Fir Café. It will be lunchtime when you arrive. Which means we can eat! Awaiting your arrival, et cetera and more—

Your grandfather Norbridge

Elizabeth pressed at her glasses, looked to the cluster of riders beside the bus, and tried to tamp down a swell of puzzled disappointment. On the one hand, she would be glad to see Norbridge once again, and it would be nice to explore Havenworth—but why couldn't they just meet at Winterhouse itself, where she was longing to arrive? Why make her wait when they could just as easily be reunited at the hotel?

She read the note again, returned it to the envelope, and then—resolving to figure this out once she was back in her seat—continued to the terminal to buy hot chocolate and a pack of cookies. If nothing else, her aunt and uncle, who had driven her to the train station in Drere the night before rather than making her walk, had given her ten dollars for the long journey by train and bus to Winterhouse. Their generosity (for this sum of money was the greatest they had ever given Elizabeth by far) had surprised her, as had the touch of sadness she thought she'd noticed in them. The whole thing had been so strange and so unlike them, Elizabeth hadn't known what to make of it. She still had $7.36 left, though, and she was hungry.

Five minutes later, when Elizabeth returned to the bus and made her way to her seat, she found it occupied by a boy about her age. The book she had been reading—*The Secret of Northaven Manor* by Damien Crowley—and that she had left on the seat itself to indicate it was taken, was nowhere in sight. She stood in the aisle waiting for the boy to look up. His black hair swept across his forehead and shaded his face, he wore a black woolen overcoat, and he was so intent on a game on his phone he was oblivious of all else.

The diesel engine growled to a start, and the bus began to rumble. "Everyone find your seats, please!" the driver called.

"I think you're sitting in my place," Elizabeth said in her most polite tone. The boy didn't look up. She tried again. "Excuse me. That's my seat you're in."

The boy slowly raised his head. His expression was dully challenging, suggesting Elizabeth had made some mistake and he might be willing to overlook it. "What?" he said flatly.

"My seat," Elizabeth said, pointing to her backpack in the rack just above his head. "That's where I was sitting."

"Does it have your name on it?" came a voice from the row behind the boy. Elizabeth looked. A heavy woman in

a white fur coat was staring at her. Beside her, a man with a bald head and a thin mustache scowled cruelly.

"There are no assigned seats on this bus," the man said. He nodded at the woman beside him, who flashed him a proud grin.

Elizabeth looked to the riders in the rows opposite, thinking for sure one of them would confirm that, indeed, the boy had taken her seat, but no one looked up. She took a deep breath. "You're right that seats don't have names on them, but that's my backpack right there, and I've been sitting in that seat since this morning when I got on. I even left my book on it."

The boy had maintained his dry look; he appeared willing to devote only another few seconds to this distraction before resuming his game.

"Rodney," said the woman in the white coat, "you stay right there." The woman smiled falsely at Elizabeth. "First come, first served. There are plenty of other seats." The man beside her scowled more deeply.

The boy, Rodney, dropped his eyes to his phone. "For sure, Mom," he said with a yawn.

Elizabeth glanced to the back of the bus. "There are a lot of other seats," she said. "And probably nicer people, too. Please, just give me my book, and I'll be happy to move."

Rodney looked up and swiveled his head from side to side with a lazy motion. "I didn't see any dumb book," he said, before scooting over and reaching for something next to his armrest. "Oh, unless you mean this thing." He slid a book out and held it up like he was displaying a rag he'd pulled from the gutter.

Elizabeth snatched it and examined the volume for damage. She felt her face reddening and her breath tightening in her chest. "Thank you!" she said brusquely as she reached for her backpack and pulled it to her. "I definitely don't want to sit here with you anyway!"

"Oh, a mouthy girl!" the woman in the white coat said.

"I need everyone to be seated," the bus driver called. "We're departing."

Elizabeth hoisted her bag onto her shoulder; she was shaking with anger. "I hope you're happy with yourselves," she said, because nothing else came to mind. She stalked to the rear of the bus and tried to keep from muttering the insults that were bubbling up in her, when she heard the man say to the woman, "Was that a Damien Crowley book she had?"

The comment was quite unexpected, and Elizabeth was so consumed with trying to calm herself as she settled into her new seat, she nearly stopped thinking about Norbridge's note.

Twenty minutes later, Elizabeth had resumed reading *The Secret of Northaven Manor* and was only intermittently distracted by her frustration over losing her seat to such a rude family. *If only I'd said, "It doesn't matter if my name is on the seat, because you don't look like you know how to read anyway,"* Elizabeth thought, before trying again to forget all about it. She considered taking out her small notebook and starting a new list, maybe something like "Things to

Say When People Are Rude to You," but she dismissed this idea.

Creating lists was something she had perfected over the years, filling three and a half notebooks with lists such as "Foreign Cities I Plan to Live in for at Least One Year Someday," "Tastiest Cookies I've Ever Eaten," "Random Rules Aunt Purdy Makes Up and Then Forgets All About," "Teachers at My School Who Don't Really Like Kids," and "Houses in Drere That Need Fixing Up and/or New Paint and/or Complete Demolition" ("The one I live in," was the first entry on this last list). Over the past year, though, her lists had begun to change. Whereas previously such things as "Favorite Candies" or "Prettiest Dolls" had held endless fascination for her, she found herself losing interest in these and was now creating ones such as "Unhealthiest Things to Eat for Lunch," or "Things People Say That I Used to Think Were Cool but Now Don't Seem Cool," or "Things Girls at My School Do Just to Be Popular." She had even started one list a few months before, just as sixth grade had begun, that was headed "Boys at My School I Might Consider Being Friends With," a list she'd never felt moved to create in previous years.

Elizabeth sighed, glanced in the direction of Rodney and his parents, and returned to her book, a gift Norbridge had given her the year before and that she'd already read once. Just as on her previous trip to Winterhouse, Elizabeth had brought several books with her, including three she'd checked out from her school library. She loved to read, and she loved books. In fact, one of the primary reasons she couldn't wait to get back to Winterhouse was because it had the most enormous library she had ever seen, and the librarian was a kind woman about Norbridge's age named Leona Springer to whom Elizabeth had grown close. She was also looking forward to seeing Freddy, whom she'd met when his parents had left him alone at the enormous hotel last Christmas, and who would be visiting again this year. Freddy was the smartest boy she knew, and the only boy she'd ever had as a friend. They'd even stayed in touch over the previous year with at least two or three email exchanges a month.

"How long till we get to Winterhouse?" someone said loudly, interrupting Elizabeth's recollections. Rodney, the boy who had taken her seat, had stretched his head into the aisle to look back at his parents.

"Only a couple of more stops," came his mother's voice. "Play your game, and let your father and me rest."

Rodney shifted his eyes and glared at Elizabeth. "Three weeks at Winterhouse. With no losers to bother me."

"Yes, Rodney," came his father's voice. "Now, focus on your game and quiet down."

Rodney grinned cruelly at Elizabeth and then snapped his head back out of sight.

Great, Elizabeth thought. *That boy and his parents will be at Winterhouse.* She stretched, set her book down beside her, and put a hand to her sweater above where the pendant of her necklace lay. This was the one thing she owned that had belonged to her mother, an indigo circle of marble rimmed in silver and with the word "Faith" inscribed on it.

Hoping for another great vacation at Winterhouse, she thought.

The year before, Elizabeth had learned that her mother—who, along with Elizabeth's father, had supposedly been killed in a Fourth of July fireworks accident—had been Norbridge's only child. This meant that she, Elizabeth, was one of the last remaining members of the Falls family. Because of this, Norbridge had promised he would find a way to bring her back to Winterhouse for good, and when she'd first returned to Drere eleven months before, she'd expected to be back at the hotel within a matter of weeks. Things hadn't turned out as she'd hoped, however. Winter had ended and then spring had arrived and then summer, and despite Elizabeth's attempts to raise the matter with her aunt and uncle—who acted as if they didn't know what she was talking about—it seemed something had gone wrong and she would remain in Drere. This was a puzzle and an immense disappointment to her, relieved only slightly by a letter from Norbridge that had come on the longest day of the year informing her there had been some "unforeseen and difficult legal complications" that were preventing him from getting her back to Winterhouse permanently.

In any event, Norbridge had written, *while I continue trying to solve this problem, I will make sure you come see us for three weeks at Christmastime.*

At least Norbridge had kept his word about that, as frustrated as Elizabeth was over the rest of it. Whatever

Norbridge had done to persuade Aunt Purdy and Uncle Burlap to let her return, she was headed back for a visit to the very place where, the year before, she had solved a mystery involving a magical book hidden in the library. This book—or, rather, as the Falls family had known it for generations, The Book—was what Norbridge's twin sister, the evil Gracella Winters, had sought for years. It had been Elizabeth who'd defeated Gracella, using her wits and a sort of *power* that she'd discovered she possessed. . . .

"Havenworth in fifteen minutes!" the bus driver called, interrupting Elizabeth's recollections.

She glanced at the luggage rack that ran along the upper length of the bus. A sticker on its rim said PLACE ITEMS CAREFULLY! and Elizabeth began mentally rearranging "place items" into "staple mice." Anagrams fascinated her, and at times her brain formed them on its own. One of her favorites, which she'd shared with Freddy when she'd first met him, was her own name, Elizabeth Somers, transformed into "heartless zombie," though she'd since discovered "sizeable thermos" was another good one.

Rodney's bag, a ratty camouflage duffel, sat above the sticker and directly over Rodney's head; Elizabeth noticed that with all the jostling of the bus and also because Rodney had left the bag at a clumsy angle, it was drooping from the rack.

One element of *the power* Elizabeth had first developed the year before was that if she cleared her mind and focused her attention, she could—to her amazement—make objects move. That is, if she chose, and if she concentrated very hard, she could cause a drinking glass to topple on the counter or a shoe to flip-flop on the floor or even a book to tumble off a shelf. It had been this very power that had saved Elizabeth—and all of Winterhouse—from Gracella's evil, because she'd used it to wrest The Book from Gracella at a crucial moment. Afterward, Elizabeth had learned from Norbridge that every member of the Falls family had some sort of unique power; he'd also warned her that her power was not to be used for selfish or improper ends. Now, though, on her way to Winterhouse and with the thought that it would be harmless enough to get just a tiny bit of revenge on Rodney, she was curious to see if she could scoot his bag a few inches farther—and make it plop down onto him.

She stared at the bag, felt her mind clearing and her vision dimming. Her eyes remained fixed on the green duffel; a small tremor moved through the pit of her stomach. The bag above Rodney's head twitched so slightly a person looking at it might not even notice. Elizabeth kept her focus on it as the bag began a slow slide off the rack and down . . .

CHAPTER 2

A CONVERSATION OVERHEARD

STARVE

"Watch out!" Rodney's mother screamed as the duffel bag plummeted toward her son's head.

But her warning came too late, and with a loud holler from Rodney, his bag slammed onto him with a scrunchy crash. He and his parents began thrashing and yelling with so much confused fury it was as if all three of them had fallen into a swimming pool.

"Please remain in your seats!" the bus driver shouted, and despite Rodney's parents' angry protestations that a horrific accident had befallen their son, before long they simmered down and grew quiet. Elizabeth picked up her book and pretended to read as she tried not to laugh. Rodney's father kept glancing upward with a worried look, as though he thought a boulder might smash through the bus's roof, and Rodney himself couldn't stop glancing about furtively, trying to figure out just what sort of trick had been played on him. After a minute or two of this, he pivoted around slowly to glare at Elizabeth, his beady eyes suggesting he was certain she'd had something to do with it. She raised her book two inches higher to hide her eyes, but she made sure Rodney could see the satisfied smile on her lips.

Ten minutes later, as Elizabeth silently congratulated herself for saying nothing to—and not even glancing at—Rodney and his parents as she'd departed the bus, she looked around at Havenworth, the small town a few miles from Winterhouse. The bus had left her across from an enormous plaza with a white gazebo at its center, and inside it a small orchestra was playing a waltz while a crowd of at least one hundred people was listening and laughing and talking. The gazebo was decorated with twinkling lights of every color, and huge hemlock trees on either side were strung with even more lights, so that although it was not quite noon, the plaza was lit up as brightly as Christmas Eve itself. There was a low hill to one side of the gazebo, and on it children were using toboggans and flaps of cardboard to sled while their parents watched. A row of well-lit shops lined the street, all with alpine trim and decorative glass windows and ornate shutters and names like Alpenhaus or Kringle Hut. Elizabeth made a mental note to add "Havenworth" to her list of "Favorite Towns/Cities," even though she hadn't yet moved more than five paces from where she'd stepped off the bus.

She looked up; a light snow had begun to fall against the steep mountains that rose nearly at the edge of town. Piled snow lined the streets, and the air was much colder than Elizabeth had imagined. She pulled her jacket more tightly around her. The music ended, the crowd clapped, and a cluster of people made their way across the street. Elizabeth asked directions to the Silver Fir Café of a woman holding the hand of a small girl.

"Turn the second corner," the woman said, pointing. "You can't miss it."

The two blocks to the café were just as busy as the one on which the gazebo stood, and Elizabeth realized Havenworth was much larger than she'd thought—she passed two chocolate shops, a toy store, and a little place named the World-Famous Chapelaria that made hats. She noticed a bookstore, too—Harley Dimlow and Sons, Booksellers—and was tempted to peek in, but she wanted to make sure she wasn't late to meet Norbridge and fig-ured she'd be able to talk him into a visit to the store after lunch. When she reached the Silver Fir Café, she shook the dusting of snow from her hair and slipped inside. It was a large, bright place, with walls extending to a high ceiling and painted with so many birds—jays and nutcrack-ers and owls and sparrows and red-tailed hawks—the café was like an aviary or some lively, colorful forest.

"Seat, miss?" Elizabeth dropped her eyes from the

dazzling walls to see a brown-haired man in a kitchen apron standing before her.

"I'm actually meeting my grandfather. I think he's here already."

The man bowed and made a slow glide with his hand into the space behind him, inviting Elizabeth onward. "Please explore. I've never been accused of keeping a young lady from her grandfather."

Elizabeth laughed as she moved past him. It was just before she rounded a corner into a small room at the back of the café that she heard Norbridge's voice.

"Nothing exactly has *happened*," he said. "But I intend to remain vigilant. You just never know about these things. You think you know, and then something happens, and what you know is that you know you didn't know at all."

Elizabeth halted. Her grandfather was talking to someone, and although a part of her understood she should turn the corner and say hello, another part of her felt an instant curiosity about what was being discussed. Norbridge was the most reassuring person she'd ever met, and yet something in the few words she'd happened to overhear alarmed her. Elizabeth stood listening.

"Vigilance is imperative, yes," came another voice—a man's—in response, "although if nothing has happened, then perhaps you are being too cautious?"

"I don't know that there is such a thing as too much caution in this instance," Norbridge said. "If there is any possibility that she might attempt something again."

"But all you have to go on is one of these vague *feelings*

you get. I'm not discounting your powers of intuition, my good man—"

"It's exactly what I felt last year at this same time, and we all know what happened then."

Elizabeth hitched her backpack high onto her shoulder and, regretting already that she'd eavesdropped on her grandfather for even a minute, turned the corner.

At the table before her sat a black-haired man wearing round eyeglasses and a heavy brown suit. He looked to her with curiosity, and as he did, Norbridge wheeled about. When his gentle eyes rested on Elizabeth, he rose and opened his arms to enfold her.

"My dear, my dear," Norbridge said, and she dropped her backpack and wrapped her arms around him as well. "You have returned."

"Norbridge," Elizabeth said, "I'm so glad to see you!"

She stood hugging him tightly, feeling all the uncertainty drain from her. The smell of woodsmoke on his coat and the grip of his strong arms around her made her feel twice as glad as she'd expected.

He loosened his embrace and backed away a step like someone examining a painting. "Look at you! Not that you can look at yourself. But what I mean is I'm looking at you, and you look as fantastic as you did last year but with even more wonderful Elizabeth-ness about you. It's incredible! How do you do it?"

Elizabeth couldn't help laughing. Norbridge—with his snow-white beard and ruddy cheeks and thick overcoat and high-laced work boots—was laughing, too.

"Well, you also look wonderful," Elizabeth said, picturing him on his morning hike or spending an hour chopping wood. "With lots of Norbridge-ness!"

Norbridge lifted an arm and flexed his biceps beneath the heavy folds of his wool coat. "I work at it!" He dropped his arm and turned to look behind him. "But how rude of me! Elizabeth, I'd like you to meet Professor Egil P. Fowles, one of the most renowned—no, let me amend that—*the* most renowned scholar of Egyptian hieroglyphics in the entire northern region, and the headmaster of our local school. All this despite prevailing in our chess battles only a handful of times his entire life."

The man with the round glasses smiled wryly and nodded. "Your grandfather is a gentleman," Professor Fowles said, "although he fails to recall our lifetime record stands at 617 victories for me and 409 for him. I am also only a dabbler in the fascinating field of hieroglyphics, but I am guilty as charged when it comes to serving at our fine school here in Havenworth." He stood and extended a hand to Elizabeth. "And it is my pleasure to finally meet the one and only Elizabeth Somers. Hardly two sentences escape your grandfather's mouth without him uttering some sort of accolade for you. I know how glad he is—indeed, how glad we *all* are—to welcome you back to Winterhouse."

Elizabeth wasn't sure if she was going to laugh or cry, she was so overwhelmed with this reception and with finally seeing her grandfather again. At the hollow of her neck, where her pendant lay, she placed a hand, even as she shook Professor Fowles's. "It's my pleasure to meet you, sir. Returning to Winterhouse is all I've been thinking about the whole year."

Norbridge reached for a chair from the empty table beside them and was about to slide it over. "Then please sit down, and let's catch up."

Egil P. Fowles moved his hands before him, as if he were clearing away a wisp of fog. "Please take my seat. I really must be going. My wife will lock the door if I'm not home within"—he raised his watch to his eyes—"seven minutes."

Norbridge glanced at his friend, and for a moment he seemed to be deciding what to say. The two men looked at each other, and Elizabeth felt something wary and conspiratorial was passing between them. It was a look that said, *Please, let's keep to ourselves the discussion we were having.*

"I didn't mean to interrupt your conversation," Elizabeth said.

Norbridge waved a hand. "Oh, we weren't talking about anything," he said lightly. "Just the same old gossip from forty years ago."

"Right, right, right!" Professor Fowles said quickly, with a nervous laugh. "Just two old codgers repeating our tales, our stories, our stale glories! The glory days, right, Norbridge? Such good times we used to have!" He gave a slight shake of his head and then sighed before extending his hand once again to Elizabeth. "Well, I hope to see you at Winterhouse soon. Quite a pleasure to meet you—and I must be going."

He gave Norbridge a salute and strode around the corner.

"A dear friend," Norbridge said, staring into the space Egil P. Fowles had vacated. "A dear, dear friend. And someone who refuses to acknowledge how often I've checkmated him." He looked to Elizabeth and gestured to the empty chair. "And now you are here."

"I really hope I didn't interrupt anything."

Norbridge shook his head. And then he reached just behind her ear and, bringing his hand back before her eyes, presented her with a miniature rose.

"Your magic is as good as ever!" Elizabeth said, taking the flower.

"How was your journey?" Norbridge said, but before she could answer, he declared, "Let's eat!"

CHAPTER 3

UNEXPECTED REVELATIONS

TRAVELED

Over lunch, as Elizabeth ate an egg salad sandwich and Norbridge drank three cups of tea with his mozzarella and tomato panini, she told him all about the previous year—that is, the eleven-plus months since she'd last been at Winterhouse. She told him about school (uninteresting, aside from the time she spent in the library), about life in Drere (increasingly boring, especially after her visit to Winterhouse), and about her aunt and uncle (not as mean as they'd once been, but still very unpleasant). There had been times when the last year had felt endless, that the weeks until she would return to Winterhouse were moving more slowly than any period in her life; but now that she was recounting the time to Norbridge, it seemed the year had passed in a blink. What she most wanted to ask him about, though—his progress on working out a way for her to live at Winterhouse permanently—remained unspoken for now; Elizabeth figured he would mention it soon enough, and she didn't want to put him on the spot.

"You say your aunt and uncle haven't been as hard on you?" Norbridge said.

She thought back to the afternoon before, when Aunt Purdy and Uncle Burlap had driven her to the train station in Drere. "It was actually pretty unusual yesterday," she said. "They came with me to see I got on the train, and when we said good-bye, they acted sort of . . . *sad*. I've never seen them that way before." Elizabeth had been puzzling over this ever since.

Norbridge arched his eyebrows. "Maybe they *were* sad. I'd think anyone would be unhappy to see you go."

"For three weeks? I'd think they'd want to throw a party!"

Elizabeth was sure Norbridge would laugh at this, but he only sat looking at her in a way that suggested there was something he knew but wasn't saying.

"Last year when you left," he said, "I asked you to give serious consideration to something. Do you recall what that was?"

She remembered their parting clearly: Norbridge had told her to be very careful about using her power, and she felt she had honored his warning as best she could. Over the past year, although she'd experimented with it during many nights alone in her room—causing a book to scoot or one of her shoes to jump—and even been tempted to use it on occasion, she'd done her best to keep it concealed. Of course, there had been the time during an argument with Aunt Purdy when Elizabeth had made a plate shatter in the kitchen sink, and it had scared her aunt and uncle so badly they'd retreated to their room and left Elizabeth alone. And there had been the time at school when she'd been so mad at Alan Kirpshaw and his endless insults she'd made his lunch tray tip over and flood his lap with chocolate milk and a bowl of chili. But these incidents had been rare, and she'd been provoked so badly each time, they seemed excusable.

"I do," she said. "You told me all of us in the Falls family have some sort of power, and it's important that we use it wisely."

"And have you?"

She thought back to the hour before, when she'd made Rodney's bag dump onto his head. "About ninety-nine percent of the time."

"Let's get that to one hundred," Norbridge said, winking. "It's not easy, I know. There have been times when I've been 'discussing' something with a difficult guest, and the impulse has come over me to make his pants drop or his glasses squeeze his head just a tiny, *tiny* bit. But, of course, I can't do those sorts of things. My sister got carried away with all of that, and you see where it led her. Dark, destructive mayhem and misery and . . . and more."

Elizabeth was thinking back to several strange moments from the year before when she'd experienced a small flicker of that "carried away" feeling. She'd felt it especially when Gracella herself, during their battle in the library, had tempted her to dismiss Norbridge and Winterhouse and join her instead. The possibility had been fleetingly—and oddly—attractive, as much as she had tried to forget about it.

"I understand," Elizabeth said as she took a bite of her blackberry pie. She was dying to ask about just when, exactly, she might be able to live at Winterhouse—or if he thought it was going to happen at all.

"You know," Norbridge said, "after you came last year and I learned how your aunt and uncle were connected to your mother, Winnie, I began putting some pieces together."

Elizabeth became still; she was eager to learn about her parents.

"We'll have time at Winterhouse for me to explain everything, but your aunt and uncle filled in several gaps for me." Norbridge stroked his beard. "I told you last year that your mother decided to leave Winterhouse because she felt she was in danger over The Book and what Gracella might attempt. She felt it was best to leave, cut all ties, at least temporarily. I lost contact with her completely—by her design—and I can only suppose she thought that was the safest approach." He paused. "But there was something more."

Elizabeth put her fork down.

"She had confided in me—she was thirteen or fourteen at the time—that she occasionally felt . . . I don't know how to put it other than she told me that she sometimes felt tempted by the story of The Book and Gracella."

"What do you mean *tempted*?" Elizabeth was fully alert.

"Evil is a powerful thing," Norbridge said. "And a very attractive thing, too. I think what she meant was that the power Gracella represented spoke to her." He leaned forward once more, and Elizabeth felt sure he was choosing his words very carefully. "I would say it's something many of us at Winterhouse have felt before and have struggled with. I think what Winnie wanted me to know was that she feared her own inclinations. So she ended up leaving Winterhouse until she felt certain she wouldn't succumb."

Elizabeth felt confused. Norbridge was describing a picture that was only half complete. "Did you find out anything more about her?"

Norbridge reached into the breast pocket of his wool shirt and removed an envelope. From it he took out a folded square of newspaper and reached across the table to hand it to Elizabeth. "Take a look. This is something I found a few months ago as I checked into things."

She opened the clipping carefully, the way a person removes delicate wrapping paper from a gift, and stared at the headline of the article: MOTHER AND FATHER PERISH IN AUTO ACCIDENT; CHILD SURVIVES. She flicked her head up and met Norbridge's eyes. He made a motion with two fingers, urging her onward. "It's from the newspaper near where your parents lived."

Elizabeth took a deep breath and returned to the article.

December 17, 2009—On Tuesday evening just after eleven o'clock, the Northside Fire and Rescue team responded to an anonymous motorist's call reporting a vehicle in flames on Highway 17 five miles east of Verano. The crew found a smoldering Toyota Camry and, inside, Ferland Somers, 28, and Winifred Somers, 26, residents of Verano, both of whom were declared deceased at the scene. Their daughter, Elizabeth, 4, was recovered from the backseat of the car and sustained no injuries.

"We have no idea what could have caused this," said William Bexley, crew chief. "We're guessing mechanical failure because there were no other vehicles involved. But honestly, if I didn't know any better, it almost looks like something struck the car."

An investigation is ongoing; Child Protective Services will retain custody of the couple's daughter pending identification of relatives.

Elizabeth turned the clipping over but found nothing more of importance there. As she tried to keep her eyes from filling with tears, she read the article one more time and then, without looking at him, handed it back to Norbridge. She felt numb and wasn't sure just what she wanted to say. *Declared deceased at the scene.* The words made her feel that her blood had stopped. She almost wished she hadn't read them.

"I never knew what happened until I located this article last April," Norbridge said.

Elizabeth picked up her fork and poked at a stray blackberry seed on her plate, and then another and another. She was only half listening to Norbridge; she kept seeing those words before her: *Declared deceased at the scene.*

"I looked into the investigation that was conducted and—"

"I wish you hadn't shown me that," Elizabeth said. A man and woman at the closest table glanced at them before returning awkwardly to their meals. Elizabeth's eyes were overflowing with tears.

Norbridge's mouth fell open. "I . . . I thought you would want to know. I had this notion that you might find it easier to talk about it here first. That's why I had you meet me."

"But I just wanted to come and see everyone!" Elizabeth said. "You, Freddy, Leona! I just wanted to . . ."

"I'm sorry." Norbridge looked stunned, as though he was overwhelmed to see Elizabeth suddenly so sad. "I'm afraid I've made a terrible mistake. I thought here in Havenworth would be the better place to discuss it."

Elizabeth grew more confused the more Norbridge spoke. She wanted to know everything about her parents it was possible to know, but to be ambushed like this, to have the excitement and anticipation she felt about finally coming back to Winterhouse sidetracked by this revelation when all she'd wanted to do was return, was distressing. She didn't even know what she wanted to say to Norbridge, and she felt that if another word escaped her mouth, she might burst into a fit of sobbing she couldn't control.

"I'm sorry," Norbridge said, rubbing his forehead. "It's clear I made the wrong decision on this."

"We could have talked about it later," Elizabeth said, pressing her hands to her face as she began to cry again. "I'm just here for three weeks, and . . . and . . ."

"You're not here for three weeks."

Elizabeth halted in mid-sob and looked up. "What?"

"You're not here for three weeks," he repeated, this time softly. "I apologize for that newspaper article. That was too much right away, I can see. But what I was leading up to was . . ." He scrunched his face, gave a little grunt of exasperation, and reached across the table with his napkin. "Here. Wipe your eyes with this, dear, and I'll explain."

CHAPTER 4

A STRANGE BOOK

BEGAN

Norbridge put a hand to his breast pocket, patted it to make sure the newspaper article was safely stored away, and then cleared his throat. "First off, my sincere apologies. I absolutely didn't mean to upset you. But where I was going with all this is, well, there's a connection between the auto accident and then with your aunt and uncle and then with the ongoing discussions I have been having with some lawyers and then again with some negotiating with your aunt and uncle and then more discussions with the lawyers. . . ." Norbridge pinched his eyes closed and moved his hands in front of his face like someone swatting at invisible flies. "I'm getting off track. What

I mean to say, and what I was winding my way up to is: I've worked it all out, and you're going to live at Winterhouse now. Forever. Or as long as you'd like. Whichever comes first, you might say." He dropped his hands. "That is—Winterhouse is your home now." He tugged at his beard. "If you want it to be."

Elizabeth's shoulders slumped; the sad anger of a moment before vanished. She had the feeling of having exhaled something awful in one puff, so that now her head was clearing.

"Really?" she said.

Norbridge nodded quickly. "Winterhouse. It's your home now," he repeated. "I've taken care of everything. There were some last-minute details, but your aunt and uncle finally agreed to . . . Oh, forget about that! You're here."

Elizabeth sat in silence, watched her grandfather grinning and nodding, before words returned to her. "Can it be true?"

Norbridge laughed. "Yes, it's true! I'm just sorry it took so long." Norbridge stood, came around the table, and knelt in front of her, enfolding her once again in an embrace. "Welcome back, Elizabeth. And welcome home."

After a long moment he let go and she sat in a daze, wondering if maybe there was some mix-up. But Norbridge continued nodding, and Elizabeth tried to soak up his words and what they all meant. She felt that her most secret prayers had been answered.

"You look like you're trying to wake up from a dream!"

Norbridge said with a chuckle. "I knew the news would be surprising, but are you okay?"

"Am I okay?" Elizabeth said. "It's the best news ever! I can't believe it. It's fantastic."

Norbridge lifted his mug of tea. "To many, many years of happiness at Winterhouse."

Elizabeth began crying once more—and then she started to laugh, too.

One hour later, Elizabeth was exploring the thousands of books inside Harley Dimlow and Sons, Booksellers, even as she felt she hadn't yet touched the ground since Norbridge had explained that, really and truly, she would now be living at Winterhouse. He had detailed a bit about how Aunt Purdy and Uncle Burlap had signed the papers just the week before, how all of Elizabeth's possessions would be shipped north, how she would now be attending the school in Havenworth—all this and two dozen more things were discussed as Norbridge steadily worked through the story of this new chapter in Elizabeth's life. But at a certain point, as Elizabeth tried to stop shaking her head in wonderment, Norbridge said he had one errand to run and that it was impossible for either of them to eat any more pie or drink any more tea. He also told her that Jackson, Winterhouse's head bellhop and Norbridge's right-hand man, would be in front of the gazebo in forty-five minutes to pick them up.

"Let's meet there," Norbridge had said. "Feel free to poke around for books while I pick up a thing or two."

Elizabeth had expected the bookstore to be cheerful and bright, perhaps because Havenworth overall felt so festive. And it wasn't so much that Harley Dimlow and Sons was dingy. It was just *gloomier* inside than she would have guessed, with its dark oak paneling, overstuffed bookcases, and pale ceiling lights set a little too far apart.

"Good afternoon," the clerk said softly from behind the stacks of books on his high desk. He was gray-haired and stooped, and for a moment Elizabeth thought to ask if he was Harley Dimlow himself or one of his sons, but she merely greeted him in return and then surveyed the looming rows of bookcases that were crammed so full they appeared near to toppling.

The man craned his head forward from the shadowy space where he sat. Elizabeth wasn't sure if the creaking sound came from the man's ancient desk, the floor beneath his feet, or his own crooked spine, but something gave out a slow crackling noise. The man fixed two bulging and bloodshot eyes on her through his thick glasses.

"Looking for something in particular?" he said, his voice a whisper.

"Do you have any books by Damien Crowley?" *The Secret of Northaven Manor*, Norbridge's gift and a story about a girl who finds a secret gem in an old mansion, had entranced her, and she wanted to read more. She'd also noticed a book by Damien Crowley when she'd sneaked into Gracella's girlhood room the year before, a strange coincidence she intended to discuss with Norbridge some-day. The odd thing was that the librarian at her school had been unable to locate any books by the same author because, apparently, no bookstores or book suppliers carried them anymore. Elizabeth herself, on a trip to the nearby town of Smelterville with her aunt and uncle in midsummer, had stopped in the local bookstore there and been told by the owner that he hadn't had a book by Damien Crowley in his store in several years. All of which had left Elizabeth intrigued at the prospect of finding something else Crowley had written.

The man's dull eyes gave a split-second flash. He tilted his head warily to regard her. "Nothing by Damien Crowley at the moment," he said. "Not many requests for him anymore."

"Would you happen to have anything on secret codes?" Later, Elizabeth would wonder why she had made this request. There were so many other types of books she was interested in.

The man lifted a bony finger and pointed to the far corner of the shop. "Aisle 13. In the back on the right."

Elizabeth looked in that direction and then leaned to one side and the other to glance down the aisles directly before her. She turned back to the man.

"You have the place all to yourself," he said, and then he eased back on his chair into the dimness, like an ancient turtle pulling its head into its shell for a long nap.

The section she was seeking was tricky to find, given that the store was in disarray, with books wedged in here and there and the labeling on the shelves something less than accurate or systematic. She also made several stops along the way to look at a book of beautiful paintings by a man named Maxfield Parrish; an illustrated volume of Robert Louis Stevenson's *Kidnapped* she wished she could buy but that cost eighteen dollars; and a book in which a doctor claimed people could train themselves to live on air alone without eating any food at all. But she finally made her way to the rear of aisle 13. There were shelves labeled ESPIONAGE, UNEXPLAINED MYSTERIES, ANCIENT MIRACLES, all of which seemed a bit random. At the bottom of the huge bookcase, Elizabeth found a section labeled CODES, CIPHERS, AND SECRET WRITING.

As she scanned the titles, a tremor moved through her: The strange *feeling* she'd begun experiencing well over a year before and that she'd worked so hard to control. It was the very heart of her still-developing power; only now it very rarely flared up without her summoning it. She felt it at this moment—and then her hand moved to a drab book that she slid out of its shelf and examined: *The Wonderful World of Words!* by Dylan Grimes, a thin volume with a copyright date of 1886, though the edition she held had been republished in 1956.

She scanned the table of contents: "The Alberti Disk," "The Scytale," "Great Seals," "Ambigrams," "The Playfair Cipher," "Inks That Glow," "The Polybius Checkerboard," "The SINISTER Connection."

Freddy would love this book, she thought. She looked at the price and winced: $22.50.

She thumbed through it, stopped at the section on "Great Seals," and studied pictures of a United States dollar bill that showed pyramids and Latin words. She skipped ahead to a page entitled "Ambigrams," a word with which she was unfamiliar, and began to read:

Although there are many types of ambigrams, the most common ones are those where someone writes or draws a word in such a way that when it is turned upside down, another word—or even the same one!—appears. If that sounds confusing, look at this example, and it will most likely make sense—just turn the picture upside down, and you will see what I mean:

It took a moment for Elizabeth to realize she was looking at the word "faith," but once she did, she was astonished, even more so when she turned the book upside down and saw the same word. She touched her necklace and thought of the strange coincidence of seeing her pendant's inscription being featured in such a curious way in this book. But what astonished her most of all was the realization that Marcus Q. Hiems, a man who'd assisted Gracella—his mother-in-law—in her evil plots the previous Christmas, had used this very same device on a business card he'd once presented to Elizabeth. His card had looked like this:

At one point during her investigations the year before, Elizabeth had noticed Marcus's signature, turned upside down, was "Sweth," the middle name of the man who'd written The Book, a clue that had helped her understand Marcus and his wife, Selena, were in league with Gracella.

Very strange, she thought. *Faith, ambigrams, Marcus Q. Hiems.*

"Finding everything all right?"

Elizabeth looked up; the old clerk was silhouetted at the far end of the aisle.

"Oh!" Elizabeth said. "Yes, I'm finding everything, no problem, thanks!"

The man turned away in silence. Elizabeth glanced at the clock on the wall and realized she needed to depart, and so she took out her notebook and wrote down the title of the book before reshelving it, jotted "Ambigrams" on her list of "Ingenious Puzzles or Word Games," and then hurried to the door of Harley Dimlow and Sons.

"Thank you," she said to the clerk, wanting to depart quickly because she found the man more than a little creepy.

"Come back soon," the old man whispered as she reached the door. "I'll see if I can find any Damien Crowley books for you."

CHAPTER 5

A CEMETERY TO AVOID

MEET

Norbridge and Jackson were standing in the lightly falling snow just beside the gazebo when Elizabeth spotted them.

"Miss Somers!" Jackson said. He wore a bright red jacket—the same color as his bellhop suit and the pillbox hat on his head—and he stretched out his arms to Elizabeth as she rushed to hug him. He had been, hands down, the most helpful and most chipper person she'd met at Winterhouse the year before—and Norbridge, she knew, trusted him without fail.

"Jackson!" she said. "So great to see you!"

He turned to Norbridge. "Couldn't let Mr. Falls walk home," he said, and then nodded to Elizabeth. "Nor you. I understand you're coming to stay with us for a while." Elizabeth told him how much she'd missed him and how glad she was to return—and now live at Winterhouse.

"Find any good books?" Norbridge said.

"That store is incredible," Elizabeth said, and the thought came to her that she could visit it again whenever she liked, despite the strange man behind the counter.

Jackson glanced skyward. "Perhaps we can talk it over while we drive back to Winterhouse, Miss Somers. If we leave now, we can outrace the storm heading our way."

Once they were in the small blue car and departing the heart of Havenworth, Elizabeth wanted to talk about Winterhouse and the bookstore and the book she'd found, but as she was about to start in, Norbridge pointed out the window to a low brick building beside a snowy field.

"Your school," he said. "Where Professor Fowles is the headmaster."

The building was trim and neat, with rows of windows. Her school in Drere was made of concrete and looked like a mini-prison. Although some of the teachers were nice enough, and although the librarian was particularly kind to her, Elizabeth usually kept to herself and found it hard to be excited about her classes or make close friends. Living in the shabbiest house in Drere and with the poorest couple—as well as always having her nose in a book—had tended to isolate Elizabeth, something that over the past year had made her feel lonely in a way she'd never truly recognized before. And in all of this she allowed herself a slight throb of optimism, the thought that a new start at a new school would be exactly what she needed.

"The school is on holiday now, of course," Norbridge said. "Classes resume after the New Year—and you'll be in attendance."

Elizabeth kept staring at the brick building as they passed.

"Do you think you'll like that, Miss Somers?" Jackson said.

"I think so," she said, but then a thought came to her. She saw herself once again, just as in Drere, somehow not making friends with the new kids in Havenworth, maybe feeling, as always, outside and on her own. *What if I don't fit in?* she thought.

"Are there a lot of students there, Norbridge?"

"It's quality, not quantity!" he said. "Havenworth Academy is on the small side, but it's a wonderful place. Jackson went to school there, and he turned out all right."

Jackson laughed, honked the car horn for no reason, and then turned a corner onto a road that began to climb uphill and away from Havenworth.

Elizabeth launched into all sorts of questions about life at Winterhouse—if she would have her own room ("You'll be back in Room 213 for now," Norbridge said, "but we'll get you something more permanent after the holiday."), if she would be taking a bus to school ("Yes, at 6:52 sharp every morning," Jackson said.), and if she could help Leona in the library as much as she liked ("She'll badger me nonstop if I don't let you," Norbridge

said, "so—yes."). She sat looking idly at her notebook throughout, and as excited as she was about reaching Winterhouse, she kept thinking back to the Grimes book and the chapter on ambigrams and Marcus Q. Hiems. One very disconcerting fact was that Marcus and his wife had disappeared after Gracella was defeated in the library.

"Did you ever find out what happened to the Hiemses?" Elizabeth said.

The two men remained silent for a moment before Norbridge turned to Jackson, who pursed his lips and glanced at Elizabeth in the rearview mirror.

"Mr. Hiems is no longer with us," Jackson said softly.

With a stab of realization, she considered his words. "Like, permanently?"

Norbridge nodded. "Marcus Hiems died. Last year. Right after the incident on New Year's Eve. Very unpleasant thing, and so I never mentioned it to you or Freddy. But he died here in Winterhouse that very night."

"New Year's Eve?" Elizabeth said softly as she

considered this news. She looked at her notebook and thought about the strange man who'd always worn black suits and kept his black, gleaming hair slicked. She recalled how she'd once seen Marcus on the small bridge outside Winterhouse, etching strange symbols on it to allow Gracella's spirit to pass over. The memory made her shudder.

"How did it happen?" she said.

"Hard to know," Jackson said. "But it appeared to be shock. Perhaps a heart attack. Nothing seemed wrong with him, you know, just to look at him."

Elizabeth felt it was strange to receive this news after so long. "You didn't want me to know last year?"

"There was so much to absorb at that time," Norbridge said.

The car became silent, and Elizabeth looked at the falling snow. It was midafternoon, and the day's light was already beginning to fade; within an hour the sky would be dark. She thought back to the conversation she'd overheard between Norbridge and Professor Fowles.

"So I guess Marcus and Gracella died on the same night," she said.

Jackson's eyes sought Elizabeth's once more in the rearview mirror. "Quite a tragedy for that family," Jackson said.

"What about Selena?" Elizabeth said.

"Not a trace of her," Norbridge said. "By the time we sorted things out that night, she was gone. Disappeared. That's the only remaining mystery."

"The only one, sir," Jackson said. "The only one."

Elizabeth wanted to tell Norbridge she had heard what he'd been discussing with Professor Fowles, but instead she said, "Where was Gracella buried?"

"The cemetery in Havenworth," Norbridge said.

"So we could go look at the tombstone, then?" Elizabeth said.

Norbridge turned to her, his face severe. "I wouldn't advise it. In fact, I would stay as far away from that place as possible."

"But why?"

"It would be unpleasant," Norbridge continued. "Unhappy recollections." He turned to look forward. "You have a whole new life about to start here, Elizabeth, and the dangers of a year ago have passed."

Elizabeth felt there was something less than convincing in Norbridge's words. "Have they really, Norbridge?" she said. "Gracella isn't coming back?"

Norbridge flicked his mouth into a gentle smile; he put a hand to his beard. "I wouldn't trouble your mind with any of it."

Jackson looked at her in the rearview mirror. "That sounds like good advice to me," he said. An odd silence had descended on the car. "Now, tell me, Miss Somers, what new book are you reading?"

The good mood returned as the three broke into easy conversation. And when, ten minutes later, Winterhouse— gleaming gold in the afternoon light, with Lake Luna behind it and the snow-covered mountains in the distance—rose into view, Elizabeth was overcome with gladness and relief. She had imagined this moment so many times, she could hardly believe it had arrived: Winterhouse, her home now in the truest sense, was before her.

"The old place is still standing," Norbridge said as they pulled up. Elizabeth would have laughed if she hadn't been distracted: far off, on the same bridge where Marcus Q. Hiems had carved evil symbols to allow Gracella to cross over to Winterhouse, she saw someone studying the brickwork. She looked more closely through the car window, and although she couldn't be completely sure, she thought the person there was the very boy who had stolen her seat on the bus that morning.

"Welcome back, Miss Somers," Jackson said. "I'm certain this hotel will be thrilled to have you stay."

But Elizabeth heard him only distantly. She was staring at the boy on the bridge.

CHAPTER 6

FRIENDS REUNITED

SURE

When Elizabeth stepped into the lobby of Winterhouse, she was almost bowled over by Freddy as he rushed to give her the biggest high five of her life.

"Freddy!" Elizabeth yelled, slapping hands with him high above their heads.

"You're back!" Freddy said, grinning wildly at Elizabeth as if she'd just won a race. He began to do a little dance in front of her, barely in rhythm to the light sounds of a string quartet that came from the lobby's ceiling speakers.

"You're crazy!" Elizabeth said with a laugh as Norbridge and Jackson entered the lobby and conferred by the check-in stand.

"See how glad I am to see you?" Freddy said. "I even put my dancing shoes on!"

Aside from being two inches taller, he looked about the same: His black hair was still thick, his face was still bright, and he wore the same clunky glasses he'd always worn. He even dressed in the same clothes—brown corduroy pants and a baggy wool shirt.

"Look at this," he said. He pulled a note card from his back pocket.

"What are you doing?"

"Just watch." He displayed the card, which had the word "ROOM" written on it.

"A word ladder!" Elizabeth said, recalling the letter-changing puzzles they had shared with each other so often. "Okay, go ahead."

"If there's a loud explosion, you hear a . . ."

"BOOM!" Elizabeth said as Freddy whipped out another card with this very word on it.

"And if Elizabeth is doing her favorite thing in the world, she has her nose in a . . ."

"BOOK! That one's almost too easy."

"And if you are watching something, you are giving it a . . ."

"LOOK!"

Freddy stood holding this card and nodding giddily at Elizabeth.

"Keep going," she said.

"That's it. 'ROOM' to 'LOOK.' You did the whole thing." He kept nodding.

"I don't get it." Usually Freddy's word puzzles added up to something clear, but she couldn't make sense of this one.

"You will!" Freddy leaned forward and whispered, "It has to do with my new project."

On each of the three previous years when Freddy had stayed at Winterhouse, Norbridge had set him to work on a project that took advantage of Freddy's ingenuity as an ace inventor. Last Christmas it had been the Walnut WonderLog, a fireplace log of shells discarded in the hotel's candy kitchen during the making of Flurschen, Winterhouse's world-famous confection.

"So what's it going to be this year?" she said.

"Elizabeth Somers," someone said before Freddy could answer. Elizabeth had been so focused on Freddy, she hadn't looked around the enormous lobby. But now she turned to see, behind her, a short, white-haired woman who'd approached silently.

"Leona!" she said, opening her arms to hug Winterhouse's one and only head librarian.

"I understand you're here to stay for good," Leona said. She put a hand to her mouth and glanced with mock fright at Norbridge, who was still standing just inside the large glass doors of the lobby entrance. "Oops! Was that not supposed to be common knowledge?"

"What?" Freddy said, pushing at his glasses. "'For good'?"

Elizabeth turned to Norbridge, seeking his approval with a look. He lifted his chin in a way that indicated *it's all right*.

"I'm going to live here from now on," Elizabeth said to Freddy. "Norbridge worked it out, and this is going to be my home now."

Freddy's eyes became enormous as he pressed his head forward. "No way!" he said. He looked to Norbridge, who was nodding in confirmation. "That's incredible!" He threw his head back and looked at the ceiling. "I'm so jealous!" he said as everyone began to laugh.

"Then you'll have more time to assist us with our puzzle," someone said.

Elizabeth looked across the lobby to where the voice had arisen. There, beside a long table, stood Mr. Wellington and Mr. Rajput, the former (who'd called to Elizabeth) tall and bald, the latter short and round and with a thick mustache. The two men, who visited Winterhouse with their wives several times a year, were working to complete a thirty-five-thousand-piece puzzle that had once belonged to Norbridge's grandfather, Winterhouse's founder, Nestor Falls. Elizabeth had assisted them often during her previous stay, and she had proved to be an outstanding discoverer of pieces as the men made their way—very slowly—to completing the puzzle.

Mr. Wellington lifted a hand. "The main thing, though, is we are very glad to see you again, Miss Somers."

"Despite your return," said Mr. Rajput wearily, "and although it is undoubtedly nice to see you again, we will most likely still find many obstacles along the way."

Elizabeth rushed over to them—the pleasant Mr.

Wellington and the perpetually gloomy Mr. Rajput—and gave them both quick hugs.

"Are your wives with you again?" she said as she studied the puzzle; the men had made good progress and were nearly two-thirds through.

"They are," Mr. Wellington said. "This is our third visit since we last saw you."

"And you're getting a lot closer!" Elizabeth said. The developing picture, which matched the painting on the huge box that had once housed the pieces, was of a beautiful temple in the Himalayas where Nestor Falls had once lived.

Mr. Rajput sighed. "Still a formidable road to travel. Many, many long days ahead. Dark days. Trying days."

Norbridge, Jackson, Leona, and Freddy joined the other three at the puzzle table.

"Oh, come now, Mr. Rajput," Leona said. "Allow yourself some pleasure at how much you've accomplished."

Freddy nudged Elizabeth with an elbow and whispered, "They're still completely obsessed with this thing!"

Elizabeth, though, was continuing to study the puzzle. Something like *the feeling* began to stir again, a sensation she had grown accustomed to experiencing when she helped the men. It seemed some part of her mind could, at times, select just the right piece and somehow determine where it fit. At these moments, something guided her hand. Now, as she looked at the picture of the temple, she felt drawn to one particular tiny shape on the table before her.

"Elizabeth?" Freddy said.

"She's got the scent!" Mr. Rajput said in a rare display of excitement. "She's got the scent!"

"We've seen that look many times before!" Mr. Wellington said.

And, sure enough, Elizabeth plucked a piece from a spread before her. She inspected it, and then she moved around the table to a portion of the puzzle's blue sky and snapped the piece into a cluster at the upper right corner.

"Extraordinary!" Mr. Wellington said.

"The young lady has just doubled our output for the entire afternoon!" Mr. Rajput said.

"How do you do that?" Freddy said.

The momentary feeling faded. Elizabeth examined the section to which she'd just added and then gave a shrug. "I don't know," she said, which was the absolute truth. "But I can't wait to finish this puzzle."

Mr. Wellington laughed lightly. "Well, we can't, either!"

"Why don't the two of you catch up?" Leona said, looking to Elizabeth and Freddy before turning to Norbridge. "I'm sure your grandfather has an important nap he needs to work through."

Norbridge wagged a finger at her. "I believe I hear a book calling you from the library," he said before looking to Elizabeth. "But, yes, actually, why don't you and the renowned inventor go have fun? We'll take care of getting your bag to your room." He lifted a hand in the direction of the clerk's counter, and a bellhop scurried over.

Elizabeth recognized him: Sampson, a thin young man of about twenty with slightly buck teeth who had been unfailingly friendly to her the previous Christmas.

"Great to see you back here, Elizabeth!" Sampson said. "And a famous full-fledged Falls family female now here forever!"

Everyone laughed, and Sampson clamped his lips tightly.

"Great to see you again, too," Elizabeth said.

"Please, budding poet, can you take her bag up to 213?" Norbridge said, and Sampson hefted Elizabeth's backpack and departed with a wave as Mr. Rajput and Mr. Wellington drifted back to their puzzle.

"What is that?" Elizabeth said, looking to an enormous diorama in the corner nearly ten feet square and enclosed on all sides by sturdy glass. It looked like a model of a small town, with tiny buildings and hills and bridges and trees everywhere, all set on a broad table and frosted with artificial snow. Elizabeth couldn't help but notice it, given its size and the fact that it hadn't been in the vast lobby last Christmas.

"You have to check this out!" Freddy said, and he darted to the glassed-in town as the others followed.

"A gift from Javier Withers," Norbridge said with pride. "Perhaps the greatest artist of miniature figurines and landscapes the world has ever known. He stayed at Winterhouse many years ago and has been wanting to share one of his works with us ever since."

Elizabeth, Freddy, Norbridge, and Leona stood before

the diorama, which was just in front of a plaque mark-ing the exact spot where, in 1919, Archduke Leopold Ferdinand Protz proposed to—and was accepted by—Lynette d'Oreille, the greatest opera singer of her age. Inside the glass walls was the most magnificent and realistic miniature town Elizabeth could imagine, with every detail—the trim on the houses, the sweep of the tree branches, the sparkle on the river ice—so lifelike it seemed as though an actual town had been shrunk and dropped down before her.

"Show her the fun part," Leona said to Freddy, and he placed his hand on a small blue dot on the glass. Instantly, a train began to chug along a track that ran through the town.

"You do the other one, Elizabeth," Freddy said, nod-ding to a second blue dot on the glass in front of her—and when she placed her hand on it, sure enough, a second train began gliding along a bridge that spanned two hills just above the town.

"That is too cool!" Elizabeth said, and she moved her hand on and off the dot to make the train start and stop along its way.

"And the two of you can play around with this thing anytime you like," Norbridge said. "Now, why don't you enjoy what's left of the afternoon and see what else is new around here? And Elizabeth, if I'm unable to visit with you later today, I'll be sure to look for you tomor-row morning or even at lunch."

"I understand," Elizabeth said, keeping an eye on her train as it entered a long tunnel.

"Hey, I can show you what I'm working on!" Freddy said. He took his hand from the glass, and so did Elizabeth, and with a wave and some good-byes, the two of them left the lobby.

<hr />

"You're going to live here!" Freddy kept repeating as they walked. "I can't believe it!"

They strode down the hallway, which was lined with black-and-white photographs from Winterhouse's early years: lumberjacks in the forests nearby, mountain climbers scaling the surrounding peaks, celebrities and politicians who had stayed at the hotel over the years. Elizabeth had enjoyed studying these photographs when she'd been at the hotel the year before. They connected her to a history and a place that was timeless, and she loved the feeling.

"I can't, either," Elizabeth said. "Norbridge arranged it. He just told me this afternoon." She was dying to talk more about it, but she also didn't want to feel she was rubbing it in—Freddy loved Winterhouse as much as she did.

"So how is it with your parents here?" she said, wanting to change the subject. This was Freddy's fourth Christmas at Winterhouse, but during the previous visits his parents—who were very rich—had arranged to have Freddy stay on his own, something that had only confirmed Freddy's belief that they didn't really care for him. This year, though, they had planned to come with him. Elizabeth knew all of this because she and Freddy had remained in touch through email, although Elizabeth's opportunities to get on a computer were few. She was able to spend one hour twice a month—the first Monday and the third Monday, during lunch hour—on the computer in her school library, and during that time the thing she looked forward to most was reading the mail Freddy sent, without fail, and then responding to him. They shared their thoughts about all their adventures at Winterhouse, how school was going, and much more. Elizabeth knew Freddy, although somewhat anxious about having his parents join him at "his" hotel, was glad they wanted to spend Christmas with him.

Freddy stopped walking, turned to Elizabeth, and frowned. "They didn't come."

"What?"

"Yeah, they went off somewhere on their own. Again." Freddy lowered his gaze to the floor and shook his head. "I don't really care anyway," he said, looking up. "I love Winterhouse, and if they were here, they would probably just ruin things. They told me a few days ago that they decided not to come." He shrugged. "They said maybe we'd come for Easter."

Elizabeth was stunned. She'd taken it for granted that Freddy's parents would be here, and now that she heard his voice and saw his face, she understood Freddy had been looking forward to it.

"Wow," Elizabeth said softly. "I don't know what to say. I'm just really sorry."

"I told you they hate me," Freddy said.

"I don't think they do. Maybe something came up for them that was important." Even as the words left her mouth, Elizabeth realized it was the wrong thing to say.

Freddy sighed. "You're lucky. You get to live here now. With your family."

As glad as she was about that, Elizabeth felt awful for Freddy. She wished the right words would come to her, but all she could do was look at her friend in silence.

"Hey, let me show you something really cool," Freddy said, pointing ahead and beginning to walk. It was clear he didn't want to discuss his parents. "It's right up here."

As they approached the doors to the enormous auditorium of Grace Hall, Elizabeth saw something on the marble floor.

"What's that?" she said, and they stopped in the very center of the hallway—like being at the middle of a four-way intersection—and stared down at an enormous seal done in purple and silver tile on the floor.

"That's the Winterhouse seal," Freddy said.

Elizabeth was completely baffled. "But it wasn't here last year."

"There was a carpet over it then. The floor had gotten all beat-up, and they wanted to protect it during Christmas

before they fixed it. That's what Jackson told me." Freddy ran his eyes over the huge design. "Pretty strange, huh?"

"That's for sure." It was all Elizabeth could do to keep *the feeling* from welling up in her as she moved around the seal and read the inscriptions. This was a genuine Winter-house riddle, and she was instantly captivated.

"*Snow-Rioter?*" she said. "*With sinister starts that end at gate?*" She stared at Freddy.

"I see that look. You're thinking there's something to figure out."

"Well, isn't there? It looks like it could have been in *The Egypt Game.*"

Freddy rolled his eyes. "You really should write your own book someday. I think you've read all the ones already written."

Elizabeth lifted her chin and smiled as if she'd been named the mayor of Havenworth and wanted to make sure Freddy understood it. She resumed studying the seal. "Did Jackson tell you anything more about this thing? Or Norbridge?"

But before Freddy could answer, a small stab of certainty—like what she'd felt all those hours earlier, just before the bus messenger had called her name—came over Elizabeth, and she knew something was about to happen.

"Freddy!" someone called.

Elizabeth looked behind her. There, racing down the corridor toward them was a black-haired girl—tall and slim—dressed in white leggings, a white skirt, and a white blouse.

"I thought that was you!" the girl said as she came to a stop before them. She was out of breath as she stood looking expectantly from Freddy to Elizabeth and back to Freddy again. With an expression of deep interest—and one a careful observer might almost have said bordered on unease—the girl said, "Is this your friend Elizabeth?"

CHAPTER 7

A MEETING, A MYSTERY

TEAMING

"Elana, hey," Freddy said. "I didn't know you were around." He pushed at his glasses and darted his eyes in Elizabeth's direction.

The girl looked to Elizabeth. "This *must* be your friend!" she said in a chipper voice. She held out her hand. "Elana Vesper. It's a pleasure to meet you."

Her eyebrows were thin, and in her long black hair was twined a white ribbon. Elizabeth looked closely. This girl had makeup around her eyes and, on her mouth, a touch of lipstick. Elizabeth knew girls like this at school. She was never quite sure if she was jealous of them for being able or daring enough to wear makeup in sixth grade, or if she felt there was something too grown-up about it. The main thing, though, the most obvious thing, was that the girl before her was, undeniably, very pretty.

Elizabeth shook her hand. "I'm Elizabeth," she said, not knowing what more to say. This girl had introduced herself as if the two of them were adults meeting at a party.

"Freddy's told me so much about you!" Elana spoke warmly and nodded. She shifted her gaze to Freddy. "Hey, did you still want to go to the lecture tonight?" Elizabeth felt herself recoil; these were exactly the sort of plans she and Freddy usually arranged for themselves.

"Oh, yeah, for sure," Freddy said. He pushed at his glasses again.

Elana put a hand to her forehead as though she'd forgotten something. "What am I saying? Of course, all three of us should go. It's such a cool subject—some sort of rock-carving code thing—and, well . . ." She looked to Elizabeth. "You ought to come with us."

"Sounds interesting," Elizabeth said uncertainly. Elana was speaking as though she and Freddy were the ones with plans in motion and she, Elizabeth, could join in if she liked.

"But if you're too tired . . ." Elana said tentatively. "Still, I hope you'll come."

"Elizabeth loves codes and that kind of stuff," Freddy said. He glanced at her. "So do I."

Elana flashed him a glance before smiling again. "Then we definitely all have to go."

"Sounds like fun," Elizabeth said, distracted by Elana's made-up eyes. "Are you staying here for Christmas?"

"We got here a few days ago, and we're staying till January," Elana said. "It's the coolest place!" She smiled at Freddy, whose face went red.

"Elana's here with her grandmother," he said.

"For an old lady, she's really nice. I can do pretty much whatever I want," Elana said.

Elizabeth felt this was an odd thing to say about your own grandmother; in fact, she was feeling there was something *too much* about Elana overall.

Elana looked at the seal. "This thing is weird, huh? It doesn't make any sense."

Just then, Elizabeth realized where she'd seen something similar. "You know what?" she said, more to Freddy than Elana. "I was in the bookstore in Havenworth today, and there was a book I found there about words and puzzles and codes. It had a chapter on seals just like this."

Elana looked at her with genuine curiosity. "I think all those things are so interesting."

"That book was very cool." Elizabeth studied the seal on the floor. She was already thinking of a way to return to the store and was wishing she'd taken a closer look at the book.

"Elizabeth loves books," Freddy said.

Elana looked to Freddy and widened her eyes. "Hey, are you going to show her the—"

"Don't!" Freddy said, cutting her off. "It's a surprise."

"Wow," Elana said to Elizabeth, "you are really gonna love his project. Just wait."

"We're heading there now," Elizabeth said, hoping this might end their little meeting in the corridor, though it struck her that maybe Elana wanted to join them for whatever Freddy was about to show her. She considered that this girl had seen Freddy's project before she had.

Elana seemed to be waiting for Freddy to extend an invitation, but then she turned to Elizabeth and some element of interest evaporated.

"Well, I don't want to hold you guys up," Elana said. "I need to help my grandmother with something anyway." She reached to hold Elizabeth's hand again. "I'm really looking forward to us being such good friends. It's just so great that you're going to be staying here."

"For sure," Elizabeth said, and she took the other girl's hand lightly before letting go.

Elana turned away. "Well, I'll see you guys tonight," she said with a wave. "Have a good one!" And she strode off down the corridor.

Elizabeth watched as Freddy gazed after her. He stopped, looked to Elizabeth the way he might look at someone who'd caught him cheating on a test.

"She's pretty cool," he said softly.

Elizabeth gave two quick nods. "Seems like it."

"I met her at dinner a couple of nights ago."

Something was bothering Elizabeth. "When she said she thought it was great I was staying at Winterhouse, did that sound like she meant staying *visiting* or staying *staying*?"

"How would she know you were staying *staying*?" Freddy said.

"You're right," Elizabeth said, though she didn't feel so sure. She glanced at the seal once more. "I want to know more about this thing."

"Come on," Freddy said. "Let me show you my project. I guarantee you'll be amazed."

CHAPTER 8

A VERY DARK ROOM

READY

"Why is it way up here?" Elizabeth said as they exited the elevator on the thirteenth floor and Freddy led her down the corridor. She couldn't imagine where they were going; last year Freddy had set up shop in a workroom on the third floor.

"Has to be," Freddy said with a grin.

"I don't get it."

They came to an unassuming door at the end of the hallway. Freddy unlocked it, and when he turned on the lights in the huge room, Elizabeth was disoriented by what was before her: A wooden walkway led up from the door to a large, square platform on a wooden foundation at the center of the room. Within the platform sat what looked like an enormous, shallow white bowl that was about ten feet in diameter. The arrangement reminded Elizabeth of those displays in museums where a huge map or diorama is enclosed in a square of railing, and you can walk around it and study it from all sides. But here, instead of some interesting display to view, there was only the vast white bowl within a wooden railing, all set inside a raised platform. It made no sense to Elizabeth. She looked up. A half dozen ropes hung from the ceiling to points around the platform itself, and some scaffolding rose here and there nearly to the top of the room.

Elizabeth looked to Freddy, who was gazing proudly upward.

"What is this?" Elizabeth said.

"Have you ever heard of a camera obscura?"

"Camera what?"

"Camera obscura. It means 'dark room.'" He glanced up at the ceiling. "There's a little box up on the roof, and it lets light in through a pinhole when you pull some ropes to open it. Then a mirror reflects it down here." He pointed to the large white bowl. "If it all works right and it's not cloudy outside, you see everything around Winterhouse projected clearly. It's like a video camera that puts everything on a screen, but the screen is the white disk there on the platform."

Elizabeth squinted at him. "I still don't get it."

"It's hard to explain," Freddy said. "I'll show you some

pictures later. But when I get it all fixed up, it's going to be incredible. You'll be able to see everything outside Winterhouse."

Elizabeth was intrigued; she was also surprised she'd never heard about this before.

"Camera obscura," she said, testing out the sound of the words.

"Yeah," Freddy said. "It's like the original photography. Leonardo da Vinci used it and then traced over the projections to make paintings of cities and landscapes. The pulleys are kind of busted up on this one, so I'm working with Jackson and a few of the other guys to fix it all up. Come on, let me show you."

They walked up the sloping ramp to the rail-lined platform. Elizabeth ran her fingers across the rim of the large, shallow bowl. "This is the screen?"

"Exactly," Freddy said. He was standing in a corner of the platform and untying some ropes there. "It's kind of a mess in here now, but with some cleanup and repair work over the next week or so, I think I can get it done before New Year's Eve, maybe even sooner."

"I can't believe I've never heard about this," Elizabeth said.

Freddy gazed at her in mock stupefaction. "What? What's that? Something Elizabeth Somers never came across in one of her books?" He began to laugh, and so did she.

"I'm on it now," she said. "Research time!" She kept a

list headed "Things I Want to Learn More About" and was always adding new items to it. Recent entries included hypnotism, calligraphy, crocheting, yoga, and how to select the right kind of dog for a pet.

"Seriously, it's pretty awesome," Freddy said. "This one was built by Milton Falls about eighty years ago. On days that weren't too cloudy, the hotel guests would come in the afternoons and they would get a little demonstration. Norbridge says he wants to start that up again."

Elizabeth moved to where Freddy stood beside a control panel full of knobs and levers. Etched on its metal facing plate was a single sentence:

> *This device allows one to see beyond.*
> *—Milton Falls, 1934*

"*See beyond?*" Elizabeth said.

"Just another eccentric member of the Falls family." Freddy's eyes brightened. "Your family!"

She laughed but then considered something for the first time: She would be staying here after the New Year, while Freddy would be returning home. It gave her a strange thrill.

The words on the panel drew her attention again: *This device allows one to see beyond.*

Freddy spent several minutes showing Elizabeth the camera obscura, explaining more about the device and its history and operation.

"And that's how it works," Freddy said, at last.

"Norbridge chose a great one for you this time," Elizabeth said, glancing at the writing on the control panel. "Do you still think much about last year? Everything that happened?" The two of them had discussed all of it in email, but over the past few months they had left most of that discussion behind.

Freddy gave a small frown. "Honestly, The Book and Gracella and the Hiemses . . . It was pretty scary. I try not to think about it too much."

It was understandable that Freddy felt this way, Elizabeth thought. She, too, sometimes wished she could forget about everything from the previous Christmas that had been so unnerving. Still, there were pieces of it she couldn't put out of her mind.

"Did you know Marcus Q. Hiems died here the same night Gracella did?" she said.

Freddy's eyes widened. "I never heard anything about that."

"Norbridge and Jackson told me when we were driving here this afternoon."

Freddy paused and looked at the huge white screen. "Remember how I wrote you about what happened the day after you left? How I overheard Norbridge and Leona in the library?"

"I remember," Elizabeth said. It was something she wanted to discuss with Norbridge. According to Freddy, Norbridge had told Leona something like, "*She* must have killed him," and then he and Leona had changed the subject when they saw Freddy.

"I always wondered what he was talking about," Freddy said. "Like, who was 'she,' and who got killed?"

"I overheard Norbridge today talking to a friend of his when we met in Havenworth. He was saying he was worried *she* might come back."

Freddy peered at Elizabeth. "*She*, like Gracella? Do you think that's who he meant both times?"

"I don't know. But it sounded really strange."

"You know what I'm hoping for?" Freddy said, and before Elizabeth could answer, he said, "A regular, normal, not-weird-at-all Christmas at Winterhouse."

The chimes for dinner began to ring, and Freddy tilted his head with a *we better get going* motion.

Elizabeth listened to the sound of the distant bells as she considered Freddy's words. He was waiting for her to say something.

"By the way," Freddy said, "'camera obscura' turns into 'a macabre scour,' just in case you were trying to figure out an anagram."

"That's a good one," she said, laughing, as she held out her hand to shake. "And I agree with you. I want a regular, normal, not-weird-at-all Christmas at Winterhouse." She gave his hand an extra squeeze. "At least, I think I do."

CHAPTER 9

STRANGE TALK AT DINNER

ANGER

Twenty minutes later, after Elizabeth quickly changed into the emerald dress Jackson had left her in her room—number 213, the same as the year before—she headed to Winter Hall with the crowd of guests. The Falls family tree was painted high above the doorway into the enormous dining room, and Elizabeth took a moment to study it. It looked like this:

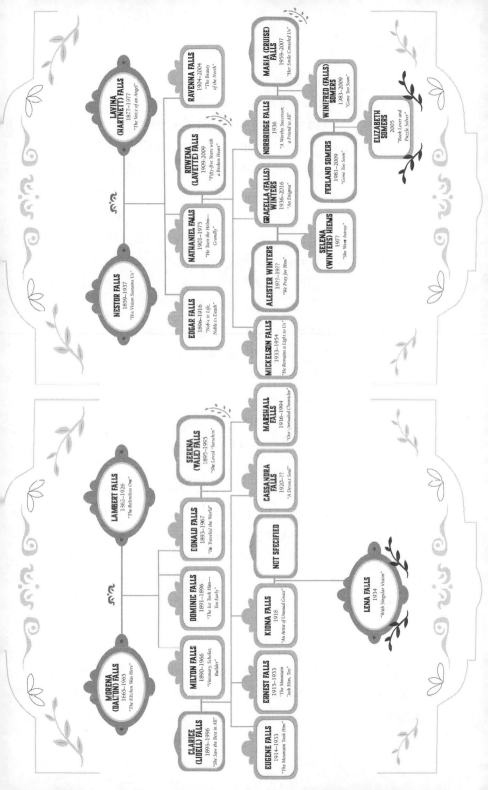

LAVINA (HARTNETT) FALLS
1877–1977
"The Voice of an Angel"

NESTOR FALLS
1859–1937
"His Vision Sustains Us"

RAVENNA FALLS
1904–2004
"The Beauty of the North"

ROWENA (CLAVETTE) FALLS
1909–2009
"Fifty-five Years with a Broken Heart"

NATHANIEL FALLS
1901–1975
"He Took the Helm—Grandly"

EDGAR FALLS
1896–1916
"Noble in Life, Noble in Death"

MARIA (CRUISE) FALLS
1958–2007
"Her Smile Consoled Us"

NORBRIDGE FALLS
1936
"A Worthy Successor, a Friend to All"

GRACELLA (FALLS) WINTERS
1936–2016
"An Enigma"

WINIFRED (FALLS) SOMERS
1983–2009
"Gone Too Soon"

FERLAND SOMERS
1981–2009
"Gone Too Soon"

SELENA (WINTERS) HIEMS
1977
"She Went Astray"

ALEISTER WINTERS
1972–1977
"We Pray for Him"

ELIZABETH SOMERS
2005
"Book Lover and Puzzle Solver"

MICKELSON FALLS
1933–1954
"He Remains a Light to Us"

LAMBERT FALLS
1862–1926
"The Relentless One"

MORENA (DALTON) FALLS
1865–1965
"The Kitchen Was Hers"

SERENA (VALE) FALLS
1895–1995
"She Loved 'Turschen'"

DONALD FALLS
1893–1967
"He Traveled the World"

DOMINIC FALLS
1891–1896
"The Ice Took Him—Too Early"

MILTON FALLS
1890–1966
"Visionary, Scholar, Builder"

CLARICE (LIDELL) FALLS
1895–1996
"She Saw the Best in All"

MARSHALL FALLS
1916–1994
"Our Unrivaled Chronicler"

CASSANDRA FALLS
1920–??
"A Devout Soul"

NOT SPECIFIED

KIONA FALLS
1918
"An Artist of Unusual Grace"

ERNEST FALLS
1915–1933
"The Mountain Took Him, Too"

EUGENE FALLS
1914–1933
"The Mountain Took Him"

LENA FALLS
1934
"With Singular Vision"

The year of Gracella's passing had been updated: Nothing had been there before. Elizabeth's eyes traveled across the spread of names—and then she started when she saw her own name beneath her parents': "Elizabeth Somers/2005/Book Lover and Puzzle Solver."

"Some nice changes, eh?" someone said in a distinctive, musical voice beside her. There, dressed in her standard black-and-white outfit, stood the kitchen helper, Mrs. Trumble, just as cheery and plump as Elizabeth remembered her.

"Mrs. Trumble!" Elizabeth said, throwing her arms around the elderly woman.

"I heard you were back! And I also heard Mr. Falls say you're staying with us for quite some time!" She lifted a finger into the air for emphasis. "*That* is *very* welcome news!"

"He just told me about it today," Elizabeth said. "I still can't believe it."

Mrs. Trumble pointed to the family tree. "You see your name up there?"

Elizabeth shook her head in wonder. "It doesn't seem real. I know it's my name, but it doesn't seem real."

Mrs. Trumble laughed. "It is! It is." The echo of chimes sounded from inside Winter Hall. "But you should get in and get seated. Dinner's about to start." She gave Elizabeth a quick kiss on her forehead. "We'll catch up soon."

Elizabeth spotted Freddy when she walked into the enormous hall, with its spread of tables and glittering chandeliers and windows that stretched from the floor to the high ceilings. She'd been in the hall two or three times a day for meals the previous year, but she could never get over how ornate it was, like something from a dream about the perfect holiday celebration. This was, however, Winterhouse's standard arrangement day after day and meal after meal, everything gleaming and bright, the fireplace at the front of the hall crackling with fragrant hemlock and fir.

Freddy was craning his neck to spot her and held up a hand in greeting; Elizabeth made her way to his table, at which he was sitting all by himself.

"Why isn't anyone else at this table?" Elizabeth said. She scanned to see if she could spot Rodney, the boy from the bus, and his parents. Sure enough, she saw them sitting at a table alone by a side door of the hall.

Freddy closed his eyes as though trying to make her disappear, and then opened them and said, "Table. Bleat."

"Okay, okay," Elizabeth said. "You're still good at anagrams." She looked around. "But why'd you scare everyone off?"

"I'm saving the seats," Freddy said. "The puzzle guys wanted to sit with us."

Right then, Mr. Wellington and Mr. Rajput and their wives appeared, and everyone sat down to catch up and prepare for dinner. The six of them talked, and Elizabeth answered questions from the adults about what she'd been up to since they'd last seen her, and everyone discussed how wonderful it was to be spending the Christmas season at Winterhouse.

Suddenly, Elana approached in a shimmering white

dress. Behind her came a stooped old lady with white hair wearing a long black gown and shawl.

Freddy darted his eyes to look at Elizabeth, just as Elana said, "Hello, everyone!" The men at the table stood as Elana and her grandmother settled in.

"This is Freddy's good friend, Elizabeth," Elana said to her grandmother once they were seated, extending a hand in Elizabeth's direction. The old woman stared at her for a moment, her eyes so dark they were nearly iridescent, like oil catching a glimmer of moonlight on an otherwise black night.

"I am very glad to make your acquaintance," the woman said steadily. She didn't blink.

"Are you enjoying it here at Winterhouse?" Elizabeth said. She couldn't have said why, but she felt that this woman had taken an instant dislike to her, and she resolved to be decisive in order not to show that she was, even slightly, flustered.

"Who wouldn't enjoy being at Winterhouse?" Mrs. Wellington said with a laugh, and everyone joined in with her. Elana's grandmother seemed distracted by the laughter; she looked back to Elizabeth, but just then a man in a red suit at the front of the room announced, "Dinner is served!" and everyone settled in as a parade of servers burst from the kitchen doors with plates of roast chicken, wild rice, and steaming vegetables.

"It's a shame you weren't here last week," Mr. Rajput said to Elizabeth when the meal began to wind down. He had tucked his napkin into the collar of his shirt above his tie, and it lay draped across his ample chest and belly. He sighed. "So distressing to think you missed the lecture by . . . by that gentleman." He turned to his wife. "What was his name again, dear?"

A tall, thin lady with several strands of pearls around her neck nodded pleasantly. "His name was Ivan Hetmosskin, and he knew *The World Book of Genius Records* inside and out!"

Mr. Wellington paused and held his empty fork above his plate. "Perhaps you mean *The Guinness Book of World Records*."

Mr. Rajput flinched and gave Mr. Wellington an icy stare. "I believe that's what she said."

"What was it that was so interesting about the talk?" Elizabeth asked. She didn't want to see an argument break out.

"The lecturer informed us," Mrs. Wellington began, "in answer to a question by our dear friend Mr. Rajput, that the largest jigsaw puzzle ever created consisted of 551,232 pieces and was made at a university in Vietnam."

Mr. Wellington brandished his fork again and swept it across the table in an arc. "I was dubious about that number when he mentioned it." He turned to his wife. "Very dubious."

Mr. Rajput sniffed as he looked to Elizabeth. "That's what Ivan Hetmosskin told us, and I take him as a credible source."

"Freddy," Mr. Wellington said, "what do you think? You're good with numbers."

Freddy shrugged. "That seems like a pretty big puzzle, but I guess they could make it that size if they wanted to."

The adults debated the matter for several minutes, veering into discussion about several other facts the lecturer had provided, everything from the most toilet seats broken by a person's head in one minute to the wealthiest cat in the world, the largest bubble gum bubble, and the greatest volume of milkshake dispensed through a person's nose.

"Well, if the record for the most charming hotel is ever decided upon," Mrs. Rajput said, "I believe this one here ought to be in the running."

"Certainly one of the most interesting, that's for sure," Mrs. Wellington said.

"I was intrigued," Elana's grandmother said to Mrs. Wellington—her first words almost the entire meal—"by a comment you made this morning about some *passageways* in the hotel."

"Oh, that old story," Mrs. Wellington said with a laugh. She had visited Winterhouse decades before when she had been a girl, had even met and played with Norbridge and Gracella when they'd all been young. It was because of that long-ago three-month stay at Winterhouse and her pleasant recollections of the time that the two older couples now vacationed at the hotel on three or four occasions each year. Also because of that visit, Mrs. Wellington considered herself something of an expert on the history of the hotel. She had certainly done a lot of research on Winterhouse and was always eager to share her knowledge.

"It wasn't even taken seriously when I was here years ago," Mrs. Wellington said. "More something told to scare the children, I think. You know, *There are monsters hidden inside the walls, so you'd better be good!* That sort of thing."

"I find the possibility fascinating," Elana's grandmother said, her voice soothing and low. She took a sip of wine and examined Mrs. Wellington with her penetrating gaze. "And I was wondering about something you said. You mentioned that Nestor Falls himself had the passageways built so he could visit the kitchen and library anytime he liked. That must mean there is an entrance in his room—or, rather, in the room occupied now by Mr. Norbridge Falls himself. And another in the kitchen where they make the candy. And another in the library."

Elizabeth had become completely focused on the old woman's words.

Elana put a hand on her grandmother's forearm and then gave a tiny press with her fingers into the old woman's sleeve. This made no sense to Elizabeth; when she thought about it later, she couldn't help thinking Elana had been urging her grandmother to stop talking.

Mrs. Wellington glanced around the table as if she was looking for someone else to offer a detail or two. "I really think the whole story is just made up," she said lightly, laughing. "I don't think there's anything to it, but the children used to talk about it like it was real."

"But assuming there might be this passageway," Elana's grandmother continued, "that would mean there would be some connection between Norbridge's room, the kitchen, and the library, yes?" She turned to Elana and gave a quick, sharp glance at the girl's hand on her arm. Elana removed it.

"That would be a logical assumption," Mrs. Rajput said. "At least I believe so."

"And there could be other passageways within the walls," said Elana's grandmother.

"The way I recall it," said Mrs. Wellington, "the story

was that there were hidden passageways all around the hotel. Supposedly, there were a few doors that allowed entrance."

A chime sounded. Norbridge stood at the front of the hall before a podium, and everyone's eyes shifted to him. Elizabeth stole a quick glance at Elana and her grandmother and saw the older woman look to her granddaughter with an expression of deep satisfaction.

Within five minutes, Norbridge had worked through his standard after-dinner speech, welcoming all the new guests, urging those who'd already been at Winterhouse for more than just this day to continue enjoying themselves, and then making a few announcements about the upcoming events over the next twenty-four hours.

"And I am very pleased," he said, "to welcome Mrs. Verna Tilden-Opal to Winterhouse after a five-year absence. Mrs. Tilden Opal is a world-renowned expert on a fascinating rock carving in the Far East known as the Behistun Inscription and will be delivering an extremely lively and interesting talk on the subject this evening at eight o'clock in Grace Hall. You do not want to miss her presentation. I know I will be there and am looking forward to . . ."

Norbridge looked to the kitchen door, where Mrs. Trumble had cleared her throat and stood making a motion with her finger as though twirling an invisible strand of wet spaghetti. Some awareness registered on Norbridge's face, and he turned to the crowd once more. He lifted both hands above his head. "What I am trying to say is: Let's have dessert!"

A line of servers stepped from the kitchen doors with plates of pie and cakes and cookies as the crowd in Winter Hall began to cheer.

"And a song, as well!" Norbridge called. "Please join me in a round of 'The Winter Hall Jingle,' sung to the tune of that ever-popular favorite 'Edelweiss'! Everyone, join in!"

And with that, Norbridge led the crowd five times through a loud and lively rendition of the following song:

> *Winter Hall, Winter Hall*
> *Three times daily we eat here.*
> *Toast and jam, leg of lamb*
> *Tuna salad, and root beer!*
> *Lots of pie dough makes the kitchen glow*
> *We could eat forever.*
> *Winter Hall, Winter Hall*
> *Thank the cook—he's so clever!*

Elizabeth sang along happily with everyone else. But she was distracted by the expression of disgust that deepened on Elana's grandmother's face as the song progressed. She was even more distracted—and puzzled—when Elana and her grandmother, under cover of the noise and excitement, stood, waved in silent general farewell to the table, and headed with surprising quickness for a side door of the hall, right where Rodney and his parents were sitting. The strangest thing of all was that Elizabeth thought she noticed Mrs. Vesper give the slightest nod to Rodney's mother. It seemed something more than a simple acknowledgment, though from where Elizabeth was sitting, she couldn't be sure—and then Elana and her grandmother slipped through the door and disappeared.

CHAPTER 10

A LECTURE CONCLUDED

COUNTER

The lecture was interesting, but perhaps not as interesting as Norbridge had led everyone to expect. Elizabeth found herself wanting Mrs. Tilden-Opal, a tiny woman with glasses so thick they made her eyes look too huge for her face, to spend less time on the archaeological circumstances of the Behistun Inscription—which had been carved on a cliff face in Iran centuries before—and more on the deciphering of the previously unknown alphabet on the rock itself. But it was a pleasant enough way to spend the evening, and it was comforting to be back in Grace Hall beside Freddy, where they'd spent so many evenings listening to music or lectures or simply passing the time before an evening swim in the basement pool. If only Elana, who sat on the other side of Freddy, hadn't come. Elizabeth had been hoping for as much when she'd seen her leave dinner so quickly with her grandmother, but Elana had returned to meet her and Freddy as planned.

"Well, that was pretty interesting!" Elana said when the lecture ended. The three children remained seated while the crowd around them filed out; Elizabeth was making a mental note to add "Behistun Inscription" to her list of "Historic Places I Plan to Visit Someday."

"I'd never heard about that carving before," Elana continued, "but I love learning about mysterious things. Secret writing and codes and all that."

"I know what you mean," Freddy said. He turned to Elizabeth. "Remember how we got interested in the Vigenère Cipher last year?"

"Of course," Elizabeth said. Just why Freddy had chosen to mention this when the Vigenère Cipher—an almost foolproof system for writing secret messages—had been crucial in solving the secret of The Book the year before was unclear to her. He'd indicated he didn't want to revisit the previous year's events, and yet here he was blabbing to Elana.

"But that was last year," Elizabeth said, waving a hand before her. She didn't want to let Elana know more than was necessary about her friendship with Freddy.

"What is it?" Elana said. "The Vig what?" Freddy spent a couple of minutes explaining the code for her while Elizabeth began to think she might go settle into her room for the night and read a book.

"Interesting!" Elana said once Freddy was done. "Maybe you'll show me more later."

Freddy pushed at his glasses; Elizabeth thought perhaps he was realizing he'd gone too far. "For sure," he mumbled.

"I might head back to my room," Elizabeth said, standing. "It's been a really long day."

"Already?" Elana said. "Don't go yet."

"Yeah, already?" Freddy said. "It's not that late. Maybe we can get some hot chocolate."

"No," Elizabeth said, now even more resolved, given that Freddy was begging her. "You guys probably want to try out the cipher, and I'm sort of tired."

Elana remained sitting and pressed a long strand of hair behind an ear. "Hey, before you take off, I was thinking of something. Remember how everyone was talking about the secret passageways at dinner?"

"Was everyone talking about them?" Elizabeth said. She'd been fascinated herself, but she didn't want Elana to know this, and she also found herself not wanting to agree with her.

"A lot of people were," Freddy said. He looked to Elizabeth. "I think."

"What I was thinking," Elana said, "is wouldn't it be cool if the three of us investigated a little? Started looking around to see if we could find one of those doorways?"

Although she wasn't pleased that Elana had brought the subject up, Elizabeth couldn't deny that the prospect of finding an entrance into a secret passageway sounded unbearably fascinating—like something from *The Arabian Nights*, she'd been thinking. Still, she wasn't sure she wanted to get tangled up with Elana.

"I don't know," Freddy said doubtfully. "It was interesting to hear about passageways and everything, but I've been here four times now, and I've never found any secret doors."

Elizabeth felt herself relax; Freddy, to her surprise, had come to the rescue.

Elana frowned and looked to the floor. "I guess you're right. Well, it sounded interesting enough. Maybe it's nothing, but it would be cool to find one of those doors." She snapped her fingers. "Hey, why don't we get together tomorrow and just hang out? We can go skating."

Freddy looked to Elizabeth eagerly. "Elana told me she's a good skater."

"There's a rink by our house," Elana said. "I compete sometimes."

Elizabeth was not eager to watch Elana show off while Freddy stood admiring her, but at least she seemed willing to give up on her fascination with the secret passageways, and maybe an hour or two outside would be fun. There had been a good storm during the afternoon, and the mountains would be gleaming with a fresh layer of snow.

"That sounds good," Elizabeth said. "Let's go skating."

Freddy nodded. "I need to work on the camera obscura in the morning. A bunch of equipment's getting delivered, so I doubt I'll be in the hall for breakfast or lunch. Why don't we meet after lunch on the thirteenth floor?"

"Sounds good," Elana said. "That would be perfect!"

"Mr. Knox!" someone called, and the three kids turned to see Jackson in the doorway of Grace Hall. "A moment of your time, please."

"Jackson told me he was going to try to line up some of the staff to help with the scaffolding starting tonight," Freddy said with a wave. "See you tomorrow."

Elizabeth was about to leave as well when Elana put a hand out to hold her back.

"Okay, Freddy," Elana said, "we'll see you tomorrow!"

They watched him head for the doorway, and then Elana fixed Elizabeth with her smile once again.

"I'm really glad you're here," she said. "Freddy's great, but, you know, he's into a lot of *boy* stuff, like tools and everything." She scrunched her face. "I'm more into books and just . . . you know, other things. I think you and I will get along well."

Elizabeth felt a notch less ill-disposed toward Elana upon hearing her say the word "books," though the comment about Freddy was odd. Elana was staring at her, and Elizabeth realized once again that Elana was the sort the boys at her school would all have a crush on. She wondered if maybe, just maybe, she had been a bit unfair to Elana and was judging her too harshly, or maybe she was just annoyed because she had expected to have Freddy all to herself.

"Was your grandmother okay at dinner?" Elizabeth said. "You guys left pretty quickly."

"I think something was bothering her stomach. She's fine now."

"It's just the two of you here?" Elizabeth said.

Elana's expression became serious. "My parents passed away a few years ago. My grandmother's been kind enough to take me in and look after me. She's really a nice lady. Freddy told me a little about you. Like, about your parents and how you're related to Norbridge. But at least as far as parents go, I think you and I have the same situation."

Elizabeth felt confused—pulled between opening up to Elana and keeping silent, between asking her about her own parents or letting her keep it all to herself. She knew the pain of losing a mother and father, understood what that loss and absence felt like. Maybe Elana's odd, false ways were a cover for the kind of sadness she felt, too, Elizabeth thought. She just wasn't sure she wanted to share anything with her—or even be friends with her.

"I'm sorry about your parents," Elizabeth said.

She was considering what she might say next, when a heavy silence fell over the hall. The familiar stab of awareness fluttered inside Elizabeth, and, in expectation of something about to happen or someone approaching, she turned to look to the doorway. Mrs. Vesper stood there. With her white hair and black clothes, she looked like some sort of apparition.

Elizabeth wondered how long the woman had been watching them.

CHAPTER 11

MISHAPS IN THE LIBRARY

PAINS

"I guess I better get going," Elana said. She raised her eyebrows brightly. "Tomorrow!"

When Elizabeth was certain Elana and her grandmother had gone, she left Grace Hall and stopped to examine the Winterhouse seal in the marble floor. The words were strange: "Prison-Dodge," "Trim-Room," "Flood-Furor," and all the rest. What could they mean? And why were there so many numbers on the four surrounding rectangles? It made no sense.

She paused, too, at the puzzle table on her way to her room. Mr. Rajput and Mr. Wellington weren't there; on the table sat their sign: PUZZLE IN PROGRESS; PLEASE DO NOT TOUCH.

Elizabeth studied the temple in the picture. This was the place where Nestor Falls and his friend Riley Sweth Granger—the author of The Book, and the person she believed was behind several of the mysteries at Winterhouse—had lived for a few years before the hotel had been built. Questions that had come to her before returned. Why was the puzzle so enormous? And who had made it in the first place?

But the day had been full enough already with so many new things to absorb and so many questions—she stared at the puzzle and realized all she wanted to do was go to her room, lie in bed reading *The Secret of Northaven Manor*, and drift off to sleep. Which, aside from the reading—left unbegun because her eyes couldn't stay open—was exactly what she did.

<hr/>

After a quick breakfast the next morning in Winter Hall, Elizabeth went to the portrait gallery, its walls lined with portraits of members of the Falls family. For several minutes she stood before the painting of her mother; it showed her on a bright summer day when she was thirteen, just a year older than Elizabeth herself. A stretch of indigo mountains rose behind her; she wore a blue dress and a purple scarf. Her calm smile never failed to reassure Elizabeth, who had stood in this exact spot looking at the painting maybe fifty times the year before, especially after she'd learned that the girl in it had grown up to be her mother. She thought about the newspaper clipping Norbridge had shared with her.

I wonder what really happened, she thought.

Elizabeth moved on. At the end of the hall were portraits of Norbridge and Gracella as children. The paintings were a matching set, appropriate for twins, and they showed each child in front of Lake Luna. Elizabeth recalled that Norbridge had a kind look in his eyes even at that young age; she also remembered the distant look Gracella had, as though even then her mind had settled on something calculating and cruel.

Elizabeth was a few paces from the paintings—and then she stopped. She realized she didn't want to look at the picture of Gracella, the woman who'd been the source of so much unhappiness. She did, however, want to see Norbridge's portrait, and so she continued forward and studied the painting of her grandfather. A minute passed, and then another; she tried to focus on Norbridge's features, the ways in which the artist had captured those elements of his face and personality that had persisted over the years. And then she moved her gaze to Gracella's portrait and was surprised to discover it didn't look half as foreboding as she recalled. For a moment, she actually felt more intrigued by this painting than by the one of her grandfather. It made her wonder, for the thousandth time, why she had been tempted by Gracella the year before.

She glanced around at the four walls, at the mass of paintings staring back, and a realization came to her: A painting of herself would probably hang in this very room someday. The notion was startling—that her image might be captured and framed in this gallery, and that some future visitors might study her and wonder who she was and what she had grown up to be. And then, just as she'd wondered when Norbridge had pointed out the school in Havenworth, she thought, *What if I don't fit in?* It was one thing to visit Winterhouse, even to learn of her connection to it—but to actually live here was another thing completely. Could she really adjust to life at the hotel and become a true member of the Falls family after all her years in Drere?

She studied Norbridge's painting one last time, and then headed to the library to see Leona Springer.

⁂

The library at Winterhouse was so much larger than any other Elizabeth had ever been in or even imagined—three stories high, with scores of rooms and bookcases and so many tens of thousands of books, Elizabeth could have read them the rest of her life and still made her way through only a small fraction—that she'd been speechless when she'd first entered it. Even after all the hours she'd spent in the library, Elizabeth remained staggered by its size, by the beauty of its darkly paneled walls and the graceful atrium at its center, which allowed light in from the glass ceiling high above. The library had an ancient feeling— and Elizabeth loved it.

"Summer's here!" came a high, squeaky voice from the office behind the library's main counter. "Summer's here!"

"Miles!" Elizabeth said as she headed for the room. There, sitting at a desk piled with books, was Leona Springer, and on her shoulder perched her green parakeet, Miles, who was continuing to caw, "Summer's here! Summer's here!"

Leona, who was examining a spread of papers, looked up. "I keep telling him it should be 'Winter's here! Winter's here!'" She raised her hand and stretched out a finger, and the bird hopped onto it so that she could present him to Elizabeth.

"Remember how you thought he was saying your name the first time you met him?" Leona said, removing her glasses to allow them to hang from the delicate chain around her neck.

"I sure do!" Elizabeth said, running a finger across the bird's head in a light pat. "So great to see him again! And the library! And you, of course, Leona!"

"It's wonderful to have you back!" Leona said. She was a short woman—Elizabeth had been the same height as her the year before, but now she was nearly two inches taller. "I'm ecstatic about that, let me tell you."

"So am I."

Miles raised his small wings and fluttered to his perch in the corner. "Teatime!" he cawed. "Teatime!"

Elizabeth and Leona laughed, Leona put a pot of water on to boil, and the two of them sat down to catch up. Over the next half hour, Elizabeth detailed the year that had passed and, mainly, asked Leona about Winterhouse and Norbridge and how things had been at the hotel. They even caught up on some of their favorite books of the past year, and Elizabeth was surprised and pleased to learn that Leona had read *The Name of This Book Is Secret*, one of her recent favorites.

"Leona," Elizabeth said finally, "some people at dinner last night were talking about secret passageways here at Winterhouse. They were saying there are some doors to passageways inside the walls. Is that true?"

Leona laughed—not unkindly, just out of surprise. "Who told you that?"

"Mrs. Wellington."

"Very sweet lady, and very knowledgeable about the hotel. But she may have blown things out of proportion."

"Well, she wasn't really saying there actually were passageways. She was more explaining that it's kind of a legend."

"It's true that at one time there was a walkway between Nestor's room and the candy kitchen. They said he wanted to be able to sneak a piece or two of candy anytime he liked. But that passageway was blocked off in the kitchen and the door sealed years ago. Nestor also had a passageway put in between his room and this library. However, when they remodeled the place, that corridor was demolished." Leona smiled to indicate she felt the whole matter had been cleared up. "Why were they talking about it, anyway?"

"A woman at the table brought it up. Mrs. Vesper."

Leona's face went dark. "Mrs. Vesper. She's been here twice with her granddaughter. The girl is nice, but the older woman is somewhat peculiar. She was interested in the reference room and spent some time up there after I showed her around."

The reference room was the very place where Gracella had ambushed Norbridge and nearly overpowered Elizabeth; it was the very room, too, where Elizabeth had discovered The Book and, after defeating Gracella, rehidden it.

"The reference room is where I found—"

"The Book," Leona said, completing Elizabeth's sentence. "I remember well."

Elizabeth took a sip of tea as she thought about this. "Leona, do you think there might be other things in Winterhouse like The Book? I've been wondering if maybe Riley Granger's game with Nestor Falls might have included more . . . I don't know, *magical* objects."

"I can't say for sure, but it wouldn't surprise me. The legend of The Book was well-known to everyone here, but at times over the years I heard a whisper or two about other things."

"Like what?"

"It's interesting that you're asking me about the hotel's hidden passageways, because there was always a rumor that there was an object hidden somewhere inside one of them." Leona paused. "It wouldn't surprise me if Riley Granger had more than one trick up his sleeve."

Elizabeth was hoping she would continue; voices came from beyond the office door.

"Perhaps we should see if the guests need help," Leona said, standing. "Are you game?"

"For sure!" There were few things Elizabeth could think of that sounded more appealing than the chance to assist in the library. "In fact, I was thinking that maybe I could start helping you out here from time to time."

Leona put a hand to the glasses on her chain. "If you can manage, I'd love that. I'll teach you all I can about the place."

"Summer's here!" Miles cawed, and Leona led Elizabeth out of the office.

"Excuse me," said a woman standing at the counter. "Do you have a section on ancient history? Greece and Rome?"

"We certainly do," Leona said, and she gestured to Elizabeth. "And my assistant, Miss Somers, can show you exactly where it is."

Elizabeth turned to Leona with a look of shock. She had wanted to assist, absolutely, but she hadn't imagined she'd be given this kind of responsibility right away.

"L-16 on the second floor," Leona whispered to Elizabeth, and then, loudly, "She is very knowledgeable about the contents of this library."

Elizabeth didn't feel so knowledgeable when, twenty minutes later and after detours—and failed attempts— to find books about traveling in New Zealand and then volleyball and then a language called Esperanto, Elizabeth felt completely lost. She hadn't helped the woman at all.

"I thought you were an expert," the woman said.

"Well, I don't know everything yet," Elizabeth said. "I sort of just started." She thought for sure this would soften the woman, but instead it just deepened the scowl on her face.

"I have very limited time this morning," the woman said, "and I was assuming the staff here would provide capable assistance." She began looking left and right as if searching for someone who might do a better job of helping her.

Elizabeth couldn't believe the woman was being so impolite. However, she told herself she must be unfailingly pleasant—*I live here now*, she thought, *and I'm part of the Falls family.*

"I want to help," Elizabeth said. "If you'd just be nice about it—"

"Nice about it!" the woman said, raising her voice. "I just want to know where some books are!"

It was at this point that Elizabeth told herself not only was she was twelve years old and an official assistant librarian, she also didn't have to allow this woman to talk to her in that tone.

"Oh, well, actually, there are books everywhere," Elizabeth said. She looked in all directions. "There, and there, and over there, and on the shelves over there . . ."

The woman's mouth fell open before she found words. "Why, I have never—"

"May I help?"

Elizabeth and the woman turned to the landing at the top of the staircase; Leona stood looking at them with a gentle expression on her face.

"You certainly may," the woman said, and after several complaints about Elizabeth—with a half dozen huffy glares in her direction—she explained what she was looking for, and Leona rattled off the various sections to her and even offered a recommendation.

The woman fixed Elizabeth with one final steely gaze even as she said, "Thank you," curtly to Leona before striding off.

"I blew that one," Elizabeth said as the woman disappeared down the stairs.

"We get the cranky ones in here from time to time," Leona said. "Don't worry about it."

Elizabeth never knew what to do when someone told her not to worry about something. She felt that the recommendation itself could only compound the worry. But she recognized Leona meant well, and she told herself she hadn't done anything wrong until she got upset with the woman.

Still, the incident, as minor as it was, returned the same question to her mind that had already popped up a handful of times: *What if I don't fit in?*

"We can't lose our cool with the guests," Leona said. "They are paying to be here and enjoy the place, the library included. Even the ill-mannered ones—we have to put up with them."

"I don't believe it!" someone said loudly from the staircase. Leona and Elizabeth turned—and there, in black jeans, tennis shoes, and a black hoodie, stood Rodney, the boy who had stolen Elizabeth's seat on the bus the morning before. He pointed at her like he was pointing at a two-headed dog.

"It's you!" he called.

CHAPTER 12

A SURPRISE IN THE JOURNAL

INSPIRE

Behind Rodney, huffing from the strain of climbing a single set of stairs, his mother and father appeared.

"The girl from the bus!" Rodney said to them before looking back to Elizabeth. The expression on his face had transformed into a combination of joy and revulsion and surprise; he looked like he'd discovered some poor little animal injured in a trap and could now torment it at his leisure. "The one with the book!"

Rodney's mother put one hand to her forehead and the other heavily on the railing, all to combat a flush that appeared to have arisen from her small ascent; and his father stood with his mouth open wide in something that looked like shock.

"The one who tried to take your seat!" Rodney's mother cried, and she pointed at Elizabeth. "Right here!"

"May I help you?" Leona said calmly. "My name is Leona Springer, and you are welcome to my library here at Winterhouse."

"I am Ernest Powter!" Rodney's father said huffily. "And that girl beside you! She . . ." he sputtered. "On our journey here, she . . ." He couldn't figure out what more he wanted to say and allowed his sentence to trail off.

Leona turned to Elizabeth and said, "Yes, my assistant, Miss Elizabeth Somers. May we help you locate something?"

Rodney pushed his head forward, gaping at Elizabeth the way a person studies an eye chart on a far wall. "Your assistant? What are you even doing here?"

Elizabeth had been preparing for this question ever since that moment on the bus when she'd heard Rodney announce—and gloat over—the fact that he would be at Winterhouse.

"Oh, I'm the granddaughter of the hotel owner," she said casually. "May I help you find something in the library?"

The eyes of all three Powters went blank; it was as if Elizabeth had just informed them that all their money had been stolen from the bank or their house had disappeared.

"Granddaughter?" Mrs. Powter said softly, slowly.

"Granddaughter?" Mr. Powter said, even more softly and slowly. He resembled someone who'd never heard the word before and was simply trying to see how it sounded on his own lips after hearing someone else say it. Elizabeth was enjoying this whole thing immensely, especially seeing Rodney look like he'd just been dropped into the library from a thousand miles away and was now trying to figure out what had happened.

"Well," Mrs. Powter said brightly, recovering. "I find that very interesting." She turned to her husband; he looked as if he'd been asked to recite the Pledge of Allegiance in Bulgarian.

"Elizabeth," Leona said, "can you please go to the office and finish the filing for me?" She gave her a quick wink. "I'll join you shortly."

Elizabeth nodded, scanned the three people blocking her way to the staircase, and then strode right for them as they parted.

"I guess I'll see you around, Miss Granddaughter," Rodney said in a low snarl as she passed, but Elizabeth said nothing and just hopped quickly down the stairs.

"She was very rude to us on our bus ride," Elizabeth heard Mrs. Powter say as she continued to the first floor. The morning light streamed in through the atrium ceiling, and the high bookcases rose all around her like well-trimmed hedges. But the presence of the Powters had upset her badly, as had her first experience of helping a guest as an assistant librarian. She headed for Leona's office with a thought that threatened to make her unhappy: She might be a member of the Falls family, and she might be at Winterhouse to stay, but adjusting to all of it would not be as simple as drifting off to sleep with a good book in her hands.

❄

To distract herself until Leona returned, Elizabeth decided to peruse the journal Marshall Falls, one of Norbridge's cousins, had written and that lay on a small podium at the rear of Leona's office. The journal was enormous—over five hundred pages—and Marshall, though a writer of quirky, meandering, and convoluted sentences, had been diligent about detailing events at Winterhouse until he passed away in 1994. Elizabeth had spent several hours the year before reading portions of the journal, and she had found it both entertaining and enlightening—she had, in fact, learned many things about her mother and The Book and Gracella and Nestor and more.

Elizabeth spent a moment cooing to Miles before stepping up to the stand that held Marshall's huge book. It was open to the title page, "*A Personal History of the Winterhouse Hotel*," and beneath this, "By Marshall Falls, Inhabitant." She turned to the lengthy table of contents and found her eyes caught by some of the headings: "The Tragic Deaths of Eugene and Ernest on Mount Arbaza," "The Half-Million Dowry Offered—but Ravenna Declines!" and "The Summer with No Ice Cream." She noticed one that intrigued her: "Norbridge Makes His Way—and Then Makes His Way Back." She thumbed forward to the chapter and began to read:

It was a curious thing to us when young Norbridge, not two years after Gracella herself disappeared from Winterhouse, decided he also was going to leave. Norbridge announced his intentions broadly and, despite the protestations of parents, cousins, aunts, uncles, friends, guests, staff (kitchen, clerks, maids, et al.), former schoolmates, members of the ski club, seven visiting lecturers, and the cinema star Ruby Jarreau (who was recuperating from exhaustion here), our decent and ambitious Norbridge resolved to separate himself from Winterhouse for "an indeterminate length of time, though I shall return," as he himself informed us.

When asked what had prompted him to set out on this adventure or escapade or tour or what-have-you, Norbridge was uncharacteristically evasive, like a man who doesn't want to explain himself or perhaps has something on his mind and is intent on keeping it hidden. He was like a person in possession of a secret he will not divulge to anyone, not even to a loving second cousin, say, or anyone else in the family, for that matter, no matter how often, even in gentle tones, that person might ask him or even plead with him to make plain his motivations. It was apparent to one and all, however, that Norbridge remained deeply curious about Gracella and what had happened to her. He often spoke of her—with warmth, some would say— and seemed to go so far even as to defend her when members of the family brought up her faults, her character defects, the many times she had been impolite or downright insolent, the strange fascination she had with black magic, the disconcerting dark clothes she took to wearing at all times, and the many improper, even immoral actions she had taken, e.g., the time she stole forty-three dollars from a piggy bank in Cassandra's room or used scissors on Ravenna's favorite dress or dumped olive oil in the suitcase of a guest with whom she'd quarreled (note well: this list could be extended for pages and pages; I am offering only an extremely limited representative sampling). Some would say this defense of his twin sister was to be expected of Norbridge—he was always a loyal and generous soul. But others noted something deeper in his interest in and support of Gracella, and it was said that occasionally he, too, had expressed an interest in more serious forms of magic and was somewhat sympathetic to his sister's pursuits. I never believed this and never saw evidence of it myself. But there were those in our family who wondered if perhaps Norbridge's proposed journey was an attempt to locate Gracella, maybe to turn her away from the dark path she had sought—or even to join her on it.

Again, let me be clear that I never read anything more into his wanderlust than the simple curiosity of a young man who has been cooped up in the far north his whole life. Heaven knows many of us here at Winterhouse have experienced a similar strain of cabin fever, *and I never begrudged him his departure. I will say, however, I was surprised he ended up being gone for two years. That seemed like overdoing it to me, but far be it from me to question his judgment. When he returned, in the summer of 1956, he had put on twenty pounds of muscle, wore a thick beard, and was full of a confidence so unshakeable, everyone understood that when the time was right, he would lead Winterhouse into its next era.*

Elizabeth skimmed ahead and tried to learn what Norbridge had done while he'd been away or where he'd gone, but she found nothing. She was puzzled—and Marshall's bizarre way of describing events hadn't helped. It had never crossed Elizabeth's mind that Norbridge might have been away from the hotel for any length of time in his younger years; she couldn't imagine why anyone, once living at Winterhouse, would ever choose to leave.

"Summer's here!" Miles cawed. "Summer's here!"

Elizabeth looked up. "You funny bird," she said as Leona entered the office.

"I am very sorry to have left you on your own for so long!"

"I've just been reading." She nodded to Marshall's journal.

"Dear Marshall's 'intriguing' work," Leona said. She looked behind her to make sure no one was at the counter.

"I've never been one to pass judgment on the multitude of humanity that arrives at the doors of our humble hotel, but those Powters are among the most uncouth and ill-mannered individuals I have ever—" She stopped and put a hand to her cheek. "I suppose I'm passing judgment, aren't I?"

Elizabeth laughed. "It's all right. I met them on the bus when I was coming here. The boy stole my seat and was extremely rude to me."

Leona pasted a look of mock surprise on her face. "Shocking! Why, that is just shocking to learn!" She and Elizabeth began to laugh.

"But how do you deal with such mean people, Leona?" Elizabeth said.

"I once heard something when I was young that has always stayed with me and that has helped me a great deal. Very simple guidance, but I have found it immensely valuable. It was, essentially, that in all dealings with others, we should try our best not to take offense and not to give offense."

Elizabeth had been expecting something more compli-cated; Leona's words surprised her by their brevity.

"I'll think about that," she said. She considered the upcoming afternoon with Elana and Freddy. "It sounds like good advice." She ran a hand over Marshall's journal. "Say, Leona, last year when I left, Norbridge gave me a book by a writer named Damien Crowley."

Leona's eyes widened. "We have several of his novels

in the literature section. He was a local, actually. Norbridge knew him and loved his books. Macabre stories. Very thrilling."

Elizabeth was about to ask more, but in the broad, open space of the library's main floor, she saw Mr. and Mrs. Powter and Rodney walking slowly. All three were looking upward, scanning the walls. Mr. Powter said something to the others as he stopped and pointed. Rodney nodded and pointed to the wall in a different direction.

"What is it, dear?" Leona said.

"The Powters are out there looking around." It was odd that the three of them were so absorbed in examining the walls rather than the stacks of books.

"Strange birds!" Miles cawed. "Strange birds!"

"Hush!" Leona said. She peered through the doorway and then began to examine some papers on her desk. "Probably a good idea to stay away from that bunch."

Although she couldn't hear what the Powters were saying, Elizabeth continued to watch. Rodney said something to his mother, but the woman responded angrily; he spoke again, explaining something, while his mother grew more agitated. The woman raised her hand viciously above her head, and then she stopped herself and glanced around the library before lowering her arm. With a jerk of her head, she indicated that Rodney was to continue walking with her, and the three Powters moved out of Elizabeth's sight. The look on Mrs. Powter's face reminded Elizabeth of her aunt Purdy. Although she hadn't considered, even two minutes before, that she might ever feel any degree of sympathy for Rodney Powter, at that moment Elizabeth understood just what he had felt. And she was sorry for him.

"I think I'll go look at the Damien Crowley books," Elizabeth said to Leona, and she headed toward the office door. "I'll be back in a few."

"Stay out of trouble," Leona said, and Miles cawed, "Strange birds," once more.

Elizabeth waited until the Powters were out of sight past a line of bookcases before ducking behind a nearby row. As she drew near, she heard Mr. Powter say, "Well, if the others couldn't find it, how in the world will we?" and then Rodney said, "That's exactly what I've been saying."

"We'll just have to keep looking," Mrs. Powter said sternly.

What are they looking for? Elizabeth thought.

"Why don't I just come back later on my own?" Rodney said.

"Look at this!" Mr. Powter said with excitement. "Perhaps it's right back here?"

Elizabeth continued to listen from where she hid behind her bookcase. Without making a sound, she craned her neck just slightly and spied the three Powters examining the wall between two bookcases. Mrs. Powter ran a hand over the wall and moved her face close to it.

"Difficult to tell," she said. She wheeled on Rodney. "Climb up on the shelves a bit and take a closer look."

Rodney swept the hair from in front of his eyes and stepped up to the bookcase. Elizabeth noticed, on a nearly empty space on a shelf just beside him, a stack of a dozen large books waiting to be reshelved. She stared at them and allowed her eyes to relax, focusing all her attention on the pile of books. *The feeling* welled up inside her; the books began to quiver. For a second Elizabeth recalled Norbridge's warning to her about using her power and about the bad ends Gracella had come to by indulging it. But the Powters were clearly up to no good, and so she felt it would be okay—just this once—to go ahead with her plan to distract them. And that meant summoning *the feeling*.

"Hurry up," Mr. Powter said to Rodney, who had scaled the first row of shelves. "We don't want to be here all day."

Elizabeth continued to stare at the books as they shook harder; suddenly, the books scooted to the edge of the shelf and then plummeted to the floor with a loud crash. The three Powters turned to look, and Rodney dropped to the floor on both feet as his mother let out a yelp. Leona came running from her office, and Elizabeth retreated behind another bookcase and disappeared.

"What is going on here?" Leona called, and Rodney and his parents began talking at once. But Elizabeth didn't wait to hear what was sure to be a round of excuses and lies; she didn't want Leona to discover she'd been snooping, and she was too busy wondering just what the Powters were up to. Above all, she was trying to keep a disturbing thought from settling into her head: She'd enjoyed upsetting the Powters. Summoning *the feeling* to be used against them had made her feel powerful, and it had made her feel strong. And she liked the sensation.

She resolved to put this notion out of her mind and go talk to Freddy about what she'd overheard.

CHAPTER 13

A TOUR OF THE CANDY KITCHEN

FORTH

After a lunch of tomato soup, a roll, and some cookies in Winter Hall, Elizabeth headed to the thirteenth floor to meet Freddy and Elana. She'd looked for Norbridge during the meal, but he was nowhere to be found, and she figured he must be very busy with hotel matters or he surely would have found time to visit with her by now.

When she left the dining room, she found herself detouring away from the main lobby and up a rear flight of stairs until she came to a T in the corridor. She looked to her left down a poorly lit hallway and noticed the door that, although she hadn't fully admitted it to herself, she knew she'd been seeking: Gracella's room, locked and unoccupied for decades. On her final night at Winterhouse the year before, Elizabeth had stolen into this room with a key Freddy had lent her, though she'd fled in fright after only a couple of minutes. Now, as she stood examining the door, *the feeling* began to stir inside her, once again without her summoning it. A low buzzing sounded in her ears. She took a step toward the door.

"Elizabeth?"

She looked behind her. "Norbridge!" she said, flustered, when she saw him standing there. "I didn't hear you."

He glanced at the door at the end of the hallway before speaking. "What are you doing here?" He looked very serious, almost angry.

"I'm heading up to see Freddy, and I was just sort of taking the long way. He showed me the camera obscura, and we're gonna go skating this afternoon with a girl here who . . ." Elizabeth realized she was babbling and had lost her focus. She looked back at Gracella's door and then to Norbridge with a feeling of defeat; she felt she'd been caught in a lie.

"I know I shouldn't come by here," she said. "I just . . . something about last year . . ."

"What is it? Please, tell me."

"How did Gracella come back?" Elizabeth said, surprised by her own bluntness. She had wondered about this for so many months, and now, standing before Gracella's door and with Norbridge in front of her, she felt moved to speak her mind. "I thought she died a long time ago."

Norbridge put a hand to his forehead and pinched at

the skin there, the way a person tries to soothe away a headache. "My sister developed a very disturbing . . . ability, and I may as well tell you candidly what it was. She perfected a method for keeping herself alive. It's a very evil form of magic, and it entails . . ." He let his sentence trail off.

"Killing people?"

Norbridge nodded. "In so many words, yes—killing people. Somehow she is able to take the vitality from others and transfer it to herself."

"So if she's done it before, couldn't she do it again? I mean, what if she's not really dead this time again, and what if the way Marcus Q. Hiems died was—"

Norbridge held up a hand to silence her. "I know you're interested in all of this, but I'm asking you to stop dwelling on it. And I also don't want you to come to this room. Understood?"

Norbridge had rarely spoken to her this directly; it took her aback. She wanted to protest and explain that she deserved to know the truth about things, particularly because she had been the one to save Winterhouse. And now Norbridge was telling her she had no business probing too deeply. There was more, too—just as with Aunt Purdy and Uncle Burlap, it was suddenly plain to her that there were rules here at Winterhouse she'd need to respect. There were restrictions.

"I don't fully understand," she said, "but I won't come by here if you don't want me to."

"Thank you."

"I was just wondering—and I was thinking, too, what if there were other objects inside Winterhouse that she wanted to get? Things that could make her more powerful. I was talking to Leona, and she told me about the secret passageways inside the walls."

"There is a lot to learn about Winterhouse," Norbridge said. "And now that you live here, we'll have plenty of time to delve into it." He pursed his lips. "You're absolutely correct that there are legends about more magical objects, perhaps hidden about the hotel, and I've given all of it a lot of thought, and investigated quite a bit, to see what I can learn. The story about something maybe being inside the passageways—and there are passageways, though they're not much to speak of—is an old one, but I've actually never found anything to validate it. Also, the doorways have been sealed for some time."

There was so much Elizabeth wanted to ask Norbridge— about his departure from Winterhouse that she'd read about in Marshall's journal, about the death of her parents, about Riley Granger's elaborate game, and about the passageways themselves—but what came out of her mouth surprised her: "What does the seal mean on the floor in front of Grace Hall?"

"The Winterhouse seal? My father used to say it was a guide for . . . something indeterminate." Norbridge looked suddenly amused by his own cluelessness, and he smiled.

Elizabeth laughed. "Well, that's not much to go on."

"Nestor was very intrigued by numerology, so my theory is there is some sort of message hidden in the numbers. But about what, I just don't know. Supposedly, the numbers and words orient a person to something inside the hotel. I've been trying to uncover the secret for years." He glanced at his watch. "If anyone's going to figure it out after all this time, maybe it will be you. I need to run now, though. I'm hoping all is off to a good start for you. I'm afraid I've been so busy I haven't had a chance to catch up. And now we have a group of tourists arriving from Tajikistan, and I promised them an outing to Bruma Pass for a snowball fight before they spend the evening in the saunas."

"You're here!" Elana called when Elizabeth entered the camera obscura room. She was on the platform beside the white disk, but when she saw Elizabeth she scurried down the walkway and came to her. "I'm so glad to see you!" She looked up at the platform where Freddy was working. "Mr. Rope Man is trying to arrange something."

"It's a lot of math," Freddy called down. "Angles and tension and torque." He leaned over the side of the platform and waved. "Hey, Elizabeth! We were gonna come find you."

"Hi," she called. She was surprised to find Elana here with Freddy already; she felt that she had come late and the two of them had become busy with work on the platform.

"You guys been here awhile?"

Elana tossed her head casually. "Just got here."

Freddy was walking down to them and wiping his hands on a towel. He pushed at his glasses and gave Elizabeth a thumbs-up. "How was the library?"

"All good," she said. "I'm going to start working there in the mornings. I'll be helping Leona."

"Very cool!" Elana said. "Maybe I'll come and pitch in, too!"

Elizabeth was about to tell her it was less that she was "pitching in," and more that she would be learning how to be a genuine librarian, when Freddy spoke.

"I just needed to check a few things here," he said. "But I'm ready to go skating."

Elana looked to them in a way that suggested she'd been hiding a secret and was now thrilled to be sharing it. "So, I found out there's a tour of the candy kitchen at one thirty," she said, "and I was thinking we should all go."

Elizabeth wanted to tell her she and Freddy had both been inside the candy kitchen so many times and eaten so much Flurschen, they could probably make it themselves.

"We've been there a million times," Freddy said.

"It's only a half-hour tour," Elana said. "I'd really love to see what they do there."

Elana looked so excited, Elizabeth was hesitant to disappoint her. She thought, too, about what they had discussed the previous evening, how Elana had shared with her that she had also lost her parents.

"If you want to see the kitchen," Elizabeth said, "we can take a quick tour."

Elana looked to her with a sunny expression. "I'd love to."

"Let's do it," Freddy said. "We can get some Flurschen and then go skating."

On the way to the candy kitchen, they passed one of the strangest rooms in the entire hotel. Like all of them, it had an ornately paneled cherrywood door and a shiny bronze door handle. But on the wall beside the door was affixed a small silver plaque on which was written the following words: THIS ROOM RESERVED AT ALL TIMES FOR EDWIN AND ORFAMAY THATCHER. PLEASE DO NOT ENTER.

Elizabeth stopped and studied the plaque. "I almost forgot about this room."

"Who are they?" Elana gazed at the plaque. "Edwin and Orfamay Thatcher?"

"They're billionaires," Freddy said. "They're the ones who made all the Cattle Battle movies back in the nineties. So now they're rich enough to come here anytime they want. I guess they like this room so much they actually pay Norbridge to keep it reserved for them."

Elizabeth studied the door. "Hard to believe," she said. She thought of creating a new list: "Richest People I've Ever Met," as she fully expected to meet the Thatchers someday soon.

Elana eyed the door, looking delighted and puzzled both. "A room that's totally empty."

"Most of the time," Freddy said.

Elana laughed. "Right. Most of the time." She moved closer and then put her ear to the door while listening for a moment.

Elizabeth was puzzled. She looked to Freddy, who lowered his brow at her in a way that said, *What's up with her?*

"Hear anything?" Elizabeth said. She'd expected Elana to say something, but the other girl looked like she was all alone and suddenly in a different world.

Elana moved her eyes to Elizabeth's and tilted her head slightly in a gesture that said, *Join me.* Although Elizabeth was feeling increasingly odd about the whole thing, she placed an ear against the door and listened. After a few seconds, she backed away.

"I don't hear anything," she said.

Elana straightened up and looked at her with bright eyes. "Me neither," she said. "Completely empty, I guess."

"You seem really interested in this room," Freddy said to Elana, which was exactly what Elizabeth was thinking.

Elana sighed. "It's just, I don't know, cool to think about a room sitting here all empty." She shrugged. "Shall we get going?"

The candy kitchen was undoubtedly the most famous spot in the hotel, the place where Winterhouse's renowned candy, Flurschen, was made, and the place that drew scores of guests for a three-times-a-week tour and free samples in the front room. Elizabeth had been inside many times. She loved the sweet aroma of walnuts and powdered sugar and jelly, all of which went into the delicious little squares of confection that, from this very kitchen, were sent to candy stores all over the world. It was sometimes said you could go almost anywhere on the globe, and even if a person hadn't heard of Winterhouse itself, all you had to do was place a piece of Flurschen in their palm, and they would immediately recognize the tasty, powdery, sweet treat no one could resist popping into their mouth. Elizabeth loved the candy kitchen, with its spread of rooms where walnuts were shelled, jelly was cooked in huge kettles, and the little squares were cooled and sliced and powdered and boxed, all by a crew of proud and efficient candy masters.

The tour of the candy kitchen, led by one of the young women who tied lavender-colored ribbons on the Flurschen boxes in the last room before they were packed away for delivery, was identical to the one Elizabeth had taken herself the year before. It would have been interesting if she hadn't been familiar with the details already. Elana, however, was fascinated by everything. She asked so many questions throughout, it was like she was preparing for an exam. She asked if all the rooms had always been arranged as they were currently, why some rooms had bookcases in them and others did not, if it was possible to visit some of the back rooms without a guide, and on and on

"We have a very curious guest!" the tour guide said at one point, by way of making light of what had become an awkward number of queries.

"This place is just so interesting!" Elana whispered to Freddy.

Elizabeth found it all very disconcerting, especially when, at the end of the tour, rather than sampling some Flurschen or admiring the antique mixing pots, Elana glanced to the doorway of the kitchen with an oddly sad expression and announced she needed to go check on her grandmother.

"I thought we were going skating," Freddy said.

"Definitely," Elana said, a hint of reluctance in her voice. "I just think I need to go see how my grandmother's doing. Why don't we meet at the rink in half an hour?"

Elizabeth felt there was something very peculiar about this sudden need of Elana's; it was as though she wanted to stay with her and Freddy but for some reason felt compelled to depart.

"Okay," Elizabeth said. "We'll meet you there. I hope your grandmother is okay."

"Thanks," Elana said with a weak smile. "I'll see you soon."

"Doesn't it seem like there's something really off with her?" Elizabeth said to Freddy as they stood staring at the empty doorway through which Elana had just departed.

He turned to her and bit his lip.

"Even though she said her grandmother lets her do whatever she wants," Elizabeth said, "it's like she's afraid of her or something."

Freddy looked to the empty doorway again. "Let's go

to the rink. But I agree with you. Something's strange with both of them."

"You think something's strange with *them*," Elizabeth said as they headed outside. "Let me tell you what happened in the library this morning."

CHAPTER 14

A SHOCKING ATTACK

TAKING

Elana never did show up at the ice-skating rink, which gave Elizabeth and Freddy plenty of time to discuss the strange doings with the Powters and the possibility that there might be something hidden in Winterhouse's secret passageways. At dinner, Elana appeared alone and explained her grandmother hadn't been feeling well and she'd needed to keep her company throughout the afternoon and then would need to stay in with her for the evening.

"The plot thickens," Elizabeth said to Freddy as they headed for an after-dinner swim in the basement pool, stopping by the diorama in the lobby first to race trains.

"There's something going on with Elana that she's not tell-ing us."

"Did you know 'Elana Vesper' can be turned into 'vane leapers'?" Freddy said.

"Okay, you worked a long time on that one. Admit it."

"She's . . . different."

"I sort of feel sorry for her," Elizabeth said, though she wasn't sure just how sorry she felt. Every time she wanted to give in to sympathy, she considered that Elana was, without a doubt, prettier than any of the girls she knew back in Drere.

"You can also get 'reveal aspen,' if you work hard," Freddy said.

"Someone's been thinking a lot about Elana's name," Elizabeth said curtly.

Freddy pointed ahead. "Let's get to the swimming pool."

The next day passed quickly. Freddy worked on his cam-era obscura. Elizabeth spent the morning helping in the library and then went skiing in the afternoon after work-ing for an hour on the puzzle in the lobby. Elana remained with her grandmother in their room. Or, at least, that's what she reported over dinner, which was the only time all day Elizabeth and Freddy saw her. Norbridge had left Winterhouse on an errand. The Powters seemed to have disappeared.

After a movie in the small theater in the evening,

Elizabeth and Freddy were heading to their rooms when the moonlight beyond the large window in the hallway caught her eye. She stopped. Lake Luna was gleaming, and the mountains on its far side glowed gently.

"I love the view from here," Elizabeth said. She stared at the huge, billowing clouds that gleamed in the moonlight. "That looks like something out of *James and the Giant Peach*."

Freddy glanced up. "Those are cumulus clouds," he said. "Or maybe cumulonimbus."

Elizabeth sighed. "Okay, Mr. Science. But that doesn't sound nearly as interesting."

Elizabeth looked to the ice rink and the skaters who were gliding around it in the lamplight. On the side of the shack where people borrowed skates, standing in thin white snow pants and a white parka, her black hair pulled back by a white bandana, was Elana. Next to her, smiling at something she'd said, was Rodney Powter, his black hood resting loosely on his head as he stood at a casual angle. He spoke, and Elana lifted her chin and laughed brightly.

"Hey, look at that," Elizabeth said as she watched them talking.

"What?" Freddy said, glancing out the window.

"That's the guy, Rodney Powter, that I was telling you about, and Elana's talking to him."

Freddy frowned. "Is there something funny about that?"

Elizabeth couldn't put her finger on it, but it looked

like Elana and Rodney were already friends, and good ones at that. They were speaking so familiarly.

"I guess not." She watched them for a moment more before moving from the window.

Elizabeth passed an hour on her bed reading a book she'd found in the library, Damien Crowley's *The Lake in the Forest*; and then she sat at the cherrywood desk in the corner and opened her notebook. She had begun a new list the day before—"Things on My Mind/Things I Want to Look Into/Things I Want to Know More About"—and now she was examining it:

1. *The newspaper clipping about my parents—and my parents, in general*
2. *What Norbridge and Professor Fowles were discussing at the Silver Fir Café*
3. *What the secret passageways in Winterhouse are all about*
4. *What the Powters were doing in the library*
5. *If there might be other "powerful" objects hidden in Winterhouse*
6. *What the Winterhouse seal is all about*
7. *Why Mrs. Vesper is so spooky and why Elana is afraid of her*
8. *How a camera obscura works*
9. *What Norbridge means about something that tempted my mother*

She considered whether her list was complete but decided to leave it alone for now. The Crowley book lay on the edge of the bed, and it drew her attention. She stared at it—and immediately, with the expertise she'd gained from a year's worth of practice, allowed her thoughts to become still and her mind to focus on the book, even as her vision blurred. The familiar tremor moved within her; the room became deeply silent. With a sudden twitch, the book stirred. Elizabeth inclined her head and intensified her concentration. The book jumped from the bed as though some invisible spring had gone off beneath it, and it landed directly in Elizabeth's hands.

"Oh!" she cried out. "That's never happened before!"

She studied the book. This was something new, and all she could do was look at the volume in amazement. She was about to set it back on the bed when a thought came to her: *Maybe now that I'm at Winterhouse, the power is even stronger.*

A noise—like a person running—came from the hallway. Elizabeth jumped up and opened her door and, just as she glanced down the corridor, she saw Rodney Powter dash past at the very end, though he didn't turn his head and so did not notice her. He was gone almost before Elizabeth realized what she'd seen.

She heard voices from the direction of the candy

kitchen and headed to it. As she turned the corner, she saw a cluster of people outside the kitchen. There were five bell-hops in their red suits, three of the kitchen staff, and a few people Elizabeth didn't recognize—guests, maybe, though they looked purposeful. As she came closer, Elizabeth saw everyone was moving brusquely with anxious expressions; she thought maybe there was some mechanical problem they were addressing, a water leak, perhaps, or a small fire. Jackson was in the circle by the door.

"What's going on, Jackson?" she asked.

He turned to her, looking like someone who has just seen a bad accident. "Miss Somers," he said flatly, arranging the small hat on his head, "I must ask you to return to your room, please. Right away."

"Is everything all right?"

Jackson twisted his body to stare at her. "Please return to your room!" he said sternly.

She had never seen or heard him like this—not even close—and it alarmed her. She stood in place, not sure what to do.

"Elizabeth, please!" Jackson said.

She began to back away slowly. "Okay, I'm going."

Jackson turned to the kitchen entrance without saying anything more. Elizabeth continued to back away, still watching the group of people.

"It was Mrs. Trumble, for sure?" someone said, though Elizabeth couldn't see who.

"I hope she's all right," someone else said.

Elizabeth stopped, and at that moment Jackson glanced

in her direction. He gave her a stern if pleading look and pointed a finger down the hallway; Elizabeth raced back to her room.

One hour later, after listening at her door and spying at the peephole to see who might pass by, Elizabeth left her room and headed for the candy kitchen. The doors were closed and the lights were out, but Sampson, the young bellhop, was stationed in front.

"Hi, Elizabeth!" he said enthusiastically, the way he might if they'd run into each other on a street in Havenworth.

"Hi, Sampson," Elizabeth said, and then, not wasting any time: "I saw a bunch of people here earlier, and Jackson asked me to go to my room because something had happened to Mrs. Trumble. Is she all right?"

Sampson's expression turned serious. "You heard, huh? Yeah, she'll be all right. They're still trying to figure out what happened, Norbridge and everyone. I guess she thought she heard something when she was walking by the kitchen, and when she went to check it out, someone attacked her, and then she blacked out."

"What?" Elizabeth was alarmed to think that someone would have harmed a defenseless lady like Mrs. Trumble, and she immediately thought of Rodney Powter racing away. "I can't believe anyone would hurt her."

"I know," Sampson said, nodding. "I think she was more scared than anything. She's in the infirmary now, but I don't think she's hurt badly."

"I saw Rodney Powter running away right before it happened."

"Yeah, someone else saw him, too. Norbridge talked to him, and I guess his parents said he was just wandering around and got scared when he heard a noise, so he took off running."

Elizabeth thought that sounded very improbable, but she decided not to ask Sampson more about it. "So no one knows what happened?"

"Not that I know of. Still, if someone really broke in there, that's kind of weird. I mean, there's nothing to steal." Sampson looked left and right, lowered his head, and then spoke softly. "I think someone must have broken in, though, because there was a bookcase pulled out, like someone was trying to get into the Walnut Door there."

"The Walnut Door?"

"That's what we've always called it. The candy guys used to bring huge bags of walnuts through a back door in the old days. It was a shortcut from outside, but they walled it up a long time ago."

Elizabeth's head was spinning as she listened. "I never noticed it before," she said, trying to sound as nonchalant as possible.

"You wouldn't, because they put a big bookshelf in front of it. That's the weird thing—I don't know how anyone would know about the door even being there." He looked down the hallway again. "You can take a peek if you like. I mean, you're Norbridge's granddaughter." He stepped aside as he turned the handle of the door to let her in. "But go kind of fast, okay? It's back there in the shelling room."

Elizabeth stepped inside. She made straight for the shelling room and saw, immediately, a bookcase on the far wall pulled away at an angle. Behind it, as she drew up close to observe, was an unremarkable brown door with a brass handle; it looked like the door to a broom closet.

Elizabeth glanced behind her and then tried the handle. It was locked tight. She ran her hand across the door and studied the bookcase. There didn't appear to be much to see. She was about to leave when she noticed a small brass plaque above the doorsill. She stood on her tiptoes to get a better look, and this is what she saw on the plaque:

WINTER

THE CHARM SEEMS SUCH A COMMON THING IN FORM AS SIMPLE AS A RING

She stared at the words, moved closer, and read the lines a dozen times. When she felt sure she had them memorized, she looked away, recited the words five times, and then looked at the plaque just to make sure she had everything fixed in her mind. She was about to leave when she felt moved to put her ear to the door and listen. She couldn't say why she wanted to do this, but before she knew it, she had placed her head against the door and was straining to hear if anything from within reached her ear.

As she stilled her own breathing and listened, she heard, from far away, what sounded like a low hum, like the noise an airplane makes before it takes off or the sound you hear in an elevator as it carries you to the top of a building. Elizabeth listened for a moment and wanted to make sure she wasn't just hearing the beating of her own heart echoing in her head. And when she was certain that, indeed, there was something making a noise from somewhere deep beyond the door, she left.

"Thanks for letting me look, Sampson."

"No problem," he said. "I just hope they figure out who did this."

"Me too," she said, the lines from the plaque dancing in her head. She lifted a hand. "I better get back to my room."

Sampson smiled. "Later!"

Elizabeth ran to 213, took out her notebook, and jotted down the lines she'd memorized. And then she added two new entries to her list:

12. *What the words on the plaque above the Walnut Door mean*
13. *Is the Walnut Door one of the entrances to Winterhouse's secret passageways?*

There's a connection, she thought as she lay down on her bed. *And I'm going to figure it out.*

PART TWO

CHRISTMAS APPROACHES— AND THE ALARM CHIMES

CHARM

CHAPTER 15

A REGRETTABLE MEETING

BLAME

When Elizabeth entered Winter Hall the next morning, it was already nearly full with guests seated for breakfast. Elizabeth looked around for Sampson or Jackson, hoping for more news about what had happened the night before or how Mrs. Trumble was doing, but she didn't see anyone she might ask. She scanned the room without locating Freddy, and so she took a seat at the nearest table. Although she was troubled by the events of the night before, she was pleased to find herself sitting with a friendly family of six from Wyoming, who told her they made it a point to come to Winterhouse every year for Christmas.

"I'm going to be living here from now on," Elizabeth told them proudly, and they congratulated her and said perhaps they would see her again in future years. Elizabeth realized how glad this made her feel, that not only would she now have a real home, but that she'd have the chance to see people like this family again.

"There you are," Freddy said, appearing with a plate of food in his hands and Elana beside him. Elizabeth felt instantly deflated; what she wanted was time alone with Freddy to talk to him about what she'd discovered in the candy kitchen.

"We were looking for you," Elana said. Her cheeks were rosy, as though she'd already been outside skating that morning and the color had lingered. Without Elana noticing, Freddy flashed Elizabeth a look that said, *I couldn't get rid of her*, and then he and Elana settled in at the table and joined in the conversation with the family from Wyoming. When they left, Elana said, "I guess people come from everywhere to stay here."

Her words sounded dismissive—"silly" was the word forming in Elizabeth's mind—but Elizabeth was resolved to be as nice as possible to Elana. *Don't take offense, and don't give offense*, she thought. She took a deep breath and said, "How's your grandmother doing?"

Elana put a hand to her chest. "Much better, thank you. I think she's just tired out from being here at this cool hotel. So much going on."

"Speaking of *going on*," Freddy said, "did you guys hear some noise last night?"

"Mrs. Trumble got hurt," Elizabeth said. She wasn't sure she wanted to bring this up in front of Elana, but there seemed no point in holding off now that Freddy had asked his question.

Elana began shaking her head. "Mrs. who?"

"One of the servers," Elizabeth said. She decided not to provide too many details—and definitely nothing about the door or the plaque—in front of Elana. "She blacked out in the candy kitchen."

Elana continued to look puzzled. "Is she okay?"

"Sounds like it," Elizabeth said. "She's resting, I guess."

"Well, I should be going," Elana said abruptly. Her face had gone white, and she looked as though she needed to lie down. "I need to get some skating in this morning. I have a big competition coming up when I get home." She stood to leave.

"And I've gotta work on the camera obscura," Freddy said. "A couple of the workers are going to help me for a few hours." He stood and so did Elizabeth.

"No problem," Elizabeth said. "I'm heading to the library." An awkward silence crept over the three of them, and Elizabeth wondered just what had come over Elana.

"The book girl!" someone said, and before she even turned around, Elizabeth recognized Rodney Powter's grating, ridiculing voice. She sensed him sidling up behind her, and when she glanced over her shoulder, sure enough, there he stood wearing his black hoodie and a pair of tattered jeans. He looked like he was dressed to spend a day at the mall rather than at a hotel beside an iced-over lake and snowy mountains. "Off to the library, Book Girl?" he said.

Elizabeth wheeled on him. "That's a really dumb thing to call me," she said. An image of Rodney dashing down the corridor, away from the candy kitchen, arose in her mind.

"Whoa!" Rodney said, his slack face suddenly arranged into something that looked vaguely shocked. "That's harsh. I was just saying hello."

Elizabeth was so exasperated she couldn't even find words; she just rolled her eyes and gave Freddy an *I can't believe what a jerk this guy is* expression. She expected Rodney or Elana to say something to each other, given that she'd seen them talking the night before by the skating rink, but a moment passed and no one said a thing.

"My name's Rodney," he said to Freddy in greeting; then he turned to Elana and did the same thing. "Rodney," he repeated, for emphasis.

"'Yonder,'" Freddy said, looking to Elizabeth and hoping she would understand he had just rearranged the letters of Rodney's name.

"Your name is Yonder?" Rodney said.

"Sorry, no," Freddy said. "I'm Freddy." Elizabeth suppressed a smile.

Rodney extended a hand to him and Elana in turn, and they offered brief greetings, all as Elizabeth stood, allowing her exasperation with Rodney to melt into bafflement. She had seen Rodney and Elana talking to each other the night before; she was positive.

"You two just met now?" Elizabeth said. For a split second, Rodney appeared almost as surprised as he had been two days before when Elizabeth had informed him in the library that she was Norbridge's granddaughter.

"Yes," Elana said. "Why's that?"

"No reason," Elizabeth said. "Just wondered."

"But you two already know each other?" Elana said, looking from Rodney to Elizabeth.

"She tried to steal my seat on the bus ride up here," Rodney said.

"That's not true!" Elizabeth let out an exasperated sigh; there was no point in explaining. She turned to Freddy. "I better get to the library. I have work to do."

Rodney lifted his hand and gave her a sarcastic thumbs-up. "Very, very cool!" he said in a lazy tone.

This irritated Elizabeth so badly, she could hardly restrain herself. "Maybe I'll see you and your parents wandering around there again. Or I'll see you running down the hallway late at night, just like last night."

"What's with you?" Rodney said.

"Are you okay?" Elana said to Elizabeth in a patronizing tone. Elizabeth felt she was about to scream; her thoughts clouded with the vision of Elana and Rodney by the skating rink.

"It's kind of interesting, isn't it," she said to Elana as she considered how fascinated Elana had been by the tour of the candy kitchen, "what happened to Mrs. Trumble?"

Elana's eyes clouded with hurt. "I don't understand what you mean."

Elizabeth looked to Elana and then to Rodney and

Freddy. She was waiting for Freddy to say something—anything—to stick up for her or clarify things. But he remained silent.

"Freddy," Elizabeth said, already turning to march out the door before them, "you want to walk with me?"

"Sure," he said. "See you, Elana. And Rodney."

"She's wacko," Rodney said, just as Elizabeth moved out of earshot. She was listening to hear what Elana said in return, but by then she was already too far away.

"Well, wait up, at least!" Freddy said.

Elizabeth spun around. "Those two are seriously bad news! We need to stay away from them."

Freddy's mouth dropped open in shock. "I was trying to be nice. I just met that guy, and we already agreed Elana is weird. What's up?"

Elizabeth took in a deep breath to collect her thoughts. "Rodney is a bully. And something's going on with him that I can't figure out. The bus, the library, him and Elana talking at the rink, and then—well, what I've been wanting to tell you is that I saw him running away from the candy kitchen late last night. I'm sure he had something to do with what happened to Mrs. Trumble. Someone attacked her. And whoever that someone was, they were trying to break into the kitchen. I'm positive Rodney's involved."

Freddy looked stunned. "Someone attacked her? Wow, that's hard to believe. But why would he break into the candy kitchen? If it was him. Or hurt Mrs. Trumble?"

"I don't know, but I have an idea." She explained how

she'd found the doorway and the plaque, and Freddy listened intently. "I think someone is trying to find one of the doorways into the secret passageway," Elizabeth said. "Someone wanted to poke around in there, and then when Mrs. Trumble heard them, the person knocked her out. That's what I think happened."

"I just hope she's okay," Freddy said. He paused. "Wow, you must have found one of the doors."

"I was thinking something else, too. Leona said there really did used to be a door in the library, and both she and Norbridge said there was one in Nestor's room—Norbridge's now."

"Three doors!" Freddy said.

"But the thing I was thinking was, if the word on top of the plaque is 'winter,' doesn't it make sense that there would be four doors? One for each season?"

"Makes sense. I just wonder where it would be."

"Four seasons and four doors," Elizabeth said. "Four, four."

"I got it. What? Is there something else?"

"Just like there are four sides to the Winterhouse seal," Elizabeth said. She was thinking, again, that she wanted to take another look at the book she'd seen at the store in Havenworth.

"You think there's a connection?" Freddy said.

"Let's keep thinking about it," Elizabeth said. "But don't mention anything about this to Elana. I'm headed to the library, and I know you have work to do. I'll look for you this afternoon, okay?"

CHAPTER 16

SOMETHING IN PLACE

CLAP

Three hours later, after Elizabeth had reshelved a small pallet of books, talked with Leona about the terrible attack on Mrs. Trumble, helped with checkouts at the front desk, and shown three guests where to find what they were looking for—all without incident—she headed to the reference room. She hadn't been there yet during her return to the hotel. In fact, she hadn't gone there at all after the New Year's Eve confrontation when she'd outsmarted Gracella and rescued Winterhouse, and she'd been both dreading and longing to visit the room again. If there was one thing the events of last year had taught her, it was that she could face her fears. She'd recently told herself she wouldn't be frightened over anything, and she'd found that the more she told herself this, the more true it became. As she headed up the library stairs, she resolved to add a new entry in her notebook—"Mottoes/Sayings to Keep in Mind"—and add last year's reminder ("*That* can't scare me!") as well as the words about not taking offense that Leona had shared.

When Elizabeth reached the third floor, all was quiet. She trod without a sound down the carpeted hallway, and then entered the nine-sided reference room, spacious and dim. It was hard to believe that in this very spot Gracella had threatened to kill Elizabeth and, through possession of The Book, destroy Winterhouse. The room was as peaceful as any place she could imagine, high shelves lining the walls, and hundreds of old and interesting books sitting in silent rows.

A rolling ladder stood against a far bookcase. The last time she'd been on it was when, right after Gracella's death, she had dropped The Book back where she'd found it, this in the hope that it would lie undisturbed. Elizabeth thought of how much she still didn't know about The Book—how it seemed that as long as she possessed it and was resolved not to unleash its power, all was fine, but if Gracella had uncovered its secret, she might have destroyed Winterhouse. At least, that was how Elizabeth interpreted the strange rhyme she had solved by using the Vigenère Cipher.

A thought came to her: She was curious to see The Book. Of course, she knew it would be where she'd left it—only she and Freddy even knew what it looked like, and Elizabeth had been all alone when she'd returned it. Still, she was curious. She glanced behind her, took a deep breath, and then rolled the ladder over to the section of the bookcase where she'd rehidden The Book. She climbed, and when she reached the top rung and was even with the highest shelf, she scanned the volumes there, recognizing a few from the year before: *The Pyramids of Ancient Egypt*; *Dreams and What They Mean*; *Astrology for You!* She was about to peek behind them when she felt the strange and familiar tremor of certainty.

"Elizabeth!" Elana, in a white dress and with a white ribbon in her hair, stood gaping at her from the doorway; her grandmother, in black, stood beside her. "What are you doing?"

"You scared me!" Elizabeth called, nearly tumbling off the ladder.

"I'm sorry, I didn't mean to." Elana looked puzzled. "What are you doing up there?"

"Just finding some books for the librarian," Elizabeth said as she climbed down, all the while trying to stop shaking. She hopped onto the thick carpet, arranged her shirt, and tried to look as casually as possible at Elana, who stepped slowly into the room, examining the spot atop the ladder Elizabeth had just vacated. She kept her eyes there for a moment and appeared to have forgotten Elizabeth completely. Her grandmother moved behind her without a sound, and Elizabeth felt deeply uncomfortable— not only because of the presence of Mrs. Vesper but because Elana was before her now just a few hours after their awkward run-in when Rodney had introduced himself at breakfast.

"So what are you doing here?" Elizabeth said with a nod.

Elana slid her gaze from the high shelves to Elizabeth. She glanced warily at her grandmother; once again, Elizabeth felt Elana was afraid of the older woman. "Oh, I finished skating," she said, "and I just wanted to poke around in the library."

"This is a fascinating place," Mrs. Vesper said, though she didn't sound fascinated at all. "I find the history of this hotel so intriguing."

The old woman stood beside Elana, and Elizabeth couldn't help feeling she had something of insistence about her, that she no longer wanted her granddaughter to say a word and would now take over.

"I've fallen in love with Winterhouse," she said, and leaned forward. "Enchanted. You must know so much about this hotel. You must have learned so many things."

"A little bit," Elizabeth said. Mrs. Vesper had placed a hand on Elana's back just below her neck, and if Elizabeth hadn't known any better, it would have appeared the old woman wanted to keep a grip on her, wanted to make sure Elana didn't move away or say the wrong thing.

"The proprietor's room must be like a museum," Mrs. Vesper said. "You've been inside?"

"Sure, I've been in there," Elizabeth said. "Why's that?"

Elana laughed nervously. "My grandmother's so nosy sometimes! She's always curious about everything." Elana

wriggled slightly; the old woman dropped her hand from her back and then snapped her head in the direction of the hallway as if she had heard some noise. The speed and vitality of Mrs. Vesper's movement startled Elizabeth; it seemed the reaction of a much younger woman.

"I'll let you girls catch up," Mrs. Vesper said. "Perhaps the two of you could spend more time together during this holiday. It would be so nice for all of us, in fact, to be closer." She looked to Elana. "My dear granddaughter has been hungry for . . . companionship."

Elana fixed Elizabeth with a look that was inscrutable— embarrassed and expectant and wary—and Elizabeth could make no sense of it. She thought about Elana losing her parents, and she tried to fit that into whatever was going on at this moment; but she was left confused.

With a nod, Mrs. Vesper moved away from the girls and departed.

"My grandmother gets kind of like that sometimes," Elana said. "I'm sorry." She glanced at the doorway. "And I . . . well, nothing."

Elana seemed a notch more at ease now that her grand-mother was gone, and for a moment it seemed she wanted to say something. But then she pasted a thin smile on her face and examined the bookcase nearest her before looking at Elizabeth once more. "I guess I just wanted to apologize for what happened after breakfast this morning. That was kind of uncomfortable, and I think I was accidentally not so nice. So I just wanted to say sorry."

Elizabeth hadn't expected this at all. "It's okay. I was

actually a little impolite to you, too, so . . . I'm sorry for that. I was just surprised when Rodney showed up."

"Well, that guy was pretty rude to you. I was being nice because he was new and all, but I didn't like how he treated you."

"You know, I thought I saw you talking to Rodney last night by the skating rink."

Elana startled almost imperceptibly, her lips parting. "Last night? No, I wasn't out there last night. You must have seen someone else." She shook her head in a way that suggested the whole thing was an impossible misunderstanding. "Hey, Elizabeth, I kind of get the feeling that you and I got started on the wrong foot. I really want to be friends, okay? If you want to."

Once again, Elizabeth wasn't sure what to say. She didn't want to be rude, but she also didn't trust Elana; she was certain there was something about her that didn't add up. "Well, no hard feelings or anything on my side."

Elana touched a hand to her forehead. "Whew! That's a relief. My grandmother likes you, too. Maybe you could spend some time with us. Or we could go into town, go shopping, something like that. There was that bookstore, too, you mentioned. I love books. Like you." She glanced at the bookcase. "But I don't want to keep you from your work. It looked like you were right in the middle of something." She smoothed her hair behind her ears.

"No problem," Elizabeth said.

Elana was mulling something over. "It would be fun to go to Havenworth. So, you know, just think about it. My grandmother and I—we do a lot of fun things together. Maybe you'd like to be a part of it."

Despite Elana's assurances that there was a lot of fun to be had in spending time with her and her grandmother, she actually didn't sound all that enthusiastic.

"A part of it?" Elizabeth said. "I don't know what you mean."

"Just . . . well, it's hard to explain. If you come with us sometime, I can explain better."

Elizabeth was lost and felt certain there was something behind Elana's words, but just what it was she couldn't be sure.

"I'll see," she said. "I better get back to work, though."

"Okay," Elana said, smiling again. She glanced up at the top shelf once more. "I guess what I really wanted to say was . . . just, you know, watch out." She laughed lightly and then added awkwardly, "I mean, on the ladder, and stuff like that."

"I've climbed the ladder lots of times," Elizabeth said, though she wasn't entirely sure she had caught Elana's meaning.

Elana fixed her with a deep stare. "I wouldn't want you to get hurt."

The moment seemed to stretch out, and Elizabeth felt it was the oddest part of the morning yet. "I'll be fine," she said.

Elana tossed her head gently. "Maybe I'll see you later today." She left the room.

Elizabeth considered what had just happened. Elana

had made some sort of invitation to her as well as offered a warning, but why? It was bizarre, she thought, but she decided to put it out of her mind. She climbed up the ladder, peered behind the row of books on the top shelf, and spotted what she was looking for: *A Guide for Children: Games, Secrets, Pastimes, and More.* The thin brown volume lay at the rear of a row of books, looking drab and ordinary. The Book was still there—though, with a tremor of uncertainty, like hearing a clap of distant thunder, Elizabeth wondered if perhaps it was in a slightly different position than she'd left it.

"Stay there," she said, dismissing the thought and pointing to The Book. "Forever."

She climbed down the ladder, went downstairs, and left to find Freddy for lunch.

CHAPTER 17

QUESTIONS—AND A TELESCOPE

ELATED

After a long discussion with Freddy over lunch and then an early afternoon spent sledding with him, Elizabeth helped Mr. Rajput and Mr. Wellington for an hour, finding four pieces that fit in the temple puzzle. She inspected the Winterhouse seal for a bit and then read in her room before heading to dinner.

"We should check out the ice castle tomorrow," Freddy said as the two of them ate their grilled salmon and rice dinners. "I guess Norbridge has it all fixed up for Christmas."

Elizabeth closed her eyes for a moment and then turned to look at Freddy. "Castle," she said. "Cleats."

"You haven't lost the touch!" He glanced around. "No sign of Elana or her grandmother."

Elizabeth looked, too. "Or the Powters. Doesn't it seem odd to come to Winterhouse and stay in your room so much?"

"Maybe they all like to watch TV or something." Freddy leaned into Elizabeth with bug eyes and assumed a creepy voice. "Or maybe they're all into black magic."

"Don't joke," she said. "There's something going on. I'm sure of it. I just don't understand why Elana seems so afraid of her grandmother. I also feel like . . . I don't know. Like she wants to tell me something but she can't bring herself to do it."

Freddy lifted his head and looked to the kitchen doors. "I hope they serve pie tonight."

The huge dining room was becoming more filled with Christmas decorations each day, and now it was glistening with ceiling streamers and green-and-red banners on the walls and huge wreaths above the windows and ornately decorated trees in all corners. The hall was alive with color and music, and the enormous fireplace crackled with a bright fire. Norbridge, however, wasn't at dinner, and Elizabeth was becoming concerned about him.

"Hello, you two," someone said as Elizabeth and Freddy stood to leave Winter Hall. And there, entering from the rear doors, was Mrs. Trumble, looking as fit and pleasant as ever.

"Mrs. Trumble!" Elizabeth called as she dashed over to her. "You're all right!"

They hugged tightly, and Elizabeth explained how she'd been at the candy kitchen and seen the crowd that had gathered and had heard all about the strange events.

"I feel fine now," Mrs. Trumble said. "I had quite a scare there, but I'm fine."

"Did someone really attack you?" Freddy said.

The old woman arched her eyebrows to indicate the whole thing was a mystery to her. "I thought I heard someone in the kitchen, but when I started looking around, I didn't see anything. Suddenly there was a flash of red, and that's all I remember."

"I'm just glad you're all right."

"I'm fine as can be now, and Norbridge has been looking into the incident."

"I haven't even seen him since yesterday," Elizabeth said, thinking about the red flash.

"He needed to leave the hotel for a bit," Mrs. Trumble said, "though he returned this afternoon. He's been looking after his cousin Kiona, as well. She was feeling a bit under the weather. Perhaps you remember her?"

"I do," Elizabeth said. "She's the one about to turn one hundred next year."

"You do remember. Well, as I mentioned, Norbridge is back now and wants to talk to you. He's in the observatory."

"On the top floor?"

"Yes, dear. He sent me to find you. He'd like you to

come up." She looked to Freddy. "Just the miss, young man."

Freddy grinned. "That's okay, Mrs. Trumble," he said, turning to face the kitchen doors. "More dessert for me."

"I'm so glad to see you!" Elizabeth said when Norbridge opened the door to the observatory.

"Me too," he said, scooping her up in a tight hug. "And I'm sorry I've been unavailable."

They were in a small room on the thirteenth floor. It had very little in the way of furnishings, but it did have a huge brass telescope inside a glass-enclosed balcony extending ten feet from the building. It was on this spot that Norbridge had once shown Elizabeth a statue of Winifred set on a pedestal far across Lake Luna.

"You saw Mrs. Trumble?" he said as the two of them sat on sofas at the center of the room, a coffee table between them.

"She told me you wanted to see me. Have you found out who attacked her?"

Norbridge shook his head. "Nothing yet. But how have things been with you so far?"

Over the next ten minutes, Elizabeth caught Norbridge up on everything that had happened and everything she had learned—the passageways, the strangeness of Elana and her grandmother, her time in the library, and how she'd seen Rodney running down the corridor on the night of the attack. What she didn't mention—because she knew

Norbridge wouldn't approve—was how she'd spied on and startled the Powters and also that she'd investigated in the candy kitchen and seen the strange inscription on the plaque.

"I think someone knows about the secret passageways," she said, "and they want to get in, so they broke into the candy kitchen. One of the doors is even supposed to be in your room, from what Leona said." She hadn't been sure how to bring this up. "Is it?"

Norbridge drummed his fingers on the arm of the sofa. "There is a door. Absolutely."

"I knew it!" She tried to picture where it might be, given that she didn't recall seeing any extra door in Norbridge's room on those occasions when she'd visited.

"However," he said, "I locked and secured it years ago. The others, too. There are a few gloomy old tunnels around this place, but I felt they were a potential hazard. So—all locked."

"But someone wanted to get in. Maybe because there's something else magical in there, right? Leona told me there was a story that there might be another object waiting to be found."

Norbridge looked to the ceiling as if to discover what to say. "I'm of the opinion," he said, when he looked at her again, "that it's not completely out of the question that there couldn't be some question regarding the question of the questionable existence of the object in question."

Elizabeth rubbed her temples to avoid the onset of a headache. "So I might be right."

"Correct."

"I just don't get why The Book or any special objects exist. Why did Riley Granger create these things or hide them here? You told me he had this idea that whoever found the things would have to decide if they were going to do something good or bad with them. But I just don't get why."

"My theory is that Riley enjoyed creating games with Nestor. It was part of something they'd learned during their time at the temple. And, yes, if I had to guess, I'd say there's another object or two in this hotel. I don't think Riley stopped at The Book."

Elizabeth adjusted her glasses. "Do you think my parents' death was really an accident? Maybe Gracella came looking for my mom—maybe she caused the accident."

Norbridge nodded. "It has crossed my mind more than a few times. That would have been a way for her to snuff out the Falls line. I'm sure if she did cause the accident, she probably thought she had killed the last of us." He dipped his head toward Elizabeth. "Or, at least, the youngest of us."

"But I was the only one who could find The Book, right? So, if she had killed me, she never would have found it." Elizabeth shook her head in confusion.

"I think Gracella changed the whole equation when she accumulated her powers over the years. Maybe she could have found The Book on her own, but you were the surest route to it. Once she killed Winnie and her husband, Ferland—*if* she did—maybe her powers diminished. Then she located you and tried to use you to secure The Book. She was always hungry for more power, more knowledge."

"Is that why you left Winterhouse when you were younger? To learn more about magic?"

"Someone's been reading Marshall's journal," Norbridge said. "Or talking a lot with our chatty librarian." He made a small check mark in the air with a finger.

"I read that chapter about you leaving."

Norbridge sighed. "I left in part because I wanted to find Gracella, maybe convince her to change her ways. But I never found her. I did some backpacking, worked on a ranch, rode trains across the country. I suppose I was something of a hobo. And then I came back to Winterhouse."

"Sounds adventurous."

"Most of it was. But do you recall what I mentioned to you about Winnie and what she went through? When I left the hotel, I had similar questions. Also, something about Gracella's curiosity and her interest in darker things seemed a bit intriguing to me back then." He paused and then said, his voice low, "How much have they developed?"

Elizabeth wasn't sure she'd heard him correctly. "How much . . ."

"Your powers," Norbridge said. The room grew silent. "Can you call things up at will?"

This was the first time he had spoken to her so directly about this—and she was glad of it. "I can, yes. Almost all the time. I'm not always totally successful, but usually."

Norbridge reached out and pulled a book from the small stack on the coffee table. He set it down. "Give it a try."

She looked at the volume: *The Gloom After Midnight* by Damien Crowley.

"Hey, that's the same writer whose book you gave me last year."

"One of my favorites. He passed away several years ago, but, boy, could he write! He used to visit us here from time to time." He pointed to the book.

Elizabeth brought her mind to a complete pause, allowed everything in it to become quiet as she stared at the volume. Her vision blurred as she concentrated, the flutters beginning deep inside. She kept her eyes locked on the book, and everything else in the room seemed to slide to the periphery. The book began to vibrate on the table; something inside it appeared to have stirred to life. A buzzing sound deepened in Elizabeth's ears, and suddenly the book popped off the table right toward her, and she caught it with both hands.

"Very nice!" Norbridge said. "That's impressive."

She examined the book for a moment and then displayed it for Norbridge. "May I read it?" she said, and he gave her a *go ahead* dip of his chin with a little laugh.

"Is that the extent of it?" Norbridge said.

"Sometimes I can tell when something's going to happen before it does or if someone is approaching or about to call me. It's not always very clear, but it happens a lot."

He nodded and invited her to continue.

"I've only been here a few days, but I think it's getting stronger." She displayed the book again. "Back in Drere, the best I could do was make a book tumble to the floor."

Norbridge stood. "As I say, I'm impressed. Just be sure to use it for proper ends."

Elizabeth felt challenged by these words; Norbridge was insisting on repeating a message. "You've mentioned that a few times. Are you worried about something?"

"It's fair to say I'm always worried about many things." He spoke slowly. "And you're my granddaughter, so I will always be worried about you."

Elizabeth glanced around the room; she knew Norbridge needed to get to work, but she chanced one last question: "Is this room just used for your observatory?"

Norbridge stroked his beard and then tilted his head in a *follow me* gesture. At the end of the short hallway off the living room was a single door he unlocked with his silver key. He gave Elizabeth a curious squint, and then he pushed the door open.

Two dimly lit standing lamps in opposite corners cast a soft glow over the carpeted room, which was dominated by the ceiling-to-floor window opposite the door. Only the black sky was visible through it at this hour. And although the enormous window was very dramatic, and the cluttered desk and the cabinets and bookshelves and two chairs at the center of the room were all cozy and inviting, what drew Elizabeth's gaze were the walls to the left and right as she followed Norbridge inside: They were covered with shiny murals done in small blue and white tiles. There were depictions—each about three feet square, so that the walls were divided into two dozen murals apiece—of climbers on mountains, skiers on trails, snowshoers on hilltops, Winterhouse beneath the full moon, and many more. The loveliness of it left Elizabeth gaping.

"They call this sort of decoration *azulejo*," Norbridge said. "It's a type of tilework from Spain and Portugal. Nestor fell in love with it and had this room decorated in the style." He studied the walls approvingly. "Good call on his part."

"Incredible," Elizabeth said as she looked more closely at a picture to her right. A caption beneath it read "The Tragic and Heartbreaking Death of Dominic Falls—Struck by an Icicle in His Youth." The picture—like all, in ornate blue upon creamy white—showed a small boy beside a cliff glancing upward at a menacing row of enormous icicles.

"My great-uncle Lambert's son," Norbridge said. "Poor boy was five years old. He never had a chance." He stood shaking his head sadly for a moment before gesturing to a scene near it. "Look at this one."

Elizabeth studied the picture: two men—one of whom she recognized as the great scientist Albert Einstein—standing beside a blackboard covered with equations. The caption read "Milton Falls and Albert Einstein—Two Geniuses, 'Relativity' Speaking, in Winter Hall." Elizabeth looked to Norbridge. "Albert Einstein came to Winterhouse?"

"He did. And that's a bad little pun there on the tiles.

My father's responsible for that. I tried to talk him out of it." He pointed to a mural on the opposite wall. "There's one you'll like."

Elizabeth examined the picture, which showed a young girl in a thick parka standing atop a snowy peak. "The Youngest Person to Make an Ascent of Mount Arbaza—The Intrepid and Fearless Winifred Falls, Eleven Years Old," read the caption beneath.

"My mother climbed that mountain when she was eleven?" Elizabeth said. She felt a surge of pride and admiration inside.

"Not only did she climb that mountain!" Norbridge said, lifting a finger and raising his voice. "At the summit she removed three bars of Kendal Mint Cake from her pack and offered them to her fellow expeditioners. We were astonished. And we polished off that candy in three minutes flat. I'll never forget it." He took a deep breath. "I had that picture made—and a few more in here. All of these depictions show a famous scene from Winterhouse's storied past." He gestured to an empty section of the wall. "Whoever takes over after I'm gone will continue."

"I'd love to spend time looking at all of these," Elizabeth said. Not only were the pictures stunning, but they were the stories of her own family.

Norbridge glanced at the walls slowly; he looked like a man in a museum sorting through his feelings for the works before him. "Nestor started this. He was subject to what is known as horror vacui. That is, 'fear of empty spaces,' and it led him to decorate these walls. Then

Nathaniel carried on the tradition, and I followed." He paused. "This is my office. First Nestor's, then my father's, now mine." He looked to her. "You're the fifth person to ever enter this room."

Elizabeth felt a chill through her. "Who was the fourth?" she said.

"Winnie. I assumed she would take over someday."

The chill Elizabeth felt deepened. There was something important occurring, though this visit had been so clearly unplanned Elizabeth didn't know what to make of it. All she could imagine was that Norbridge, on impulse, had wanted to share the magic of the room with her. Anything more than that was too much to consider, at least for now.

"It's an incredible room," she said. "I hope to see it again someday."

"I'm sure you will." He tilted his head toward the door. "I'm very sorry, but duty calls. I'll need to see you out."

When they stepped back into the living room, Norbridge gave a glance at *The Gloom After Midnight*. "Don't forget your book," he said as he hugged Elizabeth. "And maybe you want to go give Leona a hand closing up for the night."

"Thank you," she said. "For everything."

Ten minutes later, book in hand, Elizabeth arrived at the library, prepared to enjoy a visit with Leona. But as she reached for the door handle, she heard loud and angry voices within.

CHAPTER 18

A SINISTER DISCOVERY

STRIDES

"We absolutely close in ten minutes, and everyone must be out by then," Leona was saying. "I apologize if that doesn't fit your schedule, but that is how we run things." She was speaking in her "firm" voice, and Elizabeth wondered to whom she was talking—and then she entered the library and saw Leona was almost nose to nose with Rodney Powter.

"But I just got here an hour ago," he said, his voice harsh. "I want to stay for a while."

"You are very welcome to return first thing in the morning and remain the entire day, if you choose," Leona said. "But in ten minutes, these doors are closing and you will be on the other side of them."

Rodney was about to speak when he saw Elizabeth.

"Oh, and Book Girl is here now, too," he said. "I bet she gets to stay in here all night if she wants." He lifted a hand, more of a challenge than a wave. "Hello, Book Girl!"

"Young man," Leona said, "you are being disrespectful, and I must ask you to leave."

"I thought you said I had ten more minutes!"

"That was half a minute ago. Now you have been discourteous, and the library closes for you right now. If you don't leave immediately, I will speak to the management, and you and your family will be escorted from the hotel. I'm sure your parents will be very happy about that."

Rodney stood tall and straight. "You can't do that!" he said in an ugly tone.

"Just try me," Leona said. She glanced at her watch. "Forty-five seconds and counting."

Rodney glared at Elizabeth, and then he turned back to Leona. He looked about as frustrated and angry as a person could be.

"I'll be back in the morning," he said.

"You'll be welcome," Leona said. "But if you're at all ill-mannered . . ." With this, she made a slicing motion across her throat that almost made Elizabeth laugh. She had never seen Leona like this before.

Rodney glared at Elizabeth again.

"What are you looking at?" he said.

"I think the clock is still ticking," Elizabeth said.

"Fifteen seconds," Leona said.

And with that, Rodney spun on his heels and stalked out of the library, scowling at Elizabeth as he went.

Leona stood looking after him, shaking her head.

"Incredible," she said softly. "Sometimes I worry about the generation that's going to take over this world."

"It's his parents," Elizabeth said. "They're just like he is."

"Still, that is hands down the most uncouth young man I have ever had the misfortune to encounter in this exquisite library of ours."

Elizabeth looked to Leona. "Don't give offense, don't take offense."

Leona turned to her. "You're learning," she said after a moment's pause.

"Why was he so dead set on staying here?"

Leona shook her head. "Something's going on with him that I can't figure out. He's been in here the last hour-plus, just wandering around."

"Looking for books?" Elizabeth couldn't picture Rodney Powter being interested in anything in the library other than, maybe, a magazine about computer games.

"That's the odd thing," Leona said. "He wasn't looking for books at all. He just wandered around the first floor scanning everywhere. If I didn't know better, I would have thought he was looking for cracks in the walls."

"That's what I saw him and his parents doing a couple days ago." Elizabeth was thinking back to how she'd spied on Rodney and his parents and the odd things they'd said. The library walls were nearly covered with large framed paintings and old photographs and notices that had been hung years before and had remained untouched.

"Do you think he was looking for the old doorway here in the library?" Elizabeth said.

"But how in the world would that ruffian know about any of that?"

Elizabeth couldn't answer Leona's question, but that didn't stop her from feeling very anxious about the whole thing. "Do you know where the passageway was before it was destroyed?"

Leona pointed to a far wall, one where dozens of bookcases stood. The wall was entirely covered with a massive shelf and, on the wall, a spread of paintings.

"Right over there," she said.

"What if there's something still there that he's looking for?"

"Impossible. First, that he knows anything, and, second, that something is there. That door was walled up long ago, and the passageway destroyed."

Elizabeth studied the wall Leona had pointed out. "But Rodney's looking for something."

"We'll deal with him in the morning, if he returns." She checked her watch. "Closing time. But what brings you down here at this hour?" Leona locked the library doors.

"I just wanted to say hi."

"Pot of tea? And then I need to get to bed."

An hour later, after tea with Leona and then a quick stop in the portrait gallery, Elizabeth found Freddy in the camera obscura room and they decided to go for a swim. On their way to the pool, they stopped in the lobby, where Mr. Wellington and Mr. Rajput were working at their table.

"How's the puzzle going tonight?" Elizabeth said.

"Hello!" said the chipper Mr. Wellington. "All's well here."

Mr. Rajput sighed slowly without looking up. "Greetings," he murmured. "Discouraging progress. Very discouraging. There are so many other enticements for you here at Winterhouse—things more enjoyable than working on a puzzle with two old men—but I'm certain we would be so much further along if you could spare a bit more of your time now and again. Our efforts are so plodding, and it creates so much unhappiness."

"Oh, come now, Mr. Rajput," Mr. Wellington said. "The girl's entitled to her fun."

"It's all right," Elizabeth said. "I love working on the puzzle. I'll help tomorrow for sure. There's just been so much to do since I got here." She moved closer to the puzzle. "You've really done a lot," she said, studying the stone temple, the rugged mountains behind it, and the deep blue sky above. "I'll bet you'll finish in a few more visits."

"If we had more help, yes," Mr. Rajput said. "This puzzle is difficult enough with just the two of us putting in the time." He shook his head in incomprehension and despair.

"Mr. Rajput, enough!" Mr. Wellington said. "Chin up!

Face forward! Be manly about it, goodness! Hut, two, three, four! March, march, march, march! Sin, dex! Sin, dex!"

Mr. Wellington was teasing his friend mercilessly, and Elizabeth and Freddy couldn't help but laugh as Mr. Wellington continued. "Sin, dex! Sin, dex!" he chanted.

"It's all an enormous joke to you, isn't it, Mr. Wellington?" Mr. Rajput said.

The other man put a hand to his bald head and laughed loudly.

"What does 'sin, dex' mean?" Freddy said. "I've never heard that before."

"Old Roman marching orders," Mr. Wellington said.

"I take it they don't teach Latin at your schools," Mr. Rajput said. And before either Elizabeth or Freddy could answer, he said, "It means 'left, right, left, right.'"

"In abbreviation, that is," Mr. Wellington added. "'Sinister' means 'left,' and 'dexter' means 'right.'"

Elizabeth felt herself freeze. "Can you say that again?" She looked to Freddy, who had an expression on his face that mirrored hers.

"It's Latin," Mr. Wellington said. "The Latin word for 'right' is 'dexter,' and the Latin word for 'left' is 'sinister.'"

Elizabeth turned back to Mr. Wellington and, without thinking about it, put a hand to her necklace. "That's what I thought you said."

Freddy looked as though he might jump out of his skin. "We better get to the pool!" he said, and he and Elizabeth began to dash off.

"Isn't the pool that way?" Mr. Wellington said, but the kids had already disappeared around the corner.

Two minutes later, Elizabeth and Freddy were examining the Winterhouse seal on the marble floor at the center of the four-way corridor.

"'With sinister starts that end at gate,'" Elizabeth said as she studied the inscription. "This has something to do with the left side of . . . of what?" She glanced around, even held out her left arm because she thought it might help her discover whatever unknown thing she was seeking.

"I don't know," Freddy said, just as absorbed in peering at the seal as Elizabeth was.

They spent a few minutes examining each rectangle in turn, reading the words and numbers aloud.

"If you ask me," Freddy said, tilting his head even as he kept his eyes on the seal, "something starts on the left side somewhere, and then ends at a gate. But I don't know what it all adds up to."

Suddenly, the slightest tremor of the familiar feeling came over Elizabeth, and then, almost as quickly as it had arisen, it vanished. She glanced around, half expecting to see someone turning a corner, though no one appeared.

"You okay?" Freddy said.

"I'm fine." She allowed her momentary premonition to fade, but even as it did, she realized she had the urge to mention *the feeling* to Freddy. In fact, she'd been thinking for some time—throughout the year as they had emailed each other—that she might tell him about the power she'd first recognized at Winterhouse during the previous Christmas. The one piece about the fight with Gracella she'd never told Freddy was how she herself had made The Book move simply by focusing on it, and this had allowed her to rescue it from Gracella. She wondered now, as she had wondered for months, if it was maybe wrong to keep this from her friend.

"I wish I'd spent more time with that book in Havenworth," she said, dismissing these thoughts. "Someone named Dylan Grimes wrote it, and I have a feeling there might have been something in there that could help us out in his chapter about seals."

"Hey!" Freddy said. "Do you think a 'gate' could be the same thing as a 'doorway'?"

"You might be right," Elizabeth said; it felt as though a light was flicking on so that everything could be seen clearly. "That would mean something starts on the left side and ends at each doorway. And it would also mean there definitely are four doorways."

"What about all the other words on this seal?" Freddy said. "And the numbers?"

"No idea yet. But let's keep this quiet around Elana."

"She and her grandmother were so interested in the passageways," Freddy said. "And then Elana wanted to know everything about the candy kitchen."

"There has to be some connection," Elizabeth said. "With Rodney, too. He definitely wasn't just running away that night because he was scared."

"It would be so cool to figure out this seal and whatever else is going on," Freddy said.

Elizabeth laughed. "What happened to the regular, normal, not-weird-at-all Christmas at Winterhouse?"

"Weird. Wired. Wider." Freddy pushed at his glasses and raised his arms in triumph. "The anagram king still rules!"

All at once, *the feeling* descended on Elizabeth—it was like the sensation of a window opening and cold air pressing on her. She looked to the far corridor. Mrs. Vesper turned the corner and, seeing them, stopped in place.

"Hello," Elizabeth said, a bit too quickly.

"Good evening," the old lady said, without changing her expression. She nodded to them as she approached. "Have either of you seen my granddaughter?"

"I haven't seen her," Freddy said, looking to Elizabeth.

"Me neither," Elizabeth said. She was trying to calm herself, but she felt sure she was blushing.

Mrs. Vesper's black eyes flickered. She inclined her head toward Elizabeth. "This seal is fascinating, isn't it?"

Elizabeth felt her resolve building; the last thing she wanted was for Mrs. Vesper to see that she was rattled. "Very," she said. "There are all sorts of fascinating things at Winterhouse, that's for sure."

Mrs. Vesper stared at her. "As I've come to learn." She paused. "Good evening." She gave a nod and then resumed walking.

Freddy watched her as she moved silently away, and then he whispered to Elizabeth, "That woman freaks me out."

"Me too," Elizabeth said, and as she stood watching, she replayed in her mind the conversation she and Freddy had been having before they'd been interrupted. An alarming thought came to her. "Do you think she heard what we were talking about?"

Freddy bit his lip. "I hope not." He looked to the corridor. "Come on, let's get going."

CHAPTER 19

THE RIPPLINGTON SILVER CORRIDOR COVER

Elizabeth reported to the library at nine o'clock the next morning. After half an hour—with, thankfully, no sign of Rodney Powter—Elizabeth noticed a lady on the first floor looking this way and that.

"Hi," Elizabeth said. "May I help you find something?"

The woman, middle-aged and wearing a brown sweater and plaid skirt, gave her an indulgent half smile. "Thank you, but I'm looking for the librarian."

"I'm the assistant. Maybe I can help you."

The woman nodded dismissively. "I need to talk to the real librarian. I'm looking for some very specific items."

Elizabeth felt her chest tightening but tried to keep

herself calm. *Don't give offense, and don't take offense,* she thought.

"Miss Leona Springer is the head librarian," Elizabeth said. "But as her helper, I can assist you."

The woman was scanning the far corners of the library, perhaps hoping to catch sight of Leona. When Elizabeth remained standing before her, the woman lowered her gaze and said, "Please stop badgering me." She looked away.

All of Elizabeth's resolve fled. "Oh, you're looking for a book on badgers?" she said. "Yes, that makes a lot of sense. Section C-28 on the second floor. Tons and tons of books on animals, and even a few with photographs of badgers in them, in case you just wanted to look at the pictures."

"You've got to be kidding!" the woman said, fixing Elizabeth with a glare; just then Leona came from around the nearest bookcase.

"Kidding, yes!" Leona said with a laugh. "Our lovely assistant, Miss Somers, is a great kidder!" She came and put an arm around Elizabeth's shoulders. "Would you mind finishing the filing in our office, dear, and I'll join you shortly?" She turned to Elizabeth with the sternest look she had ever given her, and even gave a firm press on her back to send her on her way.

"I . . . I will," Elizabeth said, suddenly feeling foolish. She looked to the woman in the plaid skirt. "I'm sorry. I didn't mean to say what I said."

The woman sighed with annoyance. "It's quite all right," she said tersely.

Elizabeth headed for the office, feeling terrible not only for what had just happened but for being unable to shake the sense that she wasn't really learning the basics about being a librarian—and was having trouble keeping her cool.

"That assistant of yours was very rude," Elizabeth heard the woman say to Leona.

"I appreciate the observation," Leona said curtly. "Now, may I help you locate a book?"

When Elizabeth entered the office, she decided to read Marshall's journal—maybe she could forget about how poorly she'd behaved—and, with any luck, learn something more about the secret passageways. She opened the enormous book and scanned the contents to see if anything stood out; Miles bobbed on his perch but remained silent. She skimmed over chapters titled "The Most Foul-Mannered Movie Star in the World Spends Eleven Days Too Long at Winterhouse: Chas Calloway's Twelve-Day Stay with Us," and "My Sister Becomes a Nun," and "Ice on Lake Luna till August!" and then found herself intrigued by a chapter named "The Complete and Total Blocking Off of the Ripplington Mine Shafts." She began to read:

As you will recall from earlier chapters, the Ripplington Mining Company at one time dominated the landscape and countryside and region in the area around Winterhouse, with their operations, which were mines, i.e., holes dug into the ground from which were carved or hewn or hacked out all manner of minerals and other things.

However, in 1887, after careful investigation coupled with lengthy study, the president of the Ripplington Mining Company, Mr. Wilhelm Balsa Ripplington, determined that because of the tenacious permafrost throughout the region and the fact that temperatures in the region typically remained below freezing for four or five or even six months out of the year, his mining operations were unduly difficult, and his company had lost seven million dollars over its fifty years of existence. With this, he decided to relocate to warmer climes where the ground was softer and much easier to dig into, which is why the Ripplington Mining Company is now located in the deserts of Arizona and New Mexico. Before departing the area here, though, Mr. Ripplington had all of his mines plugged up so that people and animals wouldn't stumble and fall into an open pit or a dangerous hole. . . .

Elizabeth, amazed as always by Marshall Falls's unique way of explaining things, skimmed the next two pages of the journal, in which Marshall tediously described the filling in of twenty-two separate mine shafts. And then she came to the last description:

Finally, the greatest mine of all had to be plugged up, and this was the grand and massive Ripplington Silver

Corridor, whose entrance was one and a half miles from the hotel. In fact, there is a curious legend that the twisting, winding, mazelike tunnels of the mine extended beneath Winterhouse itself and that the fabled "secret passageways" said to exist within our walls connected to this enormous silver mine.

I have never believed this, of course, but it was a persistent rumor, one discussed frequently and often within the family. The story was that there was a corridor between Nestor's bedroom and the candy kitchen—and I can vouch for this very brief walkway (though hardly a "secret passageway" at all, but more of a little tunnel that allowed our illustrious founder to pop in for a square or two or three of Flurschen whenever he desired), because I myself was inside of it on three occasions—but beyond that, there were no passageways. That is, aside from the one that led from Nestor's room to the library itself, so that he could, when he chose, make his way to the library and thus evade his wife's displeasure at the fact that he so often had his nose buried in books. She had mandated the library doors be locked at nine o'clock every evening, and so if Nestor found himself at midnight wanting to read a book about, say, popular hairstyles in ancient Mesopotamia or why whale skin is found only on whales, he could simply stroll down the passageway from his room to the library and procure whatever he desired.

This passageway, of course, was demolished when

the library was renovated as part of the expansion efforts here at Winterhouse, the campaign to "improve the place," and "make it bigger," and "allow for more guests." I should add, as well, there was the ill-advised "passageway" that led to another room and that connected with the one from Nestor's room to the candy kitchen and the library. But this boondoggle of a mistake was more of an emergency exit, and I was glad it was hidden away once Nathaniel took over. But my point is that the legend persisted that Nestor's passageway converged on a spur of the mine itself, effectively creating a veritable catacomb beneath the hotel, a twisting tomb of tunnels, an arctic ants' nest, a permafrost prairie-dog town, a mountain maze! And so Mr. Ripplington poured tons and tons of pulverized rock into the entranceway to the mine, and he . . .

Elizabeth was breathless, and she skimmed ahead over the next few pages to see if there were any more references to the secret passageways. Marshall, however, simply went on and on about the mines themselves, and then he ended the chapter by explaining an idea he had to turn the pebbles on the shores of Lake Luna into glass crystal.

There were four doors into a main passageway, Elizabeth thought. *One in Nestor's room, one in the candy kitchen, one in the library, and one somewhere else. And they all joined the main passageway, and it connected to tunnels even deeper under the hotel.* She closed the journal and stared at it. *Where is the fourth door?*

"Hello, dear," Leona said as she entered the office. Elizabeth turned. Leona did not look upset, but she also didn't have her usual bright expression. "Let's sit. I'd like to talk to you."

⚜

"Elizabeth," Leona began, after she'd made rose tea and they were sitting at the small table in the corner of her office, "you know I love you dearly and have full confidence in your ability—in time—to look after the library. But there is an additional piece to all of this, and that is learning how to interact politely and gracefully with the guests who visit us."

Elizabeth had been prepared for this and had hardly needed to work herself up to apologize to Leona, because she already knew how wrong she was.

"I lost it there," Elizabeth said. "That was my fault completely, and I'm sorry."

"But you can't let people like that get under your skin."

"But she was so rude!" Elizabeth, feeling agitated again, began hearing the woman's voice and seeing her face as she had dismissed her.

"And that's an excuse for acting the same in return?" Leona said softly. She took a sip of tea. "Is that woman in control of your emotions, or are you?"

Elizabeth was stunned. She'd never thought of it this way, and as she sat trying to come up with reasons she was justified for responding as she had, she kept coming back to the fact that she was the one who'd lost her cool—the woman in the plaid skirt hadn't moved her lips for her.

"You're right," Elizabeth said. She thought of her aunt and uncle, how they were always blaming Elizabeth when something went wrong. Even when it wasn't her fault, they would get upset with her over little things, and they would get even more upset for being upset, as if Elizabeth were responsible for all of it. "My aunt and uncle were that way, always blaming me or saying I started something."

"We all tend to do that," Leona said. "Make it seem that others are responsible if we end up acting poorly. But I need you to be pleasant to everyone in the library. If not, you're just going to end up being miserable yourself, grousing inside about how mean or discourteous other people are. There will always be reasons to justify being impolite in return." Leona lifted her glasses but didn't put them on. "Be better than that."

Elizabeth nodded and sat in silence for a long moment. "I understand. I really do."

Leona set her cup of tea down and gave Elizabeth a small, warm smile. "Come here, dear. Please."

Although she couldn't guess what Leona might want, Elizabeth stood and moved to her. "Yes?" she said.

Leona waved her forward even closer with a little inward flick of her hands, and before Elizabeth knew it, Leona was embracing her gently.

"You know how much I care about you," Leona said. "And I just don't want you to let your emotions get the better of you."

Elizabeth felt tears come to her eyes as she hugged Leona in return. "I know," she said, thinking all the while that what she wanted most was to make sure she didn't let Leona down again. "I know," she repeated.

Leona gave her a tiny squeeze that felt to Elizabeth, somehow, that her friend not only understood her but believed in her as well.

Elizabeth pulled back and wiped her eyes. "And I promise I'll do my best to be patient with everyone who visits the library," she said.

"Summer's here!" Miles cawed, which made Elizabeth laugh. "Summer's here!"

"Anybody home?" came a voice from beyond the office door. Leona and Elizabeth looked to see Freddy standing on the opposite side of the checkout counter waving his hands. "I can see you back there!"

"Freddy!" Elizabeth called, leaping up.

Leona waved him in with an arm. "Come on back here, Mr. Knox!"

Freddy strolled in, pushing at his glasses and gazing around. "Summer's here!" Miles began to squawk again.

"Hey, you, little bird," Freddy said. "Are they forcing you to read books back here?"

"What are you doing here?" Elizabeth said, laughing.

"Yes," Leona said, "your visits to the library are so rare. But always very glad to see you." She pointed to the teapot by way of offering to pour him a cup, but he shook his head. "And how is that project of yours coming along? I remember when Milton would demonstrate the camera obscura two or three times a day to interested guests."

"Getting closer," Freddy said. "It's mainly getting the scaffolding all set up and the ropes arranged. A lot of testing the pulleys and cleaning up the screen, stuff like that, but I need to take a break right now while the electrician is doing some wiring." He looked to Elizabeth. "Maybe we could visit the ice castle?"

Elizabeth turned to Leona. "I'm helping out here until noon."

Leona squinted at her. "I think today you're heading right up to your room, grabbing your jacket, and accompanying this young man outside. Understood?"

"I can handle that!" Elizabeth said with a laugh.

"Do you remember that journal by Marshall?" Elizabeth said to Freddy as they left the library.

"The humongous book with all the crazy stories in it?"

Elizabeth nodded. "I found some stuff in it about the secret passageways. Marshall says that aside from doors in Norbridge's room and the candy kitchen and the library, there's also another door somewhere, but Marshall doesn't say where it is."

"You are doing some serious detectivization."

"I knew there had to be some information in that journal."

Freddy stopped. "Hey, I just thought of something. You know that plaque you said you saw in the candy kitchen? Even if the other three doors themselves don't lead anywhere anymore, maybe the plaques are still there. Like, maybe they never got removed."

Elizabeth felt a tingle go down her spine. "You might be right. Hmm, if that's the case, there might be a plaque somewhere in Norbridge's room. I'm pretty sure the library plaque is long gone, though."

"That must be what Rodney and his parents are looking for in the library," Freddy said.

"The plaques spell out something that gives information about the hidden object!" Elizabeth said. "That's got to be it."

Freddy stopped walking and looked at her. "So all we have to do is find all four plaques."

Elizabeth examined the carpet for a moment before looking up. "I'm developing a plan."

"You know, every time you say that, something bad happens," Freddy quipped.

Elizabeth laughed. "Let me grab my coat, and we can meet outside. I want to see that ice castle!"

The two of them spent the next hour exploring the ice castle, which had been built just behind Winterhouse on the huge field between the hotel and the shores of Lake Luna. As large as Grace Hall itself, it was a marvel of architecture and whimsy, with cupolas and turrets like an actual castle, and long corridors that led nowhere at all or steered a person through a maze of passages in which it was easy to get lost and hard to get out. Most of it was roofed in like an actual castle, with some walls done in blocks of clear ice—so that you could see a friend on the opposite side, even if you couldn't get to him—and some in walls of snow. There were staircases everywhere, and long slopes at points, so that you could get from the third floor back down to the first simply by sitting and sliding, and there was one "room" on the second level where it was possible to jump off a ledge into a pile of snow kept fluffy and soft by some of the workers. The whole castle was alive with kids laughing and squealing with the fun of it all, and even plenty of adults were glad to wander the immense palace as their faces turned red with a pleasant chill.

"Norbridge has really improved this castle," Freddy said to Elizabeth after they'd finally found their way out of a tangle of ice corridors. "The first year I came, it was just a dinky little house."

Just as they left the ice castle and were heading back inside the hotel, Elizabeth looked up and saw Elana at a window at the landing on the second floor. She was looking at the two of them, but when she saw that they had seen her, she quickly turned away and disappeared.

"Did you see that?" Freddy said.

"I did. She's avoiding us, I guess." Elizabeth thought back to how oddly Mrs. Vesper had treated Elana. "Or maybe her grandmother isn't letting her hang around us."

Suddenly, a snowball whammed Elizabeth on the side of her head.

"Ow!" she yelped with shock and pain. Someone was laughing—in fact, even as she tried to make sense of what had happened, she realized she heard more than one person laughing—and she turned to see Rodney and his parents with smiles on their faces, gaping at her.

"What did you do that for?" Freddy said.

"Nice aim, Rodney!" Mr. Powter said. Rodney stood with his fist pumped before him as though he'd just scored the winning shot for his basketball team.

Elizabeth shook her head and wiped the wetness from her face. "Are you crazy?" she said, turning on the three Powters. "Why did you do that?"

"Oh, it's all in good outdoor fun," Mrs. Powter said indignantly. She wore a huge white parka that made her look like a human marshmallow. "Rodney was just starting a game."

"Well, he hit me in the face when I didn't even know it was coming," Elizabeth said. And then, before she knew it and because she was so angry, she said, "You ought to spend more time indoors looking for secret doorways, rather than bothering people outside."

Mr. Powter's face went grim. "I don't know what you're talking about."

"Yes, you do," Freddy said. He pointed at Rodney. "Rodney Powter. Nerdy Towrope."

Elizabeth continued wiping at her face; the stinging pain was subsiding. "We know a lot more about what you're up to than you think."

"Oh, is that right, Ms. Lizzy Bookworm?" Mr. Powter

said. His wife turned to him with a severe look, and he immediately put a hand to his mouth.

"That's the name from my email address," Elizabeth said faintly, her stomach dropping. "How did you know that?"

Mrs. Powter stood up straight and raised her chin. She grabbed her husband's hand and reached for Rodney. "We don't need to listen to such nonsense," she said. "Come on." She yanked at the two others brusquely, and the trio turned and stalked away.

Elizabeth turned to Freddy. "How did they know my email address?" she said.

Freddy was staring blankly at the Powters as they departed. "No idea." He turned to Elizabeth. "But you should talk to Norbridge about this right away."

CHAPTER 20

TROUBLE ON CHRISTMAS EVE

SMARTIES

The remainder of the day was uneventful, and Elizabeth tried to put the unsettling confrontation with the Powters out of her mind, even as she felt conflicted about discussing the Powter incident with Norbridge. A part of her wanted to, but another part wondered if he would respond with interest or tell her it was another thing he would "look into," and so she decided to keep the matter to herself for now. After dinner and a movie (*Bedknobs and Broomsticks*, which Elizabeth thought was a bit silly but still decided to add to her list of "Movies I Want to See Again") with Freddy in the small theater, and then cookies and hot chocolate by the fire in Winter Hall, Elizabeth retreated to her room for the night.

The next day—the one before Christmas Eve—was quiet as well. Elizabeth worked in the library; went sledding in the afternoon; and skated with Freddy (Elana finally came, for an hour only, and was unfailingly pleasant and acted as though nothing was strange about her disappearing for such long stretches of time). After dinner, Elizabeth attended a lecture with Freddy entitled "My Childhood at the World-Famous Thernstrumfk Puppet Theater," delivered by a Swedish woman whose accent was so thick it was almost impossible to understand what she was saying. Elana and her grandmother were nowhere to be found that evening; same with Rodney Powter and his parents.

And then the next afternoon, as all the preparations for Christmas Eve dinner and the big party afterward moved into full swing, the general air of anticipation in the hotel became palpable. The staff seemed to be readying for an invasion. The kitchen crew scurried every which way to bring food and decorations into Winter Hall; the bellhops raced up and down the hallways to make sure the guests were comfortable and any last-minute gift deliveries were finalized; the small orchestra shuttled instruments and equipment into both Winter Hall and Grace Hall for the evening bash; and, basically, everyone in Winterhouse—staff and guests—built up to such a pitch, Elizabeth felt the roof might shoot off the top of the hotel.

An hour before dinner, Elizabeth headed to the portrait gallery, something she did most every day, even if only for a few minutes, to admire the painting of her mother. The door to the hall was open, and as she approached she saw two people inside looking at a painting, though the always dim gallery made it difficult to see who they were. When Elizabeth reached the doorway itself, she saw Elana and her grandmother standing before the portrait of Gracella.

Elizabeth retreated slightly so as not to be seen. Mrs. Vesper pointed to something in the painting before them and whispered to Elana, who nodded throughout. After a long few minutes, during which Elizabeth stood watching in silence, Mrs. Vesper took Elana's hand, and the two of them headed for the far doorway and disappeared. Elizabeth, alone now, entered the gallery.

Why were they so fascinated by that painting? she thought. She was glad they hadn't seen her. She moved to the painting of her mother and studied it. After a few minutes, she stood before the paintings of Norbridge and Gracella, almost right where Elana and her grandmother had been. And, once again, she couldn't help examining Gracella's face and her eyes and the steady gaze she held fixed, apparently, on something intriguing and powerful. "Tempted" was the word that came to Elizabeth's mind, though she quickly dismissed this and thought of the relief she'd felt the year before when Gracella had finally been defeated. She was dead and gone, buried down in the cemetery in Havenworth.

Elizabeth pulled herself away from the portrait and set her thoughts on the evening ahead.

* * *

The Christmas Eve dinner of roasted ham, baked potatoes, steamed broccoli, and a dozen other dishes was the most delicious meal of the many delicious meals Elizabeth had eaten at Winterhouse. She sat with Freddy, the two puzzle men and their wives, and a young couple from Chile. Elana, in a spotless white gown and with a white tiara perched delicately atop her jet-black hair, sat with her grandmother at a table on the other side of the hall; Elizabeth didn't see the Powters anywhere.

During dinner, Elizabeth wondered what Aunt Purdy and Uncle Burlap were doing that evening. The idea came to her that sometime in the next day or two, after all the excitement died down, she would write them a letter to say hello and let them know she was well.

"I am so full," Freddy said, just as dessert arrived.

"Me too," Elizabeth said. "What's the opposite of 'famished'?"

"'Completely stuffed.' But this pie looks so good." He closed his eyes for a moment. "'Famished.' 'Made fish.'" He patted himself on the chest. "I'm really good at this."

"Or 'as him fed,'" Elizabeth said.

Freddy smiled. "Not a bad anagram," he said, nodding. "Not bad."

The lights dimmed, and everyone turned to see Norbridge standing at the front of the hall before the enormous, blazing fireplace. He wore what he'd worn the previous Christmas—a green dinner jacket and a red bow tie—and as the crowd slowly quieted, he moved his eyes over the entire hall the way someone surveys a far horizon.

"It's magic trick time," Freddy whispered to Elizabeth.

"Good evening, dear guests!" Norbridge said, his voice

echoing. "Tonight we are together here in Winter Hall, and we have shared a meal unlike any that will ever be served again." He paused and glanced around. "Until tomorrow night." The audience laughed.

"He said the *exact* same thing last year!" Elizabeth whispered to Freddy.

"He says it every year."

Norbridge delivered a speech, and when he finished, he lifted his hands above his head. "And now," he said as the lights dimmed even more, "a bit of magic."

Two servers from the kitchen carried a small table out and placed it in front of Norbridge. This was all so familiar, Elizabeth prepared herself to see the same trick Norbridge had performed last Christmas. She looked more closely, though, and saw that instead of the two puppets Norbridge had used to tell a story of a young girl who had saved her family from an evil witch, there was only something that looked like a brown paper bag.

"A story!" Norbridge yelled, and then, quietly, "By way of disrupting your dessert." Laughter arose from the guests. Norbridge moved his hands above the table the way people warm their hands over a fire. The room grew quiet again.

"There once was an enormous mansion far away in the snowy mountains." The thing on the table began to stir. Norbridge lifted his hands to eye level, and a many-sided Chinese lantern rose from the table, inflating almost instantly. It glowed from within and was the color of old parchment and was the size of a beach ball. And then, most amazing of all, it drifted above the table and hovered in front of Norbridge as the crowd gasped nearly as one.

"In the mansion lived a young woman with her mother and father," Norbridge said, and he snapped his fingers. "And she was the light of their lives." Within the floating lantern, a purple light came on. Elizabeth watched with astonishment.

"She was very happy," Norbridge continued, "and she had always loved exploring the mansion. When she'd been younger she enjoyed making up games and stories and all sorts of mysteries for herself. Now, however, she was at an age where she was about to leave and create a life of her own elsewhere." The purple light throbbed brightly.

"One day," Norbridge said, "not long before she was set to depart, curiosity finally got the better of the young woman and she entered a room in the mansion that had always stayed locked. She found a key and walked inside, closing the door behind her." Norbridge flicked his hand, and a red light blinked on within the lantern. "But all she found, hanging on a wall, was a painting of a woman—a portrait which, oddly, bore some resemblance to her. This thrilled the young woman—and frightened her a bit, too." The red light grew brighter.

"The young woman approached the painting, and just as she drew near, she fell to the floor in a deep sleep." The red light floated close to the purple light, and then began to dart about in tight circles. "The painting, it seemed, wanted to keep her in the room forever. And the young woman might have remained there, too, had she not heard, somewhere in her deepest thoughts, the voices of her mother and father calling to her." The purple light grew brighter and larger; the red light flickered. "It took everything inside her to escape the power of the painting. And even though she had an almost overwhelming desire to remain asleep within that room, she heard the voices more loudly and shook herself awake. The young woman escaped and was reunited with her parents!"

At this, the red light burst into a shower of sparks that flared and died, and the entire lantern glowed a rich purple. The crowd began to clap and cheer; the lantern became an even more lustrous shade of purple, and then, incredibly, it began to grow larger. Within seconds, it was twice as big and expanding quickly. Some of the people in the hall shouted in amazement, and several people laughed and yelled; the clapping swelled.

"And the girl . . ." Norbridge shouted above the noise as the lantern rose higher and higher and continued to inflate, moving to the center of the hall. "Lived happily ever after!" he yelled. The lantern was now almost touching the ceiling, and it was as big around as a small car, throbbing with a bright purple light.

"The end!" Norbridge shouted. The lantern burst with a tremendous noise, like a cannon going off, and an eruption of confetti shot to all corners of Winter Hall and descended on the crowd like a sudden squall of snow. Everyone was shouting and clapping and cheering. The hall was a riot of sound, confetti was sparkling everywhere, and the band broke into a loud rendition of "Jingle Bells."

Elizabeth was astounded. She'd seen Norbridge do his tricks before, but this one so surpassed anything thus far, she couldn't even bring herself to clap but just stood staring at her grandfather as he grinned at the front of the hall.

"Okay!" Freddy said to her. "That was beyond awesome!"

Elizabeth looked to the table where she'd seen Elana and her grandmother. The old woman was still seated, glancing at the people around her with a look of complete indifference; to her, apparently, the excitement was nothing more than a curiosity. Elana, too, had remained sitting and was adjusting her tiara with a pensive expression.

What is wrong with those two? Elizabeth thought.

"Music and dancing in Grace Hall after dinner!" Norbridge shouted. "I'll see you there! But first, join me in song!" And with that, he reared back and began to bellow, "On the worst day of Christmas, my true love gave to me, a Pop-Tart with a sardine!" The crowd exploded in laughter as Norbridge waved his hands about as if to excuse a mistake.

"Let's try that again," he shouted. "The right way!" And with that, everyone joined, and Winter Hall was filled with singing.

The party after dinner was long and raucous—Elizabeth and Freddy enjoyed the music deep into the night, and the huge crowd remained happy for hours, no one wanting to let the fun end or to return to their rooms too early.

Elizabeth looked for Elana or Mrs. Vesper occasionally, but they seemed to have left; the Powters had never appeared, and she wondered what sour spirit existed among those two families that kept them from joining in the fun.

"Quick break?" Elizabeth said to Freddy as they drank some punch near one of the hall's doors.

"Definitely," Freddy said, and they stepped into the hallway, which was relatively quiet, even with the clusters of guests talking and snacking there.

"This way," Elizabeth said, heading for the stairwell up to the second floor.

Freddy shook a finger at her. "We are *not* going to the library. No way!"

He didn't need to remind Elizabeth that exactly one year before, at midnight on Christmas Eve, the two of them had sneaked into the library, and Elizabeth, for reasons still unclear to herself, had shouted Gracella's name three times. By some residue of dark magic Gracella had left stored in Winterhouse, this had revived the sorceress's spirit and allowed her to reclaim her bodily form before making her assault on the hotel a few days later.

"No library!" Elizabeth said. "I promise!" She glanced at the stairs that wound above her. "Let's look at the lake from the window."

Freddy joined her as they climbed the stairs. "I'm not even tired yet," he said.

"Good, because the party's only halfway over," Elizabeth said.

Suddenly, they heard the sound of feet padding quickly across the carpet of a corridor, though they couldn't tell if the noise came from above or below. They stopped and listened.

"Someone's running," Freddy said, and they peered over the railing; the noise was on the level below on the second floor, and then it died away. But just as it did, the sound of someone else running arose. Suddenly a blaze of red bellhop's uniform came into view, and Elizabeth and Freddy watched as Jackson dashed beneath them and then clumped down the stairs to the first floor.

"What was that about?" Freddy said. "He was chasing someone."

Elizabeth looked to him with perplexity, and the two of them hurried down to the second-floor landing. She pointed in the direction Jackson had run.

"Maybe he saw something," Elizabeth said. "He must have come from the library."

Freddy shook his head quickly. "We're not going there. Jackson's got it covered."

"But maybe . . ." Elizabeth began before shouting, "I'll meet you downstairs in five minutes!" She turned toward the library.

"Elizabeth!" Freddy said. "Stay here!" He reached out a hand to grab her, but she was already racing down the corridor.

"Five minutes!" she shouted. "I'll be right back."

"Elizabeth!" Freddy's call died away behind her.

She turned two corners and was at the library before

she knew it. The doors were wide open—strange enough at this hour—but what was even stranger was what met her eyes when she stepped inside. There was just enough illumination across the first floor that she saw that the far wall—the very one Leona had pointed out to her two days before—was in disarray: a half dozen paintings hung at skewed and drooping angles, two large banners sagged from where they'd been torn off their nails, and three tall bookcases leaned against the ones before them, half toppled and with their books scattered across the floor. Someone had vandalized the library.

Elizabeth was in disbelief. The library was such a peaceful, orderly place that to see it in this state made her not just sad but frightened: Who would have done such a

thing? She surveyed the damage and considered that all the careful work put into maintaining things had been completely ruined. She stepped closer and looked at the wall itself. At a point where the top of a door might be, and at a spot that had been concealed behind one of the now-tumbled bookcases, was a brass plaque. It was identical in size and shape to the one Elizabeth had seen in the candy kitchen, and on it were these words:

SPRING
ITS MIGHT IS ALL BUT HIDDEN TILL IT SEES ITSELF IN GLASS YOU FILL

Elizabeth dashed over to the card catalog, grabbed a scrap of paper and a pencil, wrote the inscription down, and then, folding the paper and putting it in her pocket, turned to race out of the library. Then she stopped. Something drew her back to the plaque, to the empty wall above which it was displayed. The wall was completely bare, an expanse of white that had most likely been covered by bookcases for decades. She put her hand on it and ran her fingers across the cool surface. And then she leaned into it and placed an ear against the wall. A low, rumbling noise, once again so faint and indistinct it took her a moment to hear, sounded from somewhere deep behind the wall; it seemed to grow louder as Elizabeth stood listening.

She backed away, glanced at the plaque, and then ran for the corridor back to Grace Hall.

PART THREE

BETWEEN TWO HOLIDAYS—AND THE MAGIC HARMONY BREAKS

CHARM

CHAPTER 21

THE NINETY-NINE-YEAR-OLD WOMAN

WORLD

Christmas morning was blizzardy and ten degrees below freezing. Elizabeth understood it was likely everyone would stay inside the hotel the entire day.

The evening before, after Elizabeth had returned to the party, she and Freddy watched Norbridge and Jackson and several bellhops head with urgency to the library. She knew they would clean up, lock the doors, and try to figure out what had happened. When Elizabeth saw Norbridge an hour later in the corridor outside Grace Hall, looking anxious and distracted, she'd asked him what was wrong, and he merely informed her there had been an incident in the library. When she told him she and Freddy had heard someone running and that Jackson had been chasing the person, Norbridge thanked her for the information but said nothing more. She'd told Freddy what she'd seen, of course—that there had been a plaque behind the toppled bookcases—and although they tried to enjoy the rest of the evening, the mood had been spoiled. Elizabeth went to bed with a swirl of concerns on her mind.

Now, the next morning, after she'd opened her gifts—five books from Norbridge, six books from Leona, a kaleidoscope from Jackson, and a bag of jelly beans from Freddy—and eaten breakfast, Elizabeth found herself looking at a long day alone. Norbridge was occupied with hotel business, Freddy was feeling sick from too much cake the night before, and even Leona was going to rest most of the day—the library was closed, and she felt wrung out from the damage it had sustained the night before.

Elizabeth passed the day reading and then wandered from floor to floor of the hotel, examining the interesting objects displayed along nearly every corridor: the hulking mahogany and bronze music box on the fourth floor whose only thick metal disk played "The March of the Helvetii" with a turn of a brass knob; the astrolabe on the seventh floor, a gift from the artist Salvador Dalí that was, supposedly, a reproduction of the one Vasco da Gama used on his sea voyages; the "Tooth from the Mouth of Prizefighter Jack Dempsey—Dislodged by Donald Falls, March 17, 1930, During a 'Dispute' in the Candy Kitchen" (as announced on a small placard), which was, simply, a tooth sitting under glass on a small tea plate on the ninth floor. At midafternoon, as she was working on the puzzle in the lobby with Mr. Wellington and Mr. Rajput, Sampson approached and said Norbridge wanted to see her.

"He's in Kiona's room," Sampson said. "You can find him there."

"Right now?" Elizabeth said.

"He told me to let you know."

Elizabeth had never been in Kiona Falls's room, an apartment on the first floor she shared with her daughter, Lena, who was deaf and mute. Although Elizabeth had seen Kiona on only one occasion—during Christmas Eve last year—she knew she was the oldest surviving member of the Falls family at ninety-nine years old. She had passed Kiona's room on several occasions and often wondered just what it was the elderly woman and her daughter did all day, because it was clear they left their room only for special occasions. This year, perhaps, they'd been too ill even to attend the Christmas Eve dinner.

It was a curious thing, but—as Elizabeth remembered from the family tree on the wall outside Winter Hall—nearly every woman in the Falls family had lived to be one hundred years old. Not ninety-nine and not a hundred and one—one hundred precisely. When she'd asked Norbridge and Leona about this, there had been no explanation; it was as much of a mystery as anything else about Winterhouse.

Elizabeth knocked lightly on Kiona's door. Norbridge greeted her with a silent nod, put a finger to his mouth, and motioned her inside.

"Everything okay?" Elizabeth whispered.

Norbridge nodded again and then led her down a short hallway and pointed through an open doorway. There, sleeping soundly beneath a layer of quilts and looking as peaceful as a baby in the dim golden glow of a lamp on a low bureau across the room, lay Kiona Falls. In a bed beside her and sleeping just as soundly was Lena Falls.

Norbridge motioned with his head to Elizabeth, and they left the women to their rests.

"Quite a Christmas," Norbridge said as he settled into a stuffed chair in the living room. Elizabeth couldn't tell what he meant by this—it sounded a bit ominous—but she had spread out on a roomy sofa across from him and was admiring the walls. Every surface had been painted with pictures of people of all types and in a variety of situations—some walking outside, some sitting and reading, some praying in church, some singing or laughing, and on and on, a riot of color and scene that spread everywhere, even on the ceiling.

"This room is incredible," Elizabeth said.

Norbridge chuckled. "Kiona is quite an artist. She always loved to paint."

Elizabeth glanced at the books on the coffee table between them. "Is she okay?"

Norbridge wiggled his hand before him. "So-so," he said. "I've been having the doctor stop in more frequently,

and we've been experimenting with some herbs." He sighed. "I wanted to talk to you about last night. Along the way as I sorted out the events of the evening, I heard from one of the workers that you might have been down in the library around the time everything went haywire. Someone saw you coming from that direction. I know you told me you and Freddy heard someone running away from the library, but you didn't mention anything about being in the library yourself."

He set both elbows on the arms of the chair and clasped his hands, getting right down to business. Elizabeth was taken aback. She didn't want to lie to Norbridge or disappoint him in any way. But she also wondered if she should reveal to him what she'd learned. Would he work through the trail of clues with her or explain there was nothing to worry about? She'd prepared herself for the latter because she had seen it too often already; this time she resolved not to be deterred.

"I know something's going on," Elizabeth said. "Last night we saw Jackson running back from the library, so I went to take a look. I saw a plaque on the wall on the main floor, and I actually saw one just like it in the candy kitchen after Mrs. Trumble was attacked there. I didn't tell you about it, because I didn't want to get in trouble. But I know it's there. And the riddle tells about a hidden charm."

"I don't know whether to be impressed with your investigating or troubled by your recklessness," Norbridge said, looking to Elizabeth with weary eyes. "You've already proved how resourceful you are and how pointless it is for me to remind you what curiosity did to the cat. So tell me: What have you deduced?"

"I think there's definitely someone trying to get into the secret passageway. I just don't know why, but someone knows something and wants to get in. I think Rodney Powter or Mrs. Vesper is involved. Maybe Elana, too, and even Rodney's parents."

Norbridge sighed. "Two facts to share. The Powters and Mrs. Vesper and her granddaughter were in their rooms last night. All had room service brought to them, and the bellhop confirmed everyone had stayed put."

"Maybe Rodney snuck into the library and slammed stuff around, and then got back to his room before anyone saw him." Elizabeth began to feel desperate. As she verbalized her theories, she wondered if they were just random facts, a set of coincidences or oddities that were unrelated and that added up to nothing significant. She had to confess, even as she was explaining things, she wasn't sure if there was a connecting thread, an actual plot.

"I'm mostly concerned about your safety," Norbridge said. "If you're dashing off here and there when there's trouble afoot, you're bound to get hurt."

Elizabeth felt a flicker of anger inside her. Norbridge wasn't taking her seriously—again. "I'm twelve. I'm not a little kid."

"I'm not saying you're necessarily wrong about things. I'm only saying we should remain vigilant, but without getting distracted."

This final word—"distracted"—brought Elizabeth's

anger to the surface. It was what Uncle Burlap said whenever he mentioned a problem at work: *Oh, my boss is always correcting me, and it gets me so distracted I can hardly concentrate the rest of the day!* Elizabeth found she couldn't abide the word—and now Norbridge had used it.

"Maybe last year we didn't get distracted enough by everything Gracella was doing," she said. "And then she almost destroyed Winterhouse!"

"Elizabeth." Norbridge's tone was conciliatory. "I do take your fears seriously."

But she was too upset to hear him; she felt something like what she'd felt in the library recently, on those occasions when she had tried to assist people but had failed because she'd become frustrated or riled. A part of her knew she was being a little unfair, but she also felt she had to stick up for herself and couldn't back down now.

"I just feel like when I try to explain things, sometimes you don't believe me," she said.

The room was quiet, but Elizabeth had the definite feeling that someone in the bedroom had awakened. She looked behind her.

"Don't worry," Norbridge said. "If Kiona wants to spy on us, she'll do it."

Despite herself, Elizabeth laughed, and the tension that had grown in the room broke.

Norbridge gave a tiny smile. "And I do believe you, by the way." He gestured to a book on Kiona's coffee table entitled *The Walled City of Sehrif-Kala* and said, "Give it a try."

Just as in the observatory two nights' before, Elizabeth fixed her attention on the volume and allowed *the feeling* to gather inside her. The book leapt right into her hands.

"Oh, she's good," someone said from the corridor. Elizabeth looked, even as she lowered the book to her lap. There stood Kiona Falls in a nightgown, wearing a red scarf over her hair. Her face, though creased with wrinkles, was gentle and kind, just as Elizabeth recalled.

"She is," Norbridge said. "We've just been talking out here."

"I heard," Kiona said. "I may be about to reach triple digits, but my hearing is just fine." She raised a finger to Norbridge. "Be careful what you say around me!"

Elizabeth laughed. "It's very nice to finally meet you."

"The pleasure is all mine," Kiona said. She moved forward as both Norbridge and Elizabeth stood to greet her. She waved them down with a scowl, shook Elizabeth's hand with both of hers, and lowered herself to the sofa with a wince.

"Are you comfortable?" Elizabeth said.

"I've been better," Kiona said, "but your grandfather makes sure I'm well taken care of."

"Is that ginseng drink helping?" Norbridge said.

"I'd rather have a root beer float," Kiona said, "but I confess your drink seems to be helping." She put a hand to her forehead. "I'm not quite as worn out as I was a few days ago, so thank you for that." She looked to Elizabeth.

"Nice work with the book. I haven't seen that sort of ability since dear cousin Rowena maybe sixty years back. Impressive."

Elizabeth didn't know how to respond to this. "Thank you. I just . . . It's just something that seemed to come to me. I don't know how."

"I could see into the minds of others at one time," Kiona said. "It wasn't infallible, of course, and often it was distressing—a real curse, you know, to glimpse what's inside our fellow man. But fascinating. My daughter could read the future, though now she mostly sleeps her poor life away." She nodded to Norbridge and shifted on the sofa with a tiny look of pain. "This gentleman here is a tricky one. Things materialize, things disappear."

"As you can see," Norbridge said, "my lovely second cousin is completely senile."

Kiona took a small breath; she seemed about to adjust herself again but remained in place. She looked at Elizabeth, her tired eyes glassy and kind. "I met Riley Granger once."

"Kiona . . ." Norbridge said.

The old woman put a hand up. "He came back here for a visit forty years after he left the first time. He was over eighty years old."

"I didn't think we were going to get into this today," Norbridge said.

"I heard the two of you talking out here about things," Kiona said. "That's the only reason I brought it up."

Elizabeth had felt her hair nearly stand on end when

Kiona said Riley Granger's name. "He came back here?" she said.

"But nothing happened," Norbridge said. "It was, as they say, anticlimactic. In fact, he was more senile than this dear lady at the time. I'm not even sure he realized where he was."

Kiona nodded sadly. "You're right about that. But still, it was a thrill to meet the man. We'd all heard so much about him over the years."

Elizabeth wondered why Norbridge hadn't mentioned this before. It bothered her—he'd kept an important part of the story from her.

"Well," Norbridge said, "it was disappointing. He just wandered around the hallways babbling until we got him back to his room."

"Did he come on his own?" Elizabeth said.

"A niece or someone came with him," Kiona said. "A young woman. I wish I could remember her name. Christmas of '38 or '39."

"A long time ago," Norbridge said, sighing. "A little blip in Winterhouse's history."

Elizabeth felt certain there was more to the story.

"We should let you rest, Kiona," Norbridge said. "Just wanted to say hello, and I wanted Elizabeth to meet you."

"Maybe you're the one with the failing memory, Norbridge," Kiona said. "I requested an audience with the young lady."

This surprised Elizabeth; she hadn't considered that Kiona had asked to meet her.

"You're right," Norbridge said.

Kiona moved her head in Elizabeth's direction, and then pointed to a bureau across the room. "Third drawer down on the right side. There's something for you."

This was unexpected, and Elizabeth looked to Norbridge.

"Please," Kiona said, catching Elizabeth's glance. "You don't need his permission."

When Elizabeth slid the drawer open, the smell of lavender wafted from it and she was looking at a spread of richly colored scarves. The drawer was alive with bright, flowing fabric, like an exotic garden Kiona had somehow grown inside her bureau.

"Beautiful!" Elizabeth said. "Like your paintings. I meant to tell you I love them."

"Thank you," Kiona said, beaming. "I love beautiful things. So did your mother." She lifted a hand and began moving her finger in a circle; she appeared to be stirring the scarves from a distance. "Look under them there on the right side, and you'll find a red velvet pouch. It belonged to your mother. I want you to have it."

Elizabeth dug through the scarves. A small pouch, not much bigger than her fist, with a purple drawstring cinched tightly lay within. She lifted it from the pile of scarves and examined it before turning back to Kiona.

"For me?" she said.

"For you," Kiona said. "I could never part with it before. It's not much, really, but I've kept it all these years. She was such a sweet girl, my . . . my . . . what was the relationship again, Norbridge?"

"Winnie was your second cousin once removed."

"Yes, that's what I wanted to say. We were close. She kept that bag in here with me and would come get it from time to time when she was a girl. I think she forgot about it after she got to be about your age, and I left it there in case she ever wanted to reclaim it."

"Thank you," Elizabeth said. "I'll take good care of it." She was eager to get back to her room to examine the contents of the pouch.

"And now we really should depart," Norbridge said. "I'm going to make sure you have another round of that drink, Kiona, and maybe a light dinner, too."

Kiona ignored him. "You're a smart, resourceful girl, Elizabeth. I know all about what happened here last year. We're just so delighted to have you back with the family."

Elizabeth felt immensely happy as she looked into the old woman's eyes. She lifted the pouch slightly. "Thank you so much. I'm glad to be here, and I'm really glad I had a chance to come see you."

Kiona dipped her chin in acknowledgment. "Besides, you'll be taking over someday."

A shock went through Elizabeth at these words. They were unexpected—but they also seemed to make complete sense. She felt as she did when she found the correct piece to the huge puzzle in the lobby: Something fit.

"Taking over?" she said to Norbridge. She thought back to how he had shown her his office on the thirteenth floor. Perhaps it wasn't just that she had come to live at

Winterhouse and needed to do her best to adjust—there was something to live up to, to fulfill.

"You see?" Norbridge said with a smile. "This dear lady is still trying to wake up from her nap. But I do need to discuss something with her before I go." He winked at Elizabeth. "I'm glad we had a chance to catch up, and I'll look for you tonight, okay? Please stay out of trouble."

"I will." And with a wave and a farewell to them, Elizabeth departed Kiona's room.

You'll be taking over, Elizabeth thought as she walked down the hallway. The idea gave her a thrill, and she decided to talk with Norbridge about it when an opportunity arose.

She continued to Room 213 to examine her mother's pouch, when she thought that Leona might like to see its contents, too. And so she changed her path and headed to the library.

CHAPTER 22

THE CONTENTS OF THE POUCH

HOPE

As it turned out, Leona was examining the damage from the night before when Elizabeth arrived.

"Who would do something like this?" Leona said, not really expecting an answer as she wandered around. She looked like someone surveying the aftermath of a hurricane, although most everything had been tidied up. The huge bookcases had been put back exactly in place; the plaque was hidden once again.

"Don't you think it had to be Rodney Powter?" Elizabeth said.

"You might get me to put money on that one." Leona shook her head and clicked her tongue, something she continued to do as she wandered around. "Well, I'm glad we were closed today anyway. I'm trying to soak this all up and get things in order."

"Can I help?" Elizabeth said.

Leona pulled at the shoulders of her brown wool sweater, apparently to keep herself as warm and snug as possible—or maybe to help herself make sense of what had happened. Elizabeth thought Leona looked about as sad and lost as she'd ever seen her, and it made her feel deeply unhappy. She decided not to mention the red pouch for now.

"You know, dear," Leona said, "it's Christmas Day, and you should enjoy it. However, if you want to join me, I'm going to stay here for one hour—no more—and finish a couple of chores, and then I'm going to leave it alone myself. Probably the best thing I can do."

Elizabeth remained with Leona over the next hour, and the two of them drank tea and talked. All the while, Leona put the checkout cards in order and went through some papers on her desk before arranging them in the massive wooden file cabinet against the wall.

When Leona was done, Elizabeth displayed the pouch. "I visited with Kiona a little while ago in her room, and she gave me this. It belonged to my mother."

Leona's eyes widened. "Have you looked in it?"

"I wanted to do it with you."

"Summer's here!" Miles cawed. "Summer's here!"

"I think he wants to see, too," Leona said. "Let's take a look."

Elizabeth loosened the drawstrings on the velvet bag.

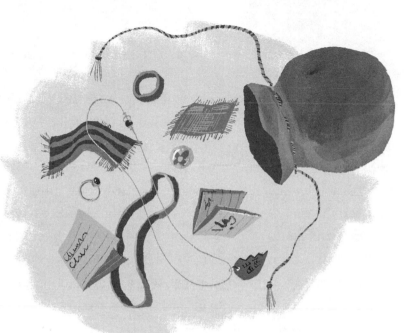

She glanced inside, saw a collection of jewelry and scraps of cloth and paper, gave the bag one jangly shake, and then turned it over to dump the treasure onto Leona's desktop. There lay a small mound of rings and necklaces and ear-rings and folded papers and squares of silk.

"Valuable stuff!" Leona said, and Elizabeth giggled.

She rummaged through the collection and, more quickly than she would have guessed, found herself slightly disappointed: It seemed to be little-kid things, the sorts of items you find in gumball machines or in boxes of Cracker Jack or at the bottom of your Halloween bag, all cheap plastic rings and fake gems and rusty silver chains. There were little patches of colored silk mixed in; Elizabeth guessed maybe her mother had once liked how they looked.

"Looks like stuff she collected at random," Elizabeth said.

"Nice, though, to have some of her private things, isn't it?" Leona pointed to three pieces of paper, folded into quarters, among the pile of plastic toys. "I wonder what those are."

Elizabeth opened them in turn carefully, half thinking they might tear. On the first was simply her mother's signature, over and over, in graceful and looping lines, as though she'd been perfecting her autograph or practicing her cursive. On the second paper was a transcription of a poem Elizabeth had seen on the family tree above the entrance to Winter Hall:

The peaks rise high, the north reels on, and mist obscures the sky
Where as one hid—denied the night!—the days of fall pass by
In winter's tempo we remain, but when fair spring returns
Soon summer's knit 'em, sky and storm, and scented heaven burns
October ear and April eye catch distant zephyr's song
The airy cloud does wet hilltop—the ancient night is long
First light, gong rang, erased the dark, the endless river crossed
The pages, pendant, picture all—where faith is never lost!

Elizabeth liked the sound of the poem, its dancing, rhyming lines; she'd liked it the first time she'd read it to herself the year before. But it was strange to her, lines that sort of made sense but that added up to nothing she understood. She'd asked Norbridge about it once, but beyond that she hadn't given it much thought. From time to time she found herself wondering about the poem. She felt, oddly, the way she felt when confronted with a crossword puzzle: There seemed to be something to solve or something to find. She wondered why her mother had copied it. Her mother's writing, though, pleased her—rounded letters all, vibrant and bright. She'd also rimmed the words with drawings of delicate flower petals.

"That old poem," Leona said. "I guess she must have liked it."

"Norbridge once told me Nestor Falls wrote it."

Leona looked puzzled. "I'd always heard Riley Granger wrote it."

The third paper was filled with writing, words here and there across the page on both sides. At first it made no sense. And then Elizabeth looked more closely and found herself startled: On the page, and surrounded by letters crossed out and scribbled, were "Snow-Rioter," "Prison-Dodge," "Trim-Room," and "Flood-Furor."

"Those are the words on the Winterhouse seal!" she said.

"They are," Leona said. "Interesting."

Elizabeth turned the paper over and examined the writing—all more of the same. "Why do you think she wrote this down?"

"If I had to guess, it looks like she was trying to figure out what those words meant."

"I think you're right." It was, of course, exactly what

Elizabeth herself had wanted to attempt, though she had no idea how to start. The words on her mother's paper, as she looked at them, weren't much help.

"Do you have any idea what the words mean?" Elizabeth said.

Leona shook her head. "That seal is a genuine riddle. I've given it a lot of thought over the years, but I still don't know its secret."

"Do you think it has anything to do with the passageways?"

"You *are* intrigued by those passageways. Why do you think there's a connection?"

"Four sides to the seal, and four doors, too, I think." She shrugged. "Just a hunch."

Elizabeth glanced at the paper and then stirred her finger through the knickknacks on the desk before returning all of it to the pouch. A thought came to her. "What happens to the guest books once they're filled up?" On a small table in the lobby, just beside the front clerk's desk, sat an enormous book in which guests could, if they chose, sign their names or write messages or make suggestions. Elizabeth had thumbed through the current one several times and enjoyed examining the comments guests left, everything from "Best place to stay—EVER!" to "The Flurschen tasted better here when I was a kid—have you changed the recipe?"

Leona turned to her file cabinet. "They're right here. Every single one since the beginning of the hotel. Why's that?"

"Kiona mentioned Riley Granger once came to visit Winterhouse when he was really old. Maybe we'd find his name in there."

"Like a needle in a haystack, I'm afraid. Unless you knew exactly when it was. That was before my time, though I've heard he paid a visit. Why are you interested?"

"It just seemed interesting. Plus, she said he came with someone."

"It would take a lot of searching—if he even jotted his name down."

"Kiona said he came at Christmas in 1938 or 1939."

Leona arched her eyebrows. "Well, that's news to me. Or if I'd heard it before I've forgotten." She stood and opened one of the drawers in her file cabinet. "Let's take a look."

She removed a thick volume from the drawer, a maroon and olive ledger in size and shape like the one on the table in the lobby. On its spine, written in black script, was a set of dates: "March 1937–August 1941."

"Maybe this is the one," Leona said, and she laid it on the table where she and Elizabeth had set their teacups. She gestured to Elizabeth. "Be my guest."

Elizabeth began thumbing through the book. The pages were yellowed with age, and the signatures and messages were both more ornate and more proper than what she found in the guest book she occasionally examined in the lobby. Maybe it had to do with the fact that people used to write in cursive much more often and much more naturally and the handwriting looked elegant, or maybe it was because the messages themselves appeared more dignified or formal—"I daresay this hotel is a model of sophistication. . . ." or "The staff are refined and anticipate one's needs in the manner of the finest hosts. . . ." or "Grace and temperate goodwill abound in this most lovely of guesthouses. . . ."—but whatever it was, Elizabeth found herself charmed just skimming the columns of notes left in the old book.

And then she came to an entry from December 21, 1938, and her heart skipped: "Riley S. Granger and Patricia P. Powter—enchanted visitors . . . We shall return."

"Look at this!" Elizabeth said. "Leona!"

The old woman read the entry, looked to Elizabeth with puzzlement, and then pressed her eyes closer to the ledger to read it again.

"Riley Granger and a member of the Powter family came to Winterhouse together?" she said. She stood straight and bit her lip. "Well, if that isn't the strangest coincidence."

"You said it." Elizabeth scanned the page again, turned it over, and looked at the one following, then the one before. "I can't believe it."

"It is definitely a stunner," Leona said. She looked in the direction of the wall where the bookcases had been toppled.

"What do you think it means?" Elizabeth said.

"Perhaps nothing," Leona said, "but it's certainly curious."

"But don't you think if there's a connection from way

back between Riley Granger and the Powters, they might know something about the passageways? And about what Riley Granger has hidden here at Winterhouse?"

Leona drummed her fingers on the open page of the guest book. "I'm going to give this one some thought, Elizabeth."

The chimes sounded for dinner.

"We better get ready," Leona said. "For now, try not to let this trouble your mind."

CHAPTER 23

A PLAN TAKES SHAPE

PHASE

"It's obvious," Elizabeth told Freddy as they sat together at dinner. He was feeling better after a day of resting, and now Elizabeth had an opportunity to catch him up about the possible connection between Riley Granger and the Powters. "Either the Powters or Mrs. Vesper is trying to find out where the doors are into the secret passageways," Elizabeth said. "I'm sure of it."

"I agree with you," Freddy said, crunching away on fried chicken, "but from everything we've heard, the passageways are all run-down and the doors are sealed. So even if they found the doors, what difference would it make?"

Elizabeth absently ran a hand across Freddy's laptop,

which was sitting on the table between them. "I'm not sure. Someone's trying to get in there, so maybe they know something we don't about how to get in or what's inside. Also, we still don't know anything about where the fourth door is. Maybe that's what they're trying to find."

"Maybe." Freddy looked distracted.

"Remember how I told you I overheard Norbridge talking about how maybe someone was returning to Winterhouse and he was getting nervous about it?" Elizabeth said.

"Something tells me you have an idea about this already."

"Well, what if Gracella is really behind all of this?" It was a notion Elizabeth had been considering for several days, something that was troubling her, given all that had occurred, not the least of which had been the red flash Mrs. Trumble had seen.

"But she's dead, Elizabeth," Freddy said. "D-E-A-D, remember? So, it's kind of hard to be behind everything if you're not actually . . . *alive*." His tone was joking, but he was serious enough that Elizabeth knew he, too, was anxious.

"Okay, but remember how she was supposedly dead, and then she came back and tried to get revenge on everyone last year? We know what she's capable of."

"But you can't just come back to life any old time!" He looked perplexed. "Can you?"

"Norbridge told me she has enough evil power to do something like that. And what if you had a bunch of people helping you out? Like, what if Mrs. Vesper and the Powters are somehow part of Gracella's . . . I don't know . . . group of helpers? Last year she had the Hiemses, and we still don't know what happened to Selena."

"But you defeated Gracella." Freddy lowered his eyebrows. "Didn't you?"

"Think about it. Why did she come back last time?"

"To get revenge on Norbridge. To destroy Winterhouse."

"And how was she going to do that?"

"By using The Book," Freddy said. "Elizabeth, is this going somewhere?"

"Yes! Listen! What if there is a different object—the charm I read about on the plaque in the candy kitchen— and it's hidden somewhere and Gracella wants it! To do . . . I don't know . . . some more magic or finally get Norbridge or something like that!"

"Or what if this is just another fantasy from one of the million books you've read?"

"No, I'm telling you! There's something going on. Oh, and let me show you something else." From her pocket, Elizabeth removed the piece of paper from the pouch that had the words from the seal written on it. She handed it to Freddy. "This is from my mother when she was about my age. It looks like she was also curious about the seal."

Freddy studied the page intently, flipping from front to back and examining all of it carefully. He looked up. "She was like you."

"What do you mean?"

Freddy held the page up before her. "Did you look at this carefully?"

"Kind of," she said, though after she and Leona had examined the paper and the other items in the pouch, she'd been so intrigued by the guest book she hadn't thought more about it.

"'Snow-Rioter,'" Freddy read, staring at the page. "Turns into 'Tower Irons,' 'Worries Not,' 'Orients Row,' 'Two Ironers.'" He raised his head from the paper and fixed her with his eyes. "She was doing anagrams. She was trying to see if there were words hidden in the seal."

Elizabeth plucked the paper from his hand and gaped at it. Sure enough, clustered around each of the four hyphenated words from the seal were combinations of letters in Winnie's graceful cursive that consisted of reworkings of the words themselves.

Elizabeth slapped a hand to her forehead. "I can't believe I didn't look at this closer! 'Prison-Dodge.' She turned it into 'Ridged Spoon,' 'Sign Drooped,' 'Eroding Pods.'" She sighed.

"But she didn't figure it out," Freddy said. He frowned. "Maybe the seal doesn't have anything to do with anagrams at all." He pushed at his glasses and glanced around Winter Hall. "Let's just assume all of this is connected and isn't just your imagination. What do you want to do about it?"

Elizabeth tapped her temple. "I've been thinking that over, and I have a plan."

Freddy shook his head. "I was afraid you'd say that."

"What if there was a way to learn more about what Mrs. Vesper is up to and see if Gracella is really buried in the cemetery? All at the same time."

Freddy tightened his lips. "I think you're about to make sure our regular, normal, not-weird-at-all Christmas gets completely un-regular, un-normal, and very weird."

⁂

After dinner, Freddy left to work on the camera obscura, and Elizabeth headed to the skating rink. Elana was there, gliding around the ice gracefully—showing off, Elizabeth thought, especially in the way she took in compliments from other skaters as she spun and leapt.

"Hey!" Elizabeth called when Elana stopped for a moment.

"Elizabeth!" She was flushed from all her skating. "How's it going?"

"Good. I thought I'd get some skating in myself." Elana said nothing, and Elizabeth continued. "I haven't seen you much lately."

"Yeah," Elana said, smoothing her hair behind her ear. "My grandmother's been tired, so I've been spending time with her in our room." She glanced around. "Freddy's not here?"

"Working on his project."

Elana glanced warily toward Winterhouse and bit her bottom lip.

"You okay?" Elizabeth said.

"Oh, yeah," Elana said. "Just tired from skating." She peered toward Winterhouse once more. "Did you enjoy Christmas?"

Elizabeth mentioned something about the Christmas Eve dinner and some of the gifts she'd received, and then, by way of trying to perk up the conversation, she asked about Elana's school and how it was where she and her grandmother lived—to which Elana offered vague responses. By then, Elizabeth had put on her skates.

"Lead the way," she said to Elana, and the two girls took to the rink.

Half an hour later, they peeled off their skates, strolled the short distance to the Winterhouse doors, and entered the long corridor leading to Winter Hall and the lobby beyond.

"I've been thinking about what you mentioned a few days ago," Elizabeth said. "About getting together. Maybe you and I and your grandmother could go down to Havenworth. There's that cool bookstore there I told you about, and seeing how you love books just as much as I do . . ."

Elana wiped her forehead. "The bookstore. That might be fun. Let me talk to my grandmother about it." She didn't sound nearly as excited as Elizabeth had expected.

"I'd love to go," Elizabeth said, perplexed by Elana's seeming indifference.

"Okay," Elana said. She continued to walk, but she kept her gaze on the carpet.

"If you're not up for it . . ." Elizabeth said.

Elana turned to her and widened her eyes. "It's not that. It's just . . . Well, it's hard to explain." She looked away.

"Is everything okay between you and your grandmother?"

"Everything's fine, really. I have a big competition coming up, so I guess I'm just nervous about it."

They came to the door to the Thatchers' room, and Elana stopped. She ran her hand over the door obliviously. And then, to Elizabeth's surprise, she leaned forward and put an ear to it. "Don't you wonder what's in here?" Elana said.

Elizabeth was feeling, once again, that there was something going on she couldn't understand, something Elana wanted to say or explain. It was another moment of perplexity in what was becoming a long list of strange events.

"Just an empty room," Elizabeth said. "Anyway, I just wanted to let you know I'd be up for a trip to town, if you want to go."

Elana backed away from the door and looked at Elizabeth uncertainly. She had the same expression on her face Elizabeth noticed when kids in her class at Drere had been daydreaming and the teacher asked them a question.

"Right," Elana said blankly.

Elizabeth decided to ask something that had been on her mind since the first night she'd met Elana. "How did your parents die?" Quickly, she added, "You don't have to tell me if you don't want to. Mine died in a car accident when I was four."

Elana looked even more uncertain, but she recovered

some of her poise before saying, "Mine, too, a few years ago. It was a bad crash on the freeway. The road was icy, and . . ."

"I was just wondering," Elizabeth said as Elana began to trail off. "It's okay."

Elana looked to her with a tiny wince; it seemed she wanted to share more but couldn't bring herself to do it. "My parents were . . . I guess I don't want to talk about it. And I better get back to my room." They began walking again; the corridor ahead diverged, and Elizabeth was about to leave Elana on her own.

"I'll see you soon," Elizabeth said. She was feeling that her attempt to put a plan in place was failing and also that she'd touched on something upsetting to Elana, who was staring away wistfully. When Elizabeth followed her gaze, she saw she was peering at the train diorama down the hallway in its corner of the lobby.

"Don't you love that?" Elana said. "It's so beautiful."

Elizabeth looked at the tiny town encased in glass. It was far off from where they were standing in the corridor, but it still looked magical even from this distance.

"It's very nice," Elizabeth said.

Elana kept staring. "I'd love to live in a place like that. Nice and peaceful." She put a hand to her cheek. "Safe. Like how you live here with everyone. They all seem to treat you so nicely. My family is—or, it was . . ."

Elizabeth felt Elana might be about to cry, though just why was unclear. And then the familiar premonition burst in on her: *The feeling* descended as if the temperature in the hallway had dropped ten degrees.

"I'll ask my grandmother if she'll take us to town," Elana said abruptly, turning away from her view of the diorama and beginning to walk again. "Maybe she—"

The two girls turned the corner and there was Mrs. Vesper. It wasn't clear to Elizabeth if the old woman had been walking toward them—by odd coincidence—or if she had, for some reason, been standing there waiting. Whatever it was, even as she tried not to show she'd been startled, Elizabeth was alarmed that, once again, Elana's grandmother had shown up silently.

"Grandmother!" Elana said brightly. "We were just talking about you."

Mrs. Vesper, in her black dress and long black shawl draped over her shoulders, didn't change her expression. She looked neither pleased nor upset, simply inscrutable. She seemed to have something on her mind and had been disturbed while considering it.

"You two have been enjoying your time together?" Mrs. Vesper said quietly.

Elizabeth stared at the woman's long hair. It was so purely white, it almost didn't look real, and Elizabeth tried to recall if she had ever seen an old person with hair quite that color. If she hadn't known any better, she might have sworn Mrs. Vesper had dyed her hair white, though it wouldn't make any sense for an older woman to do something like that.

"We were skating," Elana offered.

"Hi, Mrs. Vesper," Elizabeth said finally, because although Elana's grandmother made her uncomfortable, she prided herself on her politeness.

The old woman nodded to Elizabeth. "It's so wonderful that you live at this grand hotel. So historic here. So much to see, to experience. You must be *enchanted* by all of it."

Elizabeth shrugged. Once again, she had the feeling Mrs. Vesper had something on her mind and was trying to get at it from a distant angle. "Winterhouse is incredible," she said. "I mean, it's one of the most famous hotels in the world."

"The library is spectacular," Mrs. Vesper said. "And that elderly lady who runs it—"

"Leona?" Elizabeth said. The way Mrs. Vesper had said "elderly lady" landed on her ears like an off-key note; it didn't sound like the sort of thing one old woman would say about another. It sounded like something that would be said about someone older than yourself, which was strange because Mrs. Vesper appeared to have a few years on Leona.

"She's the librarian," Elizabeth said. "Leona Springer. I help her in the mornings."

"Elizabeth wants to take a trip to Havenworth with us," Elana said quickly. "Maybe the three of us could go tomorrow."

The old woman's eyes brightened for the first time. "Of course we can," she said. "That will give us plenty of time to get to know one another better. I've been wanting that."

She tightened her shawl around her shoulders and leaned forward slightly. "Why don't we leave right after lunch? I'll arrange a car and driver for us."

"Terrific," Elizabeth said. "I'll be ready."

Elana took her grandmother's hand. "We'll see you in the lobby, then," she said to Elizabeth.

"I want to know all about you," Mrs. Vesper said. "And perhaps you can share your knowledge of Winterhouse with us, too."

"I'm sure it will be a good time," Elizabeth said. But the two sets of eyes staring back at her weren't offering any sort of excitement; they both looked intent and severe, and Elizabeth had a moment of hesitation when she thought she might be making a big mistake in agreeing to a trip away from Winterhouse. She'd started her plan, though, and she wasn't going to back down now.

"It will be a lot of fun," Elana said, and she and her grandmother turned to leave. Elizabeth watched them for a moment, and then she headed for the corridor and her room.

Why would Mrs. Vesper want to know all about me? Elizabeth thought as she walked. She told herself that by the following afternoon, she hoped to know a lot more about Mrs. Vesper. She also planned to visit the cemetery in Havenworth.

CHAPTER 24

AN AFTERNOON IN HAVENWORTH

THROWN

Elizabeth was in the lobby the next day immediately after lunch.

"Hey!" Sampson said to her from behind the clerk's desk. "You heading somewhere?"

"I'm going to Havenworth with Mrs. Vesper and her granddaughter."

Sampson's face went from cheerful to blank. "Oh, that sounds nice." He bit his lip, very obviously keeping himself from saying anything more.

"What? Is something wrong?"

"No, no!" Sampson said quickly. "It was just kind of weird. Yesterday the grandmother was asking me to show her that room we always have reserved for the Thatchers."

"Did she say why?"

Sampson shook his head. "No, I guess she was just curious. Anyway, the Thatchers are coming soon, and they're having a bunch of their stuff shipped. It's supposed to arrive in a day or two." His eyes caught something—Jackson was approaching.

"Two of my favorite people!" Jackson said, looking bright and crisp in his spotless uniform. He always appeared very professional to Elizabeth, and she thought there could be no finer bellhop in the entire world.

"Hi, Jackson," Elizabeth said. "Say, is the afternoon shuttle running today?"

"It is, it is. It will depart Havenworth at three o'clock and five o'clock right in front of the gazebo. Why do you ask?"

"I'm heading there with Mrs. Vesper and Elana, but if I decide to return on my own—"

Jackson winked at her. "We'll see you back here at Winterhouse later today one way or another, Miss Somers."

"Buy me some jelly beans while you're there?" Sampson said.

Jackson fixed him with a level stare. "We do not request favors of our guests."

"But she lives here!" Sampson said.

Jackson considered. "You're absolutely right," he said. He handed Elizabeth a five-dollar bill. "Two bags of jelly beans, in that case."

Elizabeth laughed. "Will do!"

Jackson patted the desk sharply twice in front of Sampson. "Back to work, sir!"

Elizabeth looked to the far side of the lobby; there, fixed like statues beside the puzzle table, stood Mr. Wellington and Mr. Rajput, both examining the spread of pieces before them as though they were climbing a mountain and trying to chart a way across a dangerous crevasse. They were lost in such deep concentration, neither noticed Elizabeth approaching.

"Any luck today?" she said.

Mr. Wellington dropped his hand from his chin and regarded her with a bright smile; he looked like he'd stirred from a nap. "Miss Somers!" he said. "So very good to see you! Are you heading somewhere or coming to assist us?"

Mr. Rajput looked to Elizabeth with sad eyes. "Good afternoon. I'm guessing you are off on some adventure," he said wearily. "And we will just puzzle away here ourselves, fruitlessly."

"Enough of that, Mr. Rajput," Mr. Wellington said.

"I am heading out," Elizabeth said, "but I'll try to come this evening and help—" She stopped, noticed a piece on the edge of the table, and moved to pick it up. She studied it, scanned a section of the mountain that was already part of a cluster of more than a hundred pieces, and then moved over and pressed the piece in to join the others.

"How do you *do* that?" Mr. Rajput said, one of the few times his voice held any note other than boredom or melancholy. "Extraordinary!"

"It just felt right," Elizabeth said.

"Remarkable," Mr. Wellington said. "Absolutely remarkable." He looked to Mr. Rajput. "Well, we're up to three pieces on the day. What do you think of that?"

"No tea until we reach five," Mr. Rajput said. "As agreed upon." He had returned to his regular gloomy self. "I expect this will be a long afternoon."

"Elizabeth!" someone called. Elana and her grandmother were at the clerk's stand.

"I better get going," Elizabeth said to the two men. She glanced at the puzzle one more time, and then waved goodbye. "I'll come by tonight, okay?"

"We can only hope," Mr. Rajput said.

"Enjoy," Mr. Wellington said.

Elizabeth joined Elana and her grandmother, just as Jackson was indicating the car Mrs. Vesper had arranged was out front. Elana was dressed all in white, including a puffy white parka; Mrs. Vesper was once again all in black, though this time with a heavy overcoat.

"All set, my darling?" Mrs. Vesper said.

"This is going to be great!" Elana piped.

"I'm ready," said Elizabeth.

Mrs. Vesper leaned forward. "Let's not waste any time," she whispered.

The ride to Havenworth was uneventful. Elana's grandmother didn't say a word—perhaps because a young woman was in the car with them, something that bothered the old lady immensely when Jackson, just as the sedan pulled up and Mrs. Vesper was ushering the girls in, explained that a woman at the hotel needed to get to

Havenworth right away to handle some unforeseen emergency, and requested that she be allowed to ride to town with the three others.

"We will reimburse you for the car," Jackson explained patiently, and although Mrs. Vesper scowled and sighed, she relented and then tried her best to appear fine with the arrangement. The lady with them was anxious the entire ride; Elana prattled on about her upcoming ice-skating competition and how glad she was that her grandmother had given her new skates for Christmas. Elizabeth was relieved when the car finally reached town.

"Shall we have some tea," Mrs. Vesper said, "and a nice talk?" She looked sternly at Elana, making plain she wasn't asking what they wanted to do but, rather, explaining what they were going to do. The street where they'd been let out, just down the block from the gazebo, was bustling with shoppers and people out to enjoy the wintry afternoon. Music drifted from the gazebo and the sky was dotted with stray flakes of snow in the gentle wind.

Before Elana could agree for both of them, Elizabeth spoke up. "That sounds very nice, but there's a bookstore here that's very interesting, and I'd like to check it out first, so maybe we can meet up in a little bit, okay?" She took Elana's hand.

"Yes, but . . ." Elana said.

"It's such a great store," Elizabeth said. "You'll love it!" She looked to Elana's grandmother. "We'll meet you back here in two hours. Is that all right, Mrs. Vesper?"

The old woman put out an arm to block their way. "We've come here to discuss a few things," she said softly but firmly.

Elizabeth adjusted her glasses and looked at Mrs. Vesper. "Oh, definitely. And to have fun, too." She stared at the old woman's arm before her until the moment became so awkward that Mrs. Vesper moved aside. "I'm sure the tea place will still be open in a couple of hours."

Mrs. Vesper looked sternly at Elizabeth and then shifted her eyes to Elana. Her expression became conciliatory. "You're right, dear. You two go enjoy yourselves, and we can meet here in two hours." She smiled thinly and flashed Elana a look that indicated, *You be sure to be on your best behavior.* "And then we can talk," Mrs. Vesper said before turning and walking away.

Elizabeth realized she still held Elana's arm. Elana pulled it away slowly as she watched her grandmother depart. She seemed to be relaxing more with each step the old woman took.

"I hope I wasn't rude," Elizabeth said. "I figured it would be nice to be on our own."

Elana appeared flustered. "Yeah, well, we can just do what we want for a couple of hours and then meet back up with her." She nodded hesitantly. "Good thinking."

* * *

Harley Dimlow and Sons, Booksellers, was just as dim and overstuffed with books as it had been the week before when Elizabeth had first visited, and the man behind the counter was just as silent and weary-seeming. There were, however, a handful of people quietly browsing the shelves, and Elizabeth felt the shop was somehow warmer and more inviting than before.

"Cool place," Elana whispered, glancing around.

The clerk leaned forward to examine the two girls. "You're back," he said softly. His face was so sallow, and his hair was so wispy, he resembled someone who should have been sitting in a nursing home waiting for an afternoon snack.

"I am," Elizabeth said, pleased he remembered her.

The man nodded to her. "Ah, yes, you too," he said. "The Damien Crowley enthusiast."

Elizabeth was confused.

"It seems you're both back," he said.

Elana was shaking her head. "My first time in here," she said quickly.

The man frowned. "You bought a book a few days ago."

"Not me," Elana said brightly, shrugging. "Someone else. Sorry."

The man frowned dubiously and retreated into his little nook.

Elana turned to Elizabeth and arched her eyebrows. "You were looking for something in particular, right? There's a book you wanted?"

The encounter with the clerk had been strange enough; now Elizabeth was hoping Elana might want to drift off and find something on her own, but that seemed not about to happen. In fact, now that Mrs. Vesper had been left behind, Elizabeth realized she would need to spend the next couple of hours alone with Elana, and she wasn't sure what they might talk about or do.

"Oh, I just wanted to check out a section I was looking at when I was here before," Elizabeth said. Elana gave her a *lead the way* look, and Elizabeth headed for the back of aisle 13 to find *The Wonderful World of Words!* Several minutes later, though, after much searching and re-searching on all the shelves in the area, Elizabeth discovered the book was gone.

"Finding anything good?" Elana said. She was thumbing idly through some books on UFOs across the aisle from Elizabeth.

"Still looking," Elizabeth said.

"Oh, the Bermuda Triangle!" Elana said suddenly, yanking a book from a shelf. "This is such a cool subject. I did a report on it for school."

An idea came to Elizabeth, especially now that Elana was occupied. "I'll be right back." She moved away before Elana could object.

"Excuse me," Elizabeth whispered to the clerk when she reached his desk. She kept glancing back to make sure Elana wasn't following.

The man leaned forward, tipped his glasses up onto his forehead, and licked his lips. His ancient face was so lined with creases it looked something like a parched mud puddle, all gray and cracked. "Yes?" he said softly.

"Can you tell me where the Havenworth cemetery is?"

The man looked at her sidewise. He removed his

glasses from his forehead. "The cemetery?" he said, a bit more loudly.

Elizabeth hoped the man's voice hadn't carried to the rear of the shop. "Yes, I'd like to see it. I'm always interested in the history of a place, so I thought I would check it out."

"I see." The man blew softly on one of the lenses of his glasses and began to polish it with the sleeve of his shirt. "Are you looking for something in particular?"

Elizabeth felt uneasy. "I just wanted to see the cemetery," she said with a shrug, keeping her voice low. She glanced behind her and heard a faint swishing noise from aisle 13, the sound of steps. "Is it nearby?"

"It is," the old man said. "It is." He began to polish the other lens, and then he examined his glasses by holding them up to the light. He put them on and glanced around, apparently testing to see if his eyes still worked. "Three blocks from here. You go up Alder, take a right on Cedar, then a left on Spruce, and it's right at the very end of the street."

"Thanks." Elizabeth turned to see Elana rounding the aisle.

"Hey!" Elana said. "I thought you got lost or something."

"No, I just had a question."

"About what?" Elana said, standing before her with a perky smile.

"I couldn't find the book I was looking for." And then, to lend plausibility to her story, she removed a piece of paper from her pocket and set it on the clerk's desk. "I brought my book list with me, though."

The man peered at the sheet before him. There, folded but with some of the writing displayed, lay the page on which Winifred had worked through the words on the Winterhouse seal.

"Oh, I must have grabbed the wrong list," Elizabeth said.

The old man continued to stare at the paper. Very slowly, he moved his finger just over the words "Snow-Rioter."

"Winter or so," he said.

Elizabeth looked to him, then shook her head with incomprehension. The man jabbed a finger at the letter "w" in the words and then moved on to the "i-n-t-e" and "r" and then the "or" and "so" before repeating himself: "Winter or so."

Elizabeth was stunned: The word "winter" had been hiding right before her all this time.

"I don't get it," Elana said. "What's that all about?" She leaned in with interest.

"Nothing," Elizabeth said as she looked to the clerk. "I just grabbed the wrong paper, but thanks for helping me." She took Elana's hand. "Wanna go walk around?"

"But we just got here."

"We can come back later if we want to warm up." Her mind was racing; she'd need to wait until she was back at Winterhouse—with Freddy—to continue deciphering the words the clerk had revealed.

"I thought you wanted to look around for a while," Elana said, glancing at the rows of books.

The old man sat back slowly.

"I'm just excited to see more of the town," Elizabeth said. "And I couldn't find the book I was looking for anyway." She looked to the clerk. "It was by Dylan Grimes."

But before the old man could say anything, Elana grabbed Elizabeth's hand, moved toward the door, and said, "Well, if you want to go, let's go."

One hour later, Elizabeth had steadily guided the two of them closer to the cemetery without being obvious—she hoped. The snowfall had picked up, and the day was growing dim already. The colorful lights on the buildings of Havenworth made the first half of Spruce Street bright and welcoming; but farther down the block, the shops gave way to a few small houses set back from the road, and it suddenly felt like the warmth of the town had dwindled away.

"Let's head back," Elana said as they moved down the street.

Elizabeth peered toward the end of the block. "Hey, look. What's that?"

Elana gazed through the snowflakes. "Is that a cemetery?" She put a hand to Elizabeth's shoulder. "Come on, let's go back. Those places creep me out."

Elizabeth was determined; now that she was this close, she wasn't going to turn away.

"It looks interesting," Elizabeth said. "I love old cemeteries." This wasn't true at all, of course. She could recall being in a cemetery only once, back in Drere after the death of Aunt Purdy's friend Mabel Gulwether, when her aunt had dragged her to the graveyard to place a small bouquet of sunflowers on Mabel's grave.

Elana looked to her with alarm. "Well, I don't. Let's go back."

"But it looks so mysterious and interesting here. It reminds me of something out of *The Wolves of Willoughby Chase*. Have you ever read it?"

"No," Elana said, shaking her head and squinting into the snow. "It's pretty cold out."

It was definitely snowing harder now, and Elizabeth wasn't feeling all that chipper about traipsing around in the cemetery herself, even though she was resolved to see if there was one particular gravesite there.

"Well," she said, "if you don't want to go, just give me a few minutes to check it out, and I'll come right back."

"Why are you so stuck on going there?"

It really did sound kind of unusual, Elizabeth thought. "Five minutes," she said. She pointed to an antique shop back near the start of the block. "I'll come meet you in there, okay?"

Elana examined Elizabeth as though she'd asked her to plot out a bank robbery, but she peered at the store, took a deep breath, and said, "I'll see you there in five minutes."

Elizabeth turned and trudged toward the cemetery.

Without the bright lights of town, Elizabeth realized just how dim the afternoon had become. She stood before the wrought-iron gate, open wide between a line of brick walls that enclosed the cemetery, and looked inside. The graveyard wasn't very big, not even as big as the playground at the small school in Drere; and there were a few cedars here and there, which had been growing so long their roots created bumps and little berms all around. Some of the tombstones were so old and worn, the words carved on them were unreadable; plastic flowers lay on the snow atop a couple of graves; a few wooden crosses appeared ready to rot and fall over. Elizabeth stood in the entranceway and scanned all about to see if she could spot a relatively new tombstone somewhere. Darkness was closing in quickly.

"Not many visitors out this way," someone said. Elizabeth gasped.

From around the other side of the brick wall, a man with a thick gray beard stepped forward. He was enormous, even taller than Norbridge, and about as wide a person as Elizabeth had ever seen. He wore a tattered wool overcoat frosted with snow, his jeans were caked with dirt stains, his stocking cap clung to his head like a cowl, and his boots were laced high above his ankles and looked nearly as old as he was.

He stood blocking Elizabeth's way, staring at her with night-black eyes barely visible through his squint. The distraction of his ruddy and wrinkled face almost kept her from looking at him long enough to hold his gaze.

"Are you looking for something?" the man said.

Elizabeth was so startled she couldn't find her voice.

"I said are you looking for something?" the man repeated, more loudly. The wind moaned as it pressed through the weeds of the cemetery.

"I . . . I was just walking down here with my friend," Elizabeth said.

The man looked past her, scanned the street. "I don't see any friend." He examined Elizabeth more closely.

"She stopped in the antique store back there, and I came down here," Elizabeth said falteringly. "I'm interested in historic places, and I saw this—"

"It's not all that historic," the man said. "It's just our town's graveyard." He ran a hand across his cheek.

She thought this might be an opening. "It looks pretty old." The man said nothing. "Are you the caretaker?"

The man took three steps forward, and Elizabeth had the frightening thought that he might grab her, or at a minimum yell at her and tell her to leave him alone. He suddenly filled nearly her entire vision, looming large and dark before her as the snow fell even harder.

"I don't know why you're interested in this place," he said. "Besides, no one's been buried here in years."

With that, he turned and walked back inside the cemetery.

"No one at all?" Elizabeth said. She had a sensation of sinking and felt like she'd been standing on a patch of snow that was suddenly giving way—how could it be that Norbridge had told her Gracella was buried here, and now this man was letting her know otherwise?

The man didn't answer. He disappeared behind the wall, and then the iron gate swung into place, barring the entrance entirely. The man came into view again with an enormous chain in his hands and began winding it with a heavy clanking noise around the gate itself before fastening a thick lock on and snapping it in place. The click of the lock died quickly in the wind and darkness; Elizabeth stared at the man as he patted his hands clean.

"No one," he said, and then he retreated into the graveyard. In the darkness, he disappeared so completely Elizabeth thought she might have imagined the whole thing.

The wind stopped for a moment, everything grew quiet, and then Elizabeth went to meet Elana in the shop up the street.

CHAPTER 25

THE CAFÉ AND THE SCARAB

SCARE

One hour later, the two girls and Mrs. Vesper were seated at a booth in the Silver Fir Café, the bright paintings of birds on the high walls all around and cups of hot chocolate on the table before them. Mrs. Vesper had ordered each of them a piece of apple pie, but Elizabeth wasn't hungry and only picked at hers. The discovery at the cemetery and the awkwardness of sitting with Elana and her grandmother had ruined her appetite.

Norbridge lied to me, Elizabeth thought. She'd been hearing these words in her head since the strange man had locked the cemetery gate, and she felt so upset and hurt that any conversation with Mrs. Vesper and Elana seemed it would be merely a distraction.

Mrs. Vesper took a long sip of hot chocolate and fixed her gaze on Elizabeth. Her eyes were so penetrating and cold, and her white hair was so strangely lustrous, Elizabeth found herself unnerved. Her skin, even, had an unusual radiance, so that, despite her generally creepy appearance, there was something undeniably *preserved* about her. Even with her all-black clothing, which looked like something a woman from a hundred years before might have worn, Elana's grandmother appeared to have taken remarkable care of herself. She hadn't succumbed to the wrinkles and dishevelment typical of a woman her age. As the old woman stared at her, Elizabeth almost forgot about what she'd learned at the cemetery.

"We finally have a chance to visit," Mrs. Vesper said. "Get to know one another."

Elizabeth glanced at Elana, who was hanging on her grandmother's words.

"Thanks for bringing me here," Elizabeth said. "And for the hot chocolate and pie."

"My pleasure," Mrs. Vesper said. "My pleasure."

Elana explained how they had spent the preceding two hours—fortunately, leaving out the part about the cemetery—and gushing about how lovely Havenworth was and how they had to come back for another visit before they left Winterhouse in a few days. Mrs. Vesper asked Elizabeth about her life in Drere with her aunt and uncle. Elana mentioned a few things about her school and her skating and where she liked to go in the summer. After fifteen minutes of this, Elizabeth realized the three of them were having something close to an easy little discussion. When she thought back to it later, this part of the afternoon felt . . . *normal.*

Then Mrs. Vesper put her cup down, wiped her lips slowly, and set her hands in her lap to fix Elizabeth with a resolved expression.

"And what about church?" she said. "Did you go to church with your aunt and uncle?"

It was a completely unexpected question. Elizabeth had been preparing herself to talk about Winterhouse and then, she hoped, turn the conversation to Mrs. Vesper's interest in the secret passageways. She hadn't considered she might be asked what church she went to.

"Church? Not really. I mean, on Christmas and Easter, yes, but not much otherwise."

Elana sat up. "We don't go, either."

"It's good to believe in something," Mrs. Vesper said. "But our beliefs are, let's say, not the ones you might find in a church."

"What do you mean by 'our beliefs'?" Elizabeth said. The way Mrs. Vesper had said these words sounded very peculiar.

"Well, dear," Mrs. Vesper said, "most of what they teach in church is about getting along with everyone, no matter who they are. Even if they aren't worthy, or even if they are, say, poor or weak. It seems unusual, doesn't it? That we should try to get along with people who are beneath us? You might say it's a waste of our time, a waste of our efforts."

Elizabeth had never heard anyone talk like this, and

although there was maybe a tiny bit of logic in what Mrs. Vesper was saying, it didn't feel like it added up to the right conclusion.

"How does all that fit in with what you believe?" Elizabeth said. She was intrigued.

"We feel that if someone is fortunate to have any degree of, say, power," Mrs. Vesper said, "then he or she ought not to diminish it by sharing it with people who aren't deserving. In fact, that person should try to accumulate as much power as possible. That's the only way to keep everything moving forward in this world—by growing stronger, becoming stronger."

Elana was looking to her grandmother with something like apprehension.

Elizabeth, as unfamiliar as she was with this sort of conversation and these ideas, felt a thrill as she listened to the old woman talk. There was something alluring about her words.

"Why are you telling me all this?" Elizabeth said. "And what do you mean by 'we'?"

Mrs. Vesper looked to Elana. It was clear they had discussed something beforehand, and this was the moment when Elana would take over.

"It's our whole family, really," Elana said softly. "All my cousins and aunts and uncles, and, well, everyone. Where we live, everyone feels the way we do. And that's why I was saying, you know, I feel like it would be so nice if you and I were closer, like sisters, even." She turned to her grandmother. "Oh, I'm not saying it right at all!"

Elizabeth was confused by Elana's words, but something about Mrs. Vesper—the look in her eyes or the sound of her voice—kept her from becoming unnerved by Elana's weird speech. Elizabeth felt calm and receptive.

"What my granddaughter is trying to say," Mrs. Vesper said, "is that Winterhouse feels like a special place to us, the kind of place where a person might find herself in possession of something that had some power, something that would be even magical, you might say. It seems like an enchanted place, with many possibilities." She laughed, in acknowledgment that she was maybe veering into subjects that sounded bizarre. "Who knows? And because you live there, my hope is that you would feel close enough to us to share that. Do you understand?"

Elizabeth felt once again that the individual words she was hearing were clear, but that they didn't add up to anything coherent. She couldn't make sense of it.

"Like you were part of our family," Elana said. "You know, how people share things?"

"I guess," Elizabeth said. She felt heavy; her thoughts had slowed.

Mrs. Vesper's eyes bored into her; her voice was soothing. "In our family, no one would lie to you or scold you or anything. And you would have Elana as a friend, not just a lot of workers and old people."

Her words intertwined with thoughts already swirling in Elizabeth's mind, about Norbridge lying to her regarding Gracella's death, about Jackson most likely doing the same, about Leona being upset with her for making simple mistakes in the library, about how when Freddy was gone, there would be night after night of no one to talk to or joke around with. In a week or two, she would be alone at Winterhouse with people decades older than her who didn't really understand her and seemed, quite often, not to take her seriously.

"Does this have something to do with the story about the secret passageways?" Elizabeth said. Her words felt thick; she had the sensation that someone other than her was speaking.

"Perhaps," Mrs. Vesper said. "It may all be connected. We are just hoping we might remain close, become as close as possible, and then if there is any chance that we—"

"Miss Somers," someone said, and Elizabeth's head cleared instantly. It was like feeling a cold breeze or having loud music turned off so that your thoughts can straighten. She shook her head the way she might have if she had just awakened and wanted not to fall back asleep.

Standing beside the table and dressed in the same suit and tie he'd worn on the only other occasion they'd met was Mr. Egil P. Fowles, the headmaster of the school Elizabeth would be attending once the new year began.

"Professor Fowles," Elizabeth said with surprise. She felt as disoriented as if she was back in Drere and the headmaster had happened to walk into her aunt and uncle's house.

"I thought that was you," he said, and before Elizabeth could introduce Mrs. Vesper or Elana, Mr. Fowles was reaching a hand out to each of them and introducing himself. Mrs. Vesper looked upset at being interrupted, and Elana appeared unsure how to proceed, whether to be polite or sullen or something else entirely.

"Well," Mr. Fowles said, once the introductions had been made, "I didn't mean to interrupt your visit. Just wanted to say hello." He paused and leaned forward to look more closely at Mrs. Vesper. "Madam," he said, "that bracelet of yours."

Mrs. Vesper lifted her arm slightly and looked to her wrist at the thin, silver bracelet visible above her long black sleeve. On it was a symbol that looked like this:

"A little bauble I picked up recently," Mrs. Vesper said, and then she lowered her arm and covered the bracelet. She looked at Mr. Fowles with pressed lips.

"Do you know what it stands for?" Mr. Fowles said.

Mrs. Vesper shook her head dismissively. "Egyptian, I believe. A bit of decoration."

"I have some expertise in the area of hieroglyphics, and that, madam, is indeed an ancient Egyptian symbol." Mr. Fowles leaned forward again. "It is a scarab. Or, as we would call it, a beetle. It was the symbol for eternity, for the transformation of the body and soul."

Elana shifted her anxious eyes to her grandmother.

"And with that," Mr. Fowles said, "I must be off." He dipped his head in Elizabeth's direction. "I will look forward to seeing you when school resumes, if not sooner. And it has been a pleasure to meet you both," he said to the other two before he turned and left.

Mrs. Vesper said nothing. She merely sat looking flustered for a moment before smiling oddly at Elizabeth. "Very nice man," she said without enthusiasm.

"He's the head of the school where I'll be going," Elizabeth said. She felt uncomfortable suddenly. "And he's good friends with Mr. Falls, who runs Winterhouse."

"Before he came," Elana said, glancing furtively at her grandmother and then back to Elizabeth, "I think we were talking about how nice it would be for us to share everything."

But the mood—the spell—of a few minutes before had evaporated; Elizabeth felt she wanted to get away from Elana, her grandmother, the café, everything. She'd heard enough. "I don't know. I'll have to think it over." She looked to the doorway. "Maybe I should get going."

"We've hardly been here long," Mrs. Vesper said, a note of desperation in her voice. "Besides, I just keep thinking about how lonely you will be at Winterhouse once we're gone. I think of that poor girl who rode the bus here all by herself late at night, who—"

"What do you mean?" Elizabeth said. "I came in the middle of the day."

Elana jumped in. "I thought you said last year—"

"I never said anything about last year." Elizabeth stared at Mrs. Vesper and studied her face carefully. "How did you know I came last year at night on the bus?"

"I'm certain you mentioned it at some point," Mrs. Vesper said.

Elizabeth stood. "I better get going."

"Our car and driver won't be here for another hour," Mrs. Vesper said coldly.

"I can get home on my own."

"Elizabeth," Elana said with a pleading tone in her voice—it wasn't clear if Elana was wanting her to stay or encouraging her to leave.

"I think you're both up to something," Elizabeth said.

Mrs. Vesper narrowed her eyes at Elizabeth. "Sit down," she said grimly. "Now."

"I'm not your granddaughter, and I don't have to listen to you. I'm leaving."

"Sit down!" Mrs. Vesper said, almost snarling the words.

"I'm leaving," Elizabeth said. "And I'm going to talk to Norbridge."

"Sit!" Mrs. Vesper said, and she reached and grabbed Elizabeth's arm.

Instantly, before she even considered what she was doing, *the feeling* arose inside Elizabeth, and she glared at Mrs. Vesper. The teapot on the table began to rattle on its plate, clattering away as if the water inside had begun boiling furiously; and then it lurched off the plate, crashed to one side, and poured its remaining water across the table and onto the floor.

"What in the world!" Mrs. Vesper cried, standing abruptly as her chair fell back. But Elizabeth was already racing out the door, into the dark streets of Havenworth and away from Mrs. Vesper and Elana. When she returned to Winterhouse, she would talk to Norbridge and tell him everything—except how much pleasure she'd taken in using her power.

CHAPTER 26

THE SEAL UNRAVELED

REVEAL

"Kiona had a really rough day," Sampson said from behind the clerk's desk in the lobby.

Elizabeth had barely been able to contain her racing thoughts as the shuttle bus had carried her back to Winterhouse; and now, having dashed into the lobby and explained to Sampson that she needed to find Norbridge immediately, he was telling her Norbridge and Leona had accompanied Kiona to the hospital in Havenworth and wouldn't be back until late that night.

"They want to make sure she's all right," Sampson said somberly. "Honestly, they were pretty worried about her. I think everyone is."

Elizabeth's concerns about what Mrs. Vesper might

be up to and why Gracella wasn't really buried in the Havenworth cemetery receded for the moment.

"I guess I'll talk to him in the morning, then," Elizabeth said.

Sampson shrugged. "I wish I could be of more help."

Elizabeth thought of something. "Do you know if Jackson's around?"

"I'm pretty sure he's in Grace Hall. They're setting up for the lecture tonight."

And after she thanked him and raced off, Grace Hall was exactly where she found Jackson as he was supervising an arrangement of tables on the stage for the evening's lecture.

"Miss Somers!" Jackson said as she raced down the long aisle and rushed up the stairs to him. "What brings you here?"

"Jackson," she said, breathing hard, "I wanted to ask you about something."

He raised his eyebrows and waited.

"I went to the cemetery in Havenworth today."

Jackson looked at her with his large, friendly eyes. He adjusted the brass nameplate on his coat, made sure his pillbox hat was straight, and cleared his throat. "You found the cemetery in town?" he said, and Elizabeth nodded. Jackson rubbed his chin. "I have a feeling I know where this is going. I also know that Mr. Norbridge Falls himself advised you not to visit there."

"I'm going to tell him, too. Maybe I shouldn't have gone, but I did. I think you probably already know what I found there—or, I guess I should say, what I didn't find there."

"I see," Jackson said. He nodded slowly, taking in this new information. "Yes, I see." He held up a hand. "Before you go any further, allow me to clarify two things. First, you should discuss all of this with your grandfather. He is absolutely the one with whom you should be having this discussion. The second is that Gracella Winters indisputably perished on that night nearly a year ago in our library. Which is to say: She died. The coroner examined her, we all witnessed the body—cold, with no pulse, nothing at all. And so I can tell you with one hundred percent certainty that your grandfather's sister died. There is no question about that."

"Then why isn't she buried in the cemetery like Norbridge said?"

"This is a very disturbing part of the story, Miss Somers. I think you should take it up with your grandfather."

"Please, Jackson! Sooner or later I'll find out, and I just want to know what happened."

He sighed, looking to the curtained stage and then back to Elizabeth. "It seems someone gained access to the mortuary where Gracella lay awaiting burial. The coroner was perhaps not as diligent as he might have been. We actually had members of the Winterhouse staff stationed there with him for protection at all times. But in the middle of the night the day before she was to be buried, somehow . . . We don't know how it happened. The bellhop on duty at the mortuary fell into a sleep that lasted for hours, and when he woke up, the body was gone." Jackson looked to the floor.

"Someone stole her body?" Elizabeth said. She felt instantly chilled.

"In so many words, yes. Someone stole her body."

"It had to be Selena," Elizabeth said. "I know it! And if Gracella really has all the evil magic we know she has and she came back last year, maybe the same thing's happening again."

"As I said, you should discuss all of it with your grandfather."

"I understand. But he might not be back till late tonight?"

"I'll let him know right away that you wish to see him."

"Thank you, Jackson." Elizabeth ran her gaze over the entire hall, her eyes lingering on the enormous stage. "It's frightening, all of it." She needed to talk to Freddy.

Jackson nodded gravely. "Mr. Falls," he said. "That's who can straighten this out."

Elizabeth burst into the camera obscura room five minutes later. "Hey!" Freddy called to her. "I thought you might—"

"Freddy!" Elizabeth said as she raced up the ramp to him. "You're not gonna believe everything that's happened today. I went to the cemetery, and I had a really weird conversation with Elana and her grandmother, and you won't believe what I found out!"

"Whoa! Slow down. What happened?"

"Someone stole Gracella's body! Last year from the morgue. She was never buried."

Freddy's mouth dropped open. "What?" His glasses started to slide down his nose, and he pressed them back up. "You've gotta be kidding me!"

"I wish. And come with me. I think I figured something out."

As they headed to the Winterhouse seal, Elizabeth shared everything that had happened, and Freddy took it all in with somber interest. "Who do you think took . . ." Freddy said when Elizabeth had finished explaining everything. "You know, stole her . . ."

"Who do I think stole Gracella's body?" Elizabeth said. It felt creepy to speak those words. "I'm sure it was Selena Hiems, but I don't know how she did it."

"Maybe other people helped her somehow," Freddy said.

"There are definitely other people involved. I just don't know how many. Mrs. Vesper is for sure on my list of most suspicious people right now, and probably Elana, too. And the Powters aren't far behind. I just don't understand how it's all related, or how it connects to what happened last year."

"There has to be another object they're trying to get their hands on," Freddy said. "That's the only thing that makes sense."

"Someone wants to find the fourth door and get whatever it is that's hidden in the passageway. And I think

Mrs. Vesper thinks I can lead them to it. She's connected to Gracella; I just know it. The Powters, too. I can't quite figure out how it all fits together, but I'm going to talk to Norbridge when he comes back. He *has* to believe me now."

The two of them stood before the Winterhouse seal. "Okay," Elizabeth said. "I think I may have started to figure things out. The clerk at that bookstore noticed something that helped me, and I've been playing around with the letters in my head ever since."

She pointed to the rectangle before them, with the words "Snow-Rioter" inside. "Look at that," she said. "The word 'winter' is in 'Snow-Rioter.'"

Freddy peered at the words and then turned to Elizabeth with a look of pleasant comprehension. "But it leaves 's-o-r-o' still, and that doesn't add up to anything."

Elizabeth indicated the words on the floor again. "But add in 'Drift,' and then try it. 'S-o-r-o-d-r-i-f-t.'"

Once again, Freddy stared at the seal in deep contemplation. And then an expression of shocked awareness took over his face, and he gaped at Elizabeth. "'First door,'" he said quietly. "It says 'first door.'"

"Yep!" Elizabeth said, nodding. "You got it. 'First door winter'!"

"Have you figured out the other ones, too?"

"Not yet. But let's try."

"It seems like there's a season, a number, and the word 'door' in each one," Freddy said, his thoughts already spinning the letters around every which way.

"Let's figure out the rest," Elizabeth said.

Over the next few minutes, the remaining words in the rectangles resolved for two of them, now that they understood the key. "Prison-Dodge Scorn" became "second door spring"; "Trim-Room Shudder" became "third door summer"; and "Flood-Furor Halt" became "fourth door fall."

"It's easy once you know what's going on," Freddy said. "Now that we know what the words are, it seems sort of obvious." He became serious once more as he examined the seal. "But what does it mean? And the numbers, too?"

"That's what I can't figure out."

Freddy studied the seal with renewed interest, staring deeply at the inscriptions. "Hey," he said, "what if the word 'steps' really does mean 'steps'? And if each set of words is sort of like a title for one of the four doors, maybe the numbers are like directions to the doors."

Elizabeth's eyes widened. "You think those are the number of steps someone would take to get to each door?"

Freddy shrugged. "Let's try it out. We know where the winter door is. It's in the candy kitchen, so if we start right here on the seal and walk one hundred twenty-six steps—"

"To the left!" Elizabeth yelled. "Sinister! The left side! That's got to be it! Come on. Let's write down the numbers and give it a try."

They walked 126 steps down the corridor, at which point they came to a T and turned right to pace off 38 steps before making another turn. They followed each of the numbers in turn and counted off the steps, all leading to the candy kitchen. And although the door to the kitchen was closed when they arrived—so that they were unable to count off the final steps—it was clear the numbers would lead to the Walnut Door.

"Amazing!" Freddy said. "The seal is basically a map to the four doors."

"We'll know for sure after we try the next one," Elizabeth said. "The spring door is the one that was in the library."

They raced back to the seal, and after they started at the second rectangle and—heading left at the outset—followed the steps, it led them to the locked door of the library.

"If we could keep going, the steps would take us to the wall where I saw the plaque," Elizabeth said. "There's no doubt the seal is a map."

"Which means we can figure out the location of the two other doors now," Freddy said.

Elizabeth's eyes went bright. "Let's do it!"

The next door, however—the summer one—proved troublesome. Unlike the doors in the candy kitchen and library, of which they were already aware, the location of the third door was unknown, and so at each fork, it was unclear if they needed to turn left or right. After much backtracking and many false turns and treks up and down staircases, they worked through a path that took them to the workshop on the third floor where Freddy had perfected the Walnut WonderLog. They stood in the hall-way; Freddy didn't have his key on him.

"This can't be right," Elizabeth said.

Freddy was just as puzzled. "There's no door. I've been in there a million times."

Elizabeth studied her paper. "We must have made a mistake somewhere."

"Hey, we know the last door is in Norbridge's room," Freddy said. "Why don't we go through the steps and see if that one works? Then we can figure out this third one."

"Good idea."

Fifteen minutes later, after walking through the steps for the fourth door, they did, indeed, find themselves in front of Norbridge's apartment.

"Next time I'm in here, I'll walk off the rest of it," Elizabeth said, "and I bet I'll find the door."

"Let me get the key to my workshop," Freddy said. "At least we can look in there and see if we notice anything having to do with the other door."

The first thing they did when they were inside Freddy's workshop—still cluttered with sawhorses and tables and boards and tools—was pace off the numbers from the seal, though the final steps were blocked by several crates set against the wall.

"I never really thought much about this stuff," Freddy said as they pushed boxes aside and stacked them away from the wall.

Once they cleared all the boxes and slid two pieces of

plywood out of the way, they saw, painted white like the wall itself so that it was almost unnoticeable, a door. It was a smooth white panel of wood set within a molded sill; even its knob had been painted white.

"It was here the whole time," Freddy said. He sounded like he'd turned a corner and found that his house had appeared. "I can't believe it."

"Incredible," Elizabeth said. She put a hand to the door and ran her fingers across it lightly, the way you might check a wall you had painted the day before to test if it was dry. She pulled her hand away and studied the door before trying to turn the handle. It was fixed in place.

"I wonder why it's painted over," she said.

"Maybe they wanted to make it look like the wall," Freddy said.

Her eyes fixed on something above the top sill that was slightly raised, though just as white as the door itself.

"That's got to be another plaque," she said. "Hey, don't you have some turpentine or something in here?"

"Right here," Freddy said, grabbing a bottle of turpentine and a towel from the table.

Elizabeth slid a crate in front of the door and stepped onto it, wet one of the towels, and then began scrubbing at the paint. It washed off slowly, revealing a brass plaque inscribed with faint letters. Once she'd rubbed away the last streaks of paint, she hopped down from the crate and stood back to read what was written there:

SUMMER

THEN ALTERS TO AN OBJECT STRONG
ITS POWER USED FOR RIGHT OR WRONG

"We found the door," Elizabeth said. "If I can find the one in Norbridge's room, I'll know the entire poem. It's got to be the explanation for whatever is in the passageways."

"I still can't believe this door was here all along," Freddy said.

Elizabeth examined the plaque. And then she stepped forward, leaned into the door, and placed her ear against it; instantly, she heard the faint humming noise again, like

a motor starting in the distance. She pressed against the door more closely and listened.

"What do you hear?" Freddy said. He stepped forward and put his ear against the door. After a moment he backed away and shook his head. "Nothing," he said with a shrug.

"A low humming noise," Elizabeth said. "Don't you hear it?"

Freddy moved his head to the door again and then gave a frown. "I don't hear a thing."

"It's pretty clear," Elizabeth said. An idea came to her: *Maybe I'm the only one who can hear it, just like I was the only one who could find The Book.* And then this thought was broken by a tremor that ran through her and that made her jerk her head away from the door. Someone was approaching.

"Freddy!" she said. "Quickly! Let's cover this up!"

Within seconds, they had slid a piece of plywood in front of the door and were restacking some boxes.

"Hey!" someone said from the doorway, and when Elizabeth and Freddy looked, there stood Rodney and his parents, staring at them.

CHAPTER 27

THE VIEW FROM THE DARK ROOM
METHOD

"What are you guys doing?" Rodney said indignantly. Mr. and Mrs. Powter looked as though they'd caught Elizabeth and Freddy stealing something.

"This is my workshop," Freddy said. "And it's private." He and Elizabeth moved slowly from the stack of boxes they'd arranged.

Mr. Powter examined the room the way a person looks at a home he might want to buy. "I wasn't informed that this space was closed to guests," he said.

"Yes," Mrs. Powter said. "And we'd like to take a look around."

Elizabeth took a deep breath. "I know you're up to

something," she said, "and I know what you're looking for."

"Oh, and just what is that?" Mrs. Powter said. She began glancing to the corners of the room. "And just why are the two of you so jittery?"

"Why don't you leave us alone?" Freddy said.

"Oh! Mr. Inventor finally sticks up for his girlfriend!" Rodney said.

"She's not my girlfriend!" Freddy said. "And you all need to leave."

"Now, look here, young man," Mr. Powter said, "we are paying guests of the hotel and can go where we like."

Mrs. Powter took another survey of the room, running her eyes across the walls. "Perhaps there's something interesting in this room." She looked to Elizabeth with a cruel smile. "Don't you think?"

Rodney leered at Elizabeth like a gremlin, his eyes full of hatred. "I think so," he said.

"The lovely Powter family!" came Norbridge's voice from the corridor, and then Norbridge himself stood in the doorway. He looked to Elizabeth and Freddy. "And two more of my favorites, as well! Greetings, one and all!"

"These two *children* inform us we are not allowed in this room," Mr. Powter said, pulling himself up to full height and wheeling on Norbridge.

"They would be correct," Norbridge said gently, stroking his beard.

"And what is the reason for that?" Mrs. Powter said. "It's only a little workshop."

"A little workshop that is off-limits," Norbridge said, the wisp of a smile still on his face as he spoke calmly. "Except to my designated inventor and my granddaughter." He backed away from the door and swept his arm into the corridor. "And now I invite you to prepare yourselves for dinner." He winked. "We are serving pork chops tonight. Very tasty."

Mr. and Mrs. Powter stood as if in shock. Mrs. Powter began shaking her head in disbelief. "This is very poor treatment, Mr. Falls," she said. "Very poor."

"Let's get out of here," Rodney said. "Losers. At a stupid hotel." He stalked out the door.

"This isn't the end of this," Mr. Powter said to no one in particular before he and his wife followed their son.

Norbridge squinted at their backs as they left but said nothing. He stepped into the room and examined the wall with the boxes before it; it seemed he'd already dismissed the Powters from his thoughts.

"How's Kiona doing?" Elizabeth said to fill the heavy silence.

"She gave us a scare," Norbridge said, "but it looks like she's going to be fine." He looked to Elizabeth. "What's going on in here?"

"Why didn't you just tell me about Gracella from the start?" she said.

Norbridge inhaled deeply. "Ah, I see. Elizabeth, to be frank, it's not the sort of thing I wanted to share with my granddaughter. I'm aware you spoke with Jackson about it, and I'm hoping you can forgive me. I simply wanted to spare you unnecessary worry." He curled his lips. "Perhaps I should have told you, and I'm sorry if you feel hurt about it."

Elizabeth felt anger rising in her again. On the one hand, it made sense that Norbridge had spared her the details—and he was apologizing—but it also made her feel like a little kid, like someone he didn't trust enough to handle the truth. Her eyes began to burn, but she told herself she wasn't going to lose her temper and she wasn't going to cry.

"I think she's trying to come back somehow," Elizabeth said. "And I think Mrs. Vesper and the Powters have something to do with it. They even knew my email address, and Freddy and I think maybe they hacked my account. Maybe that's how they knew I was coming back to Winterhouse and a bunch of other things. Maybe they're helping Gracella, just like the Hiemses."

"We know where all the doors are, too," Freddy said, "and we figured out the Winterhouse seal."

Elizabeth looked to Freddy, dumbfounded—but also a little glad—he'd laid everything out so starkly.

Norbridge gave a long, loud sigh, like he'd rolled off his bed onto the floor and was trying to make sense of his condition. He put a hand to his brow and began to rub the skin there. "I'm getting too old for this," he said, with just enough lightness that Elizabeth felt reassured. And then he dropped his hand and said, "Just tell me everything."

Which she did over the next several minutes. And when

she was done, Norbridge simply nodded and said, "Three things. Stay completely away from Elana and Mrs. Vesper and the Powters. And keep the door to this workshop locked at all times."

Elizabeth was confused. "That's only two things."

Norbridge placed his hand over his heart. "And stay out of trouble. For your grandfather's sake." He fixed Elizabeth with his gaze. "I believe you, though."

The evening passed without incident—and so did the next day. In fact, Elizabeth didn't see Elana or her grandmother or the Powters at all; she and Freddy spent the time sledding, racing the trains in the glassed-in diorama in the lobby, and talking things over in the camera obscura room while Freddy worked. In the evening they attended a lecture in Grace Hall ("Five and a Half Years in Ruben Maesta's Chocolate Emporium"), and then they both turned in early.

Things calmed down—but ominously, Elizabeth felt: The days were pleasant only on the surface. There was another very interesting lecture she and Freddy attended— "The Life of Edgar Cayce—Man of Mystery," delivered by a man from India who wore a beret and spoke with a charming English accent; they also attended two of the concerts in Grace Hall, watched a movie (*The Sea Charmer*, about a doomed mermaid and a pilfered bottle of rare absinthe), and made two visits to the swimming pool. She noticed a delivery of luggage and boxes for the Thatchers, who were said to be arriving just after the New Year; she visited Kiona, too, briefly, after she returned from the hospital, and she was doing well.

Three days after the discovery of the door in Freddy's workshop, Elizabeth awoke to find a note under her door that read:

Come to the camera obscura room before
breakfast!—Freddy

She dressed quickly and headed upstairs. When she entered the camera obscura room, Freddy was on the platform with a rope in one hand and a wrench in the other.

"Elizabeth!" he called. "Come on up. I have something to show you."

"Looking pretty good in here," she said as she walked up the ramp. The scaffolding had been removed, and the room looked open and bright.

They talked for a few minutes about the movie from the night before, and all the while Freddy was distractedly fiddling with the ropes and pulleys and adjusting the huge white disk of the screen itself before them.

"So why did you want me to come here?" Elizabeth said.

Freddy said nothing, merely pointed to the ceiling. He had a glint in his eye as he turned to the panel mounted beside the platform and flipped a switch; the room went dark aside from a small, dim light in the panel itself.

"Watch," Freddy said. With a pull of the rope beside him and, high above in the ceiling, a sort of gulping sound like the noise a flue makes in a chimney when it's opened and a fire is about to be lit, the white disk in front of Elizabeth and Freddy was instantly alive with a winter scene: an ice-coated lake in the foreground and, beyond that, a line of brilliant snow-clad mountains gleaming under a blue morning sky. Elizabeth let out a gasp of astonishment. It felt less that a picture had been projected onto the disk in the style of a movie screen and more that, through some animating magic, the white surface of the shallow bowl had burst into life: a world of winter color and vibrancy and light had been waiting to press itself into the white screen and had now blossomed instantly.

"Incredible!" Elizabeth said, taking in the scene before her, so crisp and alive it seemed to be trembling, the way things look from the edge of some high cliff or mountaintop.

"I told you!" Freddy said. "Awesome, huh?"

A sudden realization struck Elizabeth. "Hey, that's Lake Luna!"

"Yeah, we're looking at what's outside Winterhouse right now. The box on the roof is like a camera, and we're seeing the video here!" He gestured to the white disk. "Watch."

He gave a tug of the rope, and suddenly the lake drew even closer, as though Freddy had swooped some airborne camera instantly nearer to the lake by a few hundred yards.

He pulled on a second rope, working the two in tandem, and the image on the disk grew smaller and then, with a blur, changed into a view of the sledding hill and, beyond it, a slope of snow-clad hemlocks.

"You can look all around," Freddy said. He tugged at the ropes again, and suddenly the sledding hill filled the entire screen. "You can zoom in"—he pulled again, and the sledding hill became a small streak in the middle of a vast spread of snow and trees—"or you can zoom out! Whatever you want. I'm just letting more or less light come in through the little hole on the box up on the roof."

Elizabeth stared in pleasant shock. It seemed Freddy had brought an entire small world to life on the disk before them, and she was overwhelmed by what she was seeing. "I didn't really know what to expect," Elizabeth said, "even after all the times you showed me this stuff. But now! Wow, this is incredible!"

They spent the next half hour looking at the world around Winterhouse, all revealed on the white screen. Twice cars approached on the road to the hotel, and Freddy showed Elizabeth a trick where, by holding a piece of paper above the disk at the point where the car was projected, it looked like Freddy was carrying it on the paper itself. He did the same thing when they noticed a bellhop walking behind the hotel toward the lake—Freddy hovered the piece of paper over the screen, and the man appeared to be walking on the paper rather than the snow outside.

"That's too funny!" Elizabeth said.

"This thing is so cool. People are going to love coming up here to check it out."

Freddy became silent for a moment. "Hey, Elizabeth," he said. "There's something I've been wondering about. Remember how when we found the door in my workshop and then you said we needed to hurry and cover it up? It was almost like you knew the Powters were coming."

Elizabeth had been wondering for so long about whether she ought to tell Freddy about *the feeling* and the power associated with it, and now he was practically inviting her to explain. Aside from Norbridge and Kiona, no one else knew about it. "It was just a kind of feeling I had," she said. "I don't know how to explain it. Sometimes I sort of sense things before they happen." She wasn't sure how much more to reveal. "I can even make things move."

"Move?" Freddy said. "I don't get it."

"Have you ever read *Matilda*?"

"You and all your books! What does that have to do with anything?"

"Well, it's kind of like how in that book she—" Elizabeth began, but just then she saw something on the screen that caught her attention: Two people had departed the back doors of Winterhouse and were heading for the ski shed.

"Hey, look," she said, pointing to the white disk.

Freddy pulled at the ropes, and suddenly the view was of the two people at close range: Elana, dressed in white, and Rodney, in a sleek black jacket and pants, were walking briskly toward the ski shed.

"Our two favorite people!" Freddy said.

Elizabeth peered at the screen in amazement. "What are they doing?"

"Breakfast just started, too. So why are they outside right now?"

Elizabeth stared intently. The two were talking about something, and then Rodney laughed and Elana broke into a smile.

Freddy adjusted the view, then backed out; Elana and Rodney reached the ski shed.

Elizabeth looked to Freddy. "The shed's not even open right now," she said. Elana and Rodney appeared with skis and poles in their hands.

"They're going skiing, it looks like," Freddy said.

"I don't get it," Elizabeth said. A bad feeling was growing in her. She watched the two by the ski shed, saw them put on cross-country ski boots, click into their skis, and then push off with their poles along the groomed tracks that led along the west side of the lake.

"They look like they have somewhere to go," Freddy said.

"I think you're right." Elizabeth guessed Freddy was thinking just what she was: Gracella's cabin, the very place from which she and Freddy had once been chased by the spirit of Gracella herself, lay a couple of miles up the trail Elana and Rodney were approaching.

"I'm going to check out what's going on," she said.

"Elizabeth, no!" Freddy said. "No way, you cannot go out there!"

She began to hurry down the ramp toward the door. "I have to," she called. "I'll see if Jackson or Sampson or someone is around, but I've gotta hurry! Let someone know I went out if you don't see me back here in an hour!"

"Elizabeth, don't! Just wait for Norbridge!"

But she was already out the door and in the corridor, racing for the stairwell so she could get to the ski shed herself, clamp on a pair of skis, and follow Elana and Rodney.

CHAPTER 28

DANGER AT THE CABIN

TARGET

Panicked thoughts raced through Elizabeth's mind as she glided along the ski trail. The morning air was brisk and sharp—her breath flashed away from her in puffs of steam, and her face felt blistered by the cold. But she was too focused on discovering where Elana and Rodney were going and what they were doing to consider how frigid the morning was. She hadn't seen Sampson or Jackson or anyone else she trusted once she'd departed the elevator on the first floor. There had been no time to waste—no opportunity to detour to Winter Hall or wander around looking for help. She'd needed to get moving right away or risked losing all hope of catching up to Elana and Rodney. Uncertainty filled her as she pushed forward along the twin tracks in the snow; she had no idea what she would say or do when—or if—she found Elana and Rodney.

After leaving the wide field along the Winterhouse side of Lake Luna, Elizabeth followed the trail into the trees that rimmed the lake along its west side. It was dim here, a world of green hemlock and white snow and blue-black shadow.

As the minutes passed and she pressed on, she kept scanning ahead for signs of the other two. Her breath pounded in her chest, and twice—ten or fifteen minutes away from Winterhouse—she stopped to recover her wind. Each time she was awed by how quiet it was in the forest, the sunlight streaming silently through the trees. She continued, calculating how far she was from Gracella's cabin, where she was certain Elana and Rodney were headed.

An ice-crusted stream came into view and, spanning the short distance across it, a snow-covered bridge. was the turnoff to Gracella's cabin. Elizabeth slowed, m forward quietly, barely gliding She came to a stop b grove of thin alders and removed her skis. Two sk led from the trail itself up the gently sloping hill directly to the small cabin that sat in a clearing atop the crest. Two pairs of skis leaned upright before its door. Elana and Rodney were inside.

Elizabeth began to walk, in sunlight again. The snow wasn't deep, and the tracks had cleared a path for her; she didn't make a sound. Slowly, steadily, one deliberate step at a time, she moved closer to the cabin.

"You need to make the lines darker over there," came a voice—Rodney's—from inside. These were the first words Elizabeth could make out now that she was ten yards from the cabin.

"I wish we didn't have to do this," came another voice—Elana's.

"Well, then don't," Rodney said with annoyance. "That's if you want Mom and Dad to get mad at us."

Mom and Dad? Elizabeth thought. *Who is he talking about?*

"Really," Elana said, "this whole thing is awful. I hate it."

"Well, do you want her spirit to come here instead of the hotel?" Rodney said. "Let's just finish the drawing like Aunt Selena told us. Then they can find the thing in the passage."

Elizabeth stood listening, straining to catch every ⎯d. She felt so stretched with tension, wanting to learn ⎯ever she could—but the cold was settling in on her ⎯y, and she was terrified she would be discovered.

⎯t Selena can stay an old lady for all I care," Elana ⎯ "She hasn't been nice to me this whole time. Not at all."

"Do you want the same thing to happen to us that happened to her? You want to turn old? Or worse? I don't like this any more than you do, but we have to help."

"I know," Elana said. "Still, I wish we didn't have to do any of it."

There was silence and then the sound of steps. "I'll be right back," Rodney said.

The thought came to Elizabeth that what she ought to do was silently retrace her steps, ski quickly back to Winterhouse, tell Norbridge and Jackson what she'd heard, and turn it over to them. She looked behind her at the trail and at her skis.

"Hey!" came a voice. Elizabeth turned to see Rodney in the doorway of the cabin gaping at her. "What are you doing here?"

For a second, Elizabeth thought to bolt for the trail. Instead, she calmed herself and then, not knowing how she managed it, she smiled and waved.

"Oh, hey, Rodney," she said, trying to make it sound like it was the most natural thing in the world to run into Rodney Powter out here when everyone else was back eating breakfast at Winterhouse.

Elana stepped out. "Elizabeth?" she said, staring in wonder.

"Hi, Elana." Elizabeth's mind was racing, trying to make sure she chose her words carefully. "I decided to go out skiing, and when I stopped by that bridge, I saw skis up here."

Rodney turned to Elana. His mouth had remained wide open, and he had an expression on his face that said, *What do you make of this?* He looked to Elizabeth.

"Well, you ought to just turn around and go back," Rodney said.

Elizabeth thought quickly. "I wanted to apologize, Elana. For what happened at the café in Havenworth."

Elana looked at her skeptically. "Okay," she said slowly before turning to Rodney. "But you should probably head back to Winterhouse."

"You were pretty rude to me and my parents, you know," Rodney said.

Elizabeth continued walking, came up to the cabin, and eyed the two others with as much sincere-looking friendliness as she could fake. "Like I said, I was just about to turn around. But when I saw this cabin, I thought I'd check it out." She peered through the doorway.

"Did you hear me?" Rodney said, fixing Elizabeth with a menacing look.

Elizabeth gave him a little frown that said, *I don't have to listen to you*, and then stepped forward another couple of steps. "Cool cabin," she said. "I wonder who it belongs to."

"I don't think you get it," Rodney said. "You need to get out of here."

Elizabeth looked him up and down, and then turned to Elana. "Are you two brother and sister?"

Elana's mouth fell open. "What are you talking about?"

"I heard you guys say something about your mother and father when I was walking up."

"Rodney and I are just friends," Elana said, stammering, "and we came out skiing."

Elizabeth felt something drop inside herself, some realization taking hold as she studied Elana's face. "You were lying when you told me your parents died," she said.

"You and Rodney really are brother and sister. And your parents are making you two do all of this to—"

"I don't know what you're talking about," Elana said. And then, pleadingly, she said, "You should get going, Elizabeth. Please." She looked to Rodney, who stared back at her with a challenging, agitated expression.

Elizabeth stared past them. The interior of the cabin—completely empty, with only two small windows—was so captivating, the presence of Elana and Rodney was only a slight distraction. "That's a bizarre picture," Elizabeth said. On the otherwise spotless wooden floor was a drawing in black ink of the same symbol that was on Mrs. Vesper's bracelet. "Norbridge will be interested in that."

"Norbridge, Norbridge," Rodney said mockingly. "That old doofus."

"I'm going to tell him everything," Elizabeth said. As the words left her mouth, she realized they sounded slightly desperate; standing beside Elana and Rodney and looking at the picture on the floor of the cabin had made her feel suddenly very frightened.

"Fine, then," Rodney said. "Why don't you run back to Winterhouse?" He looked at her with a cruel grin.

"You're a bully," Elizabeth said. "Your parents are mean to you, so you're mean to everyone else. But you don't scare me. I know way more about what you're up to than you think I do. And I know why you're out here at this cabin and who it belongs to."

Rodney folded his arms and lifted his chin in defiance. "You better be gone in ten seconds."

"Oh, do you guys need to do something more here for Gracella?" Elizabeth said. "Maybe she'll help you find the thing that's hidden in Winterhouse? The thing you're looking for? I guess I do know, don't I?"

Elana's eyes snapped wide open. "Leave! You have no idea what's going on."

"Cut it out!" Rodney snarled, turning quickly to glare at Elana. "Don't tell her anything!"

"Tell me anything about what?" Elizabeth said, but Rodney spun around in a fury and grabbed her shoulder. "Get out of here!" he yelled.

"Hey!" Elizabeth said. Pain radiated from her shoulder as Rodney dug in with his fingers. "Let go of me!"

"What's going on!" someone yelled, and the three kids came to an instant stop. Jackson and Sampson were walking up from the bridge.

"What are you guys doing?" Sampson called. Rodney let go of Elizabeth.

"Were you hurting her?" Jackson said.

"Yes, he was!" Elizabeth said.

"She pushed me!" Rodney said.

"That's a lie!" Elizabeth said, and then the two men, dressed all in red, with red stocking caps on their heads, stood before them. Elizabeth was so glad to see them she could hardly catch her breath. "He grabbed me because they're out here trying to help Gracella Winters!"

"She's crazy!" Rodney said.

Jackson looked grim, his eyes flashing to one of the

kids and then the next and the next. "Tell me what's going on," he said. "Immediately."

"We were just leaving," Elana said, glancing fearfully at Elizabeth, before addressing Jackson. "We were just getting a little skiing in." She looked to Rodney. "Come on."

The two of them stepped off the porch and snapped into their skis. Elizabeth, Jackson, and Sampson stared in silence as Elana and Rodney skied down the small hill, glided onto the trail, and disappeared into the woods.

Jackson watched until he was sure they were gone, saying nothing the entire time. Sampson came over beside him.

"Do you want me to—" Sampson began, but Jackson held up a hand to silence him.

"Not worth wasting any words over those two," Jackson said, and he turned and looked to Elizabeth. "All well with you, Miss Somers?"

She was rubbing her shoulder, trying to figure out what had just happened. "I'm fine," she said and then sighed. "I am really glad you two came when you did."

"What was he doing?" Sampson said.

"I'll have to tell you the whole thing," Elizabeth said, shaking her head. "You won't believe it." She paused, then turned to look behind her in the cabin.

"You're sure you're all right, Miss Somers?" Jackson said.

Elizabeth heard his words, but she also thought she

heard something behind her. She took two steps into the cabin and listened.

"Miss Somers?" Jackson said.

"You okay, Elizabeth?" Sampson said. "We can head back to Winterhouse."

"I think maybe . . ." Elizabeth said, though she wasn't sure what she wanted to say and was distracted by a vague feeling of dread. She looked around, to every corner of the cabin. There was nothing within—no furniture, no curtains on the windows, nothing hanging from the ceiling—only the strange drawing on the floor. Other than that, there was simply a barren, open, silent space, completely abandoned and still.

"They made that drawing," she said faintly, pointing to the scarab. "I think it's to help Gracella somehow."

She cocked her head and listened. The morning was windless and quiet, but she thought she could hear a low noise arising from somewhere, a faint rumbling sound. It struck her this was the same sound she'd heard on the three occasions she'd put her ear to the doors at Winterhouse, the ones with the plaques above them.

"Elizabeth?" Sampson said. "You okay?"

She stood listening. The sound grew; something was drawing nearer. The cabin darkened slightly, the way the sky appears when dusk is settling; the slightest tint of crimson colored the edges of her vision, a faint glow of red rimming the frame of her sight, no matter where she looked. Elizabeth shivered, more with fear than from the cold. At some level of awareness, she continued to hear Sampson and then Jackson speaking her name, asking her something or explaining something, but she was too overwhelmed by the sound and her own anxious thoughts and a sudden, growing heaviness in her limbs to take full notice.

And then, from somewhere behind the rumbling noise or over it or as part of the swelling rush it was making toward her, she heard a voice: "It is yours." Elizabeth leaned forward to make certain she'd heard the words correctly—and also because she found something . . . *tempting* in them. "It is yours," came the voice again.

As she leaned so far forward that suddenly the cabin floor seemed to rush up before her eyes, Elizabeth realized the voice was familiar. The floor had slammed into her, she thought, though this made no sense. And just as everything went black, and Sampson and Jackson were over her, calling her name, Elizabeth understood that the voice—the words just whispered to her—was the very one she'd heard in the library the year before when Winterhouse had nearly been destroyed. It belonged to Gracella Winters.

PART FOUR

THE YEAR ENDS—AND THE FAR CHAMBER CALLS

CHARM

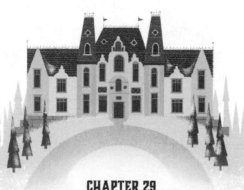

CHAPTER 29

THE FINAL DOOR

DOLOR

When she considered it afterward, Elizabeth couldn't recall the moment when she surfaced from sleep and recognized she wasn't in her own room. When she finally, fully awoke, though, she realized she was under a thick quilt on a bed in a room that was dim and still, and then she understood she was in Norbridge's apartment and her head was aching badly. She sat up with a start, fully alert. Voices came from beyond the door, which was open just enough to allow in a thin seam of pale light.

"Did you hear something?" came a voice.

That's Norbridge, Elizabeth thought.

"I think she's still sleeping," came another voice—Leona's.

"I'll check," Norbridge said. "Don't say anything about Gracella. I don't want her to be anxious."

"Well, she's going to be anxious whether we mention it or not. She knows what's going on."

Elizabeth was tense with concentration and sat listening for every word.

"Just don't make it worse," Norbridge said. "I'm worried."

"You're always worried! You should say, 'I'm *more* worried.'"

There was a silence, and then the door opened and Elizabeth was staring at Norbridge in the doorway.

"Ah, Elizabeth," he said haltingly. "You're awake." He glanced behind him. "We were just relaxing out here with some tea. Figured you might be up by now. Why don't you join us?"

She pulled the blanket off, rose, and stepped cautiously into the main room, which was lined with so many book-crammed shelves it could almost have been a library itself. Leona was sitting on a love seat and had a blanket wrapped around her; she looked tired—pale and weary, her face drawn.

"Please," Leona said, "sit down, dear. It's good to see you up and about."

But Elizabeth stood in place, looked from Leona to Norbridge and back. "What's going on? I know something's going on."

"Please sit down," Norbridge said, "and then we can talk it all over."

"Elana and Rodney are brother and sister," Elizabeth said, not moving. "And Mrs. Vesper isn't Elana's grandmother. I'm almost positive she's really Selena Hiems. They made her old somehow. And Gracella is trying to come back to find what's hidden in the passageway."

"Dear," Leona said. She said nothing more, simply looked pleadingly at Elizabeth and patted the empty spot on the seat beside her. Elizabeth moved to her and sat, and then Norbridge sat, too, on the sofa opposite.

"I don't know how she does it," Elizabeth said, "but Gracella uses people to keep herself alive, like you told me once, Norbridge. Last year we thought she was dead, but she wasn't really. I think she stole the life out of Marcus Hiems to keep herself alive, and Selena almost died, too, but not quite. She just got really old. And now she's back— she's Mrs. Vesper—and some other people in that family are with her, and they're all trying to trick us and hunt around and get into the passageways! There's something in there they want!" Elizabeth was getting more frantic as she spoke, the horror of it all coming together for her as she explained everything and felt the throbbing in her head and the ache in her body. "We have to do something!"

"I am doing something," Norbridge said. "I've had my eyes on the Powters since they arrived. Same thing with Mrs. Vesper. I don't tell you all these things, because I don't want you to worry, but I've been anxious the last two weeks, just as you have."

Elizabeth rubbed her forehead, feeling the pain in her

head expanding. "What time is it anyway? How long was I asleep?"

"It's ten o'clock," Leona said.

"Ten o'clock?" Elizabeth said. "But I left Winterhouse at eight thirty!"

"At night," Leona said. "You've been sleeping all day."

"Oh, no," Elizabeth said miserably, dropping her head into her hands before looking up at Norbridge. "We have to do something! Norbridge, you know someone stole her body. She's trying to get back here and do something. They're all trying to help her out, and—"

"Elizabeth, please," Norbridge said. "Slow down."

"But you're not listening!" Elizabeth said. "We have to do something!"

"I am listening," Norbridge said. "You just need to slow down. You had quite a fall."

"But you never really listen to me!" she said, crying now. "Every time there's something going on, you don't believe me!" Even as she said the words, she knew they weren't entirely true—but there was enough truth in them that she felt justified in saying them. "I know you're looking out for everything, and I know you probably don't want to scare me sometimes—but I'm not a little kid! You can tell me what's going on!"

"Leona and I are just as concerned as you are," Norbridge said. "Truly."

"He's right, dear," Leona said. "We had on awful scare this morning after Jackson and Sampson told us what happened."

"Can you walk me through the morning?" Norbridge said. "I've spoken with Freddy, so I know you saw Elana and Rodney leaving Winterhouse, but what happened after that?"

Elizabeth recounted the morning quickly. "They made a drawing on the floor, too. It's the same thing Mrs. Vesper has on her bracelet. I heard Rodney say it was something to make sure Gracella came directly to Winterhouse and not the cabin."

"Jackson said you mentioned that right before you blacked out," Norbridge said. "I went out there myself to take a look."

"That's good," Elizabeth said. She rubbed her temples with both hands; her head ached badly. She let out a low groan of pain, realizing how much she was hurting.

"You have a bit of a bruise," Norbridge said, setting his palm on the right side of his own head to indicate where Elizabeth had struck the floor. "Knocked yourself out pretty good."

Elizabeth closed her eyes. "There was something else. Right before I blacked out, I heard a voice."

"A voice?" Leona said. "What do you mean?"

"I don't know," Elizabeth said. "It sounded like it was in the cabin, but it was in my head, too. It said, 'It is yours.' Twice."

"'It is yours'?" Norbridge said. "What does that mean?"

Elizabeth shook her head. "I don't know. But . . . I swear—it was Gracella's voice."

Leona put a hand on Elizabeth's shoulder and gave her

a consoling rub. "Maybe it was just the fright of being out there and having such an awful encounter with those two others."

"Everything started to go red, too," Elizabeth said. "You know what that means. I'm sure Gracella is behind all of this. I know it. I heard her voice. She's here somehow!" Elizabeth leaned back heavily on the love seat; her head was throbbing so badly she felt it might burst. "Is this what a migraine feels like?"

"It's what it feels like to try to get over a blow to the head," Leona said.

"Water, aspirin, rest, and some ice for the swelling," Norbridge said. "That's what you need. I'm going to have you stay here for a night or two so we can keep an eye on you. That way we can help you out when you need it."

Elizabeth didn't move. She sat with her head resting on the back of the love seat. "I know what you're doing. You want to keep me away from Elana and Rodney and all of them."

"What I want to do is allow you to recuperate," Norbridge said.

She looked at him. "But you also don't want me to run into any of those people, right?"

"I don't think that will be a problem," Leona said.

"What do you mean?" Elizabeth said.

"She means they're all gone," Norbridge said. "Left. Departed. Checked out."

"They left Winterhouse?" Elizabeth said. "The Powters? Elana? Mrs. Vesper?"

"That's exactly what I mean," Norbridge said. "Before lunch today. Every last one of them. They cleared out of Winterhouse, and with any luck we won't see them again. I'm telling you, I believe everything you say, and I want to protect this old hotel just as much as you do."

Elizabeth felt awful when she woke the next morning; the pain in her head had worsened, and she was barely able to read or eat or do anything without feeling that her head was about to throb right off her neck if she moved it at all. She kept thinking about the departure of the Powters and Elana and Mrs. Vesper—or, as she now thought of the latter, Selena Hiems. It didn't seem possible those five had simply abandoned their scheme, had simply given up in defeat and left Winterhouse. It was much more likely they'd merely retreated briefly because they understood everyone at Winterhouse would now be watching them—or, more likely, Norbridge would have told them to check out of the hotel—and there would be no chance to put their plot into action, whatever it was. But Elizabeth was positive what was happening was merely a hiatus and not a surrender; somehow, at some time, Gracella Winters and the others would resume their attack.

Elizabeth napped during the middle of the day. When she awoke, she was finally able to read a bit; but she felt worse as the evening passed, and it wasn't until the next morning that she felt halfway back to normal. When Norbridge saw she was doing better—and after Freddy came by for a visit and she explained all that had happened—she was alone for the afternoon and found herself sitting on the sofa, glancing out the window at the snow-covered mountains above the lake. All the while, she was distracted by the half-open door to Norbridge's bedroom, which she'd been in by herself on only one occasion. That had been New Year's Eve the year before, when she'd been drawn by the massive painting that hung on the wall there depicting Norbridge, his wife, Maria, and Winifred herself when she was three or four years older than Elizabeth.

She sat reading, then glancing out the window, then looking around the room, then thinking about snacking on an apple, then trying to read some more—all the while trying to quiet an insistent thought that had sat waiting for her from the moment she had awakened in Norbridge's extra bedroom: One last door was somewhere in this apartment. She set her book down and decided she would walk off the steps of the final numbers from the Winterhouse seal to see just where, exactly, they led her. If she recalled correctly, once inside Norbridge's front door, she would need to take a few more steps inside, then three more either left or right, then eight, then four, then three. As she measured these paces, she was unsurprised to find they led directly to the door of Norbridge's bedroom, which she pushed open to peer inside.

The room was dimly lit, one wall lined with two bookcases and a large bureau. The painting—huge, almost as high as the ceiling and over four feet wide—dominated one side of the opposite wall. Elizabeth entered the room silently, the way she might have had Norbridge himself been dozing in the large bed. She counted off the remaining steps and found herself standing before the painting she recalled from the year before: Lake Luna, the mountains beyond, Norbridge in a trim black suit. Maria wore a delicate white dress, and her warm green eyes and lustrous black hair made her look beautiful and elegant. Between Norbridge and Maria stood Winifred, Elizabeth's mother, wearing a violet dress, purple ribbons strung in her hair; her gentle smile mirrored Maria's. The two of them appeared to share some secret or were glad to be standing outside on a beautiful day before Winterhouse. Elizabeth put her hand to the pendant around her own neck as she stared at the painted version of it on her mother: A gold chain lay delicately around Winnie's neck, and dangling from it was the familiar indigo circle of marble rimmed in silver, the word "Faith" etched into it.

I've followed the numbers on the seal, and the door should be right here, she thought.

As she stood examining the painting, taking in the pleasing sight of her mother and her grandparents from years before, she realized something was odd. There wasn't anything strange about the painting itself, but, still, there was something she found disconcerting, even if she couldn't figure out just what it was. She took two steps back and studied the painting again. She leaned to the left; she leaned to the right. Nothing stood out, but she found herself staring hard at the picture. *A painting like this should be in a different place in this room*, she thought. *It's so close to the corner.*

Elizabeth moved to the painting and gently, so that it didn't fall, angled it a few inches away from the wall to peek behind. There, in clear outline, was the rim of a doorway. She lowered the painting back into place and stood trembling.

The last door, she thought. She closed her eyes, rubbed her temples again, and then glanced through Norbridge's open door to make sure she was truly all alone. She put her hand on the frame of the painting and pulled it from the wall just slightly, but farther than she had before. At the top of the door, as she had expected, was a plaque, and on it were these words:

FALL
THE HOLDER, HEEDING SILENT VOICE
ALONE MUST MAKE THE FATEFUL CHOICE

Elizabeth studied the words, connected them with the words on the other plaques. And then she put her hand on the small door handle and gave it a twist. It turned easily. She pushed the handle just enough that the door creaked and began to move outward into the tunnel. Quickly, Elizabeth pulled the door closed. She glanced around and then recalled seeing a flashlight in the kitchen. She ran and grabbed it, returned, opened the door again, and

shined the light to see within. Before her was a narrow passageway with clean white walls and a high ceiling—she'd imagined something cramped and gloomy, and so she was pleasantly surprised. The air was slightly musty. She shined the light into the distance and saw the corridor leading away into darkness.

Elizabeth switched off the flashlight, closed the door, lowered the painting, and stood before it with her mind racing. And then she went and took her notebook up from the table where she'd left it, returned to Norbridge's room, and jotted down the words on the plaque, adding them to the lines from the other plaques in the order she was certain they belonged:

The charm seems such a common thing
In form as simple as a ring
Its might is all but hidden till
It sees itself in glass you fill
Then alters to an object strong
Its power used for right or wrong
The holder, heeding silent voice
Alone must make the fateful choice

Riley Granger, she thought, *why did you have to make everything so hard to figure out?* But as she stood puzzling over the lines she'd written, another part of her thought that as long as she was the only one who knew about this door and what was on its plaque, and as long as Norbridge could make certain the Powters and Elana and Selena didn't somehow find their way back into the hotel, the secret of Winterhouse was hers and hers alone.

I'm the only one who can get into the secret passageway, she thought.

A knock sounded on the apartment door, and Elizabeth jumped as though she'd heard an explosion.

CHAPTER 30

FEARS—AND AN ENTRY

SAFER

"Coming!" Elizabeth called.

She left Norbridge's bedroom, set the flashlight back where she'd found it on a shelf in the kitchen, and went to see who had knocked.

"Special delivery of Flurschen for Elizabeth Somers!" came an odd voice from the other side of the door—though the voice wasn't so odd she couldn't figure out to whom it belonged.

"Freddy!" she said with a laugh as she opened the door to see her friend standing before her in his best clothes: a white dress shirt and crisply ironed brown corduroy pants.

He held a small package out to her. "I really did bring

some candy for you. I don't know if you can go to the party tonight, so I wanted to stop by to see you. You feeling any better?"

"A little," she said. "Come in." She poured two glasses of cider, and they sat at the dining room table. She was dying to tell him about the final door but decided to wait and surprise him.

"My head's definitely better, but I'm still kind of tired," she said. "Norbridge might let me go to the party for a little while if I'm up to it later."

"I think it's going to be really boring there tonight without you. I hope you can come."

"So, still no sign of anyone? Elana? The Powters?"

"None. They're gone. The whole thing's bizarre. And to think that Elana and Rodney are brother and sister. I never would have guessed."

"I just wonder how much they've figured out about the doors. I'm positive Elana went to that bookstore and bought that book I told you about, but I don't know how much it might have helped her." A thought had been growing in Elizabeth's mind about *The Wonderful World of Words!* "There were a lot of connections in that book to Winterhouse. 'Faith' and seals and 'sinister'—all of that. I wouldn't be surprised if Riley Granger had read it."

"Yeah, but unless Elana and them unscrambled the anagrams and found the doors, none of it really matters, right?" Freddy drummed his hand on the table and shifted his eyes around the room. "And speaking of finding doors, you must have peeked around in here by now."

She lifted her eyebrows.

"You found it!" Freddy said.

"In Norbridge's bedroom," she said, taking a sip of her cider. "But no one could get in there unless they broke into this apartment, and everyone who might try has left. You have the key to your workshop, right? I'm worried about Selena or the Powters coming back."

"The key is safe," Freddy said, patting his pants pocket. "Did you go inside the—"

"Greetings, you two!" Norbridge said as he opened the door to his apartment and strode in. "Apple cider and Flurschen! That's a well-rounded meal!" He stood before them in his black suit jacket and bow tie, his hair neat and his beard bushy. "And you're looking very dapper, Mr. Knox!"

"You too, Norbridge," Freddy said.

"How are you feeling?" Norbridge said to Elizabeth.

"Better."

Norbridge plucked at his suspenders with both hands and then pulled out a chair to sit with them. "Maybe you'll feel up to welcoming the new year tonight at the big party!" He reached for a piece of Flurschen from the plate Elizabeth had set on the table. "Mind?" he said, and before she answered, he plucked a candy, popped it into his mouth, and began to chew. "I never get tired of this stuff," he said as he smacked away.

They talked for several minutes, and all the while Elizabeth wondered if maybe she had left the door to Norbridge's room open a bit wider than before and he might notice. The last thing she wanted to do was make him worry.

She also couldn't wait to tell Freddy she'd actually entered the secret passageway.

"So is this year's party really going to be the best one ever?" Freddy said.

"Since I took over Winterhouse forty-four years ago," Norbridge said, "each year's party has improved upon its predecessor by two percent on average, according to my assessment. When you compound those numbers across the decades, that means this year's party will be two and two-fifths times better than the very first party I arranged back in 1973. So, yes—this year's party will be the best one ever."

"That's very precise," Elizabeth said, though she wasn't sure it was completely scientific.

"I like it!" Freddy said, beaming. Something occurred to him, though, and he shifted his eyes to the table and fell silent. "Who will put the parties together when . . ." he began.

"Do you mean who will take over Winterhouse after I'm gone?" Norbridge said.

It was exactly what Elizabeth had been thinking—and just what she'd been wanting to discuss with Norbridge ever since their visit to his office and then the comment Kiona had made.

"I guess that's what I'm asking," Freddy said.

Norbridge leaned back and adjusted his bow tie. "I took over for my father, and he took over for his father. My daughter was going to take over for me."

Freddy whipped his head in Elizabeth's direction and

was about to say something, but she put a hand to her forehead and looked down, and Freddy remained silent.

"Your head, dear?" Norbridge said. "Hurting again?"

And although she was aching a bit, the main thing was that she wasn't sure she wanted to delve too deeply into the subject at hand just yet. It was enough to have come to Winterhouse and to try to fit in.

Elizabeth dropped her hand from her head and looked at her grandfather. "Do you think it's really all over? I mean, do you think they all just decided to leave and not do anything?"

Norbridge squinted at the plate of candy for a moment. "I think with people whose souls have been infected by evil, you never really know what they might do."

A silence descended on the room, and Norbridge set one palm down on the tabletop. It was an odd and deliberate gesture—like testing the surface for warmth—and it indicated something more to come. He stared at his hand with a strange fixity, and the two kids watched. Suddenly, beneath Norbridge's palm, as though he'd imparted a glow to the table simply by the power of touch, a golden light brightened around the rim of his fingers. He moved his hand steadily across the surface of the table, leaving a trail of amber light behind—after several swipes and curls, it became clear what he was doing: Norbridge was writing something. Even before he came to the end of his motions, Elizabeth realized what it was he was spelling. Still, when he finished, she was stunned to see the very same design she had seen in the book by Dylan Grimes nearly two

weeks before, the same word she kept on the pendant around her neck:

"No matter how you look at it, though," Norbridge said, "from any angle, we have to keep the faith." He stared at Elizabeth. "You hold it up in any light, and we'll be okay."

She felt certain he was letting her know something important, and she put a hand to the pendant around her neck. Norbridge leaned toward the table and then, as if blowing out candles on a birthday cake, gave a quick puff. The word there flared and then faded to nothing, like embers dying in a fire.

"How do you do that stuff?" Freddy said, scratching his head and inspecting the table.

An urgent knock sounded at the door. "Mr. Falls!" someone called from the corridor. "Mr. Falls!"

Norbridge answered the door to find Sampson, breathless, standing there.

"What is it, my good man?" Norbridge said.

Sampson was so distraught he didn't notice Elizabeth and Freddy sitting at the table.

"Sir!" he said. "The Thatchers just arrived. They said they hadn't sent any belongings beforehand and were just coming on the spur of the moment. All the luggage and stuff in there? They don't know who it belongs to or where it came from. But there was one big crate that was open, and it was empty! You should come right away."

Norbridge held up a hand to quiet him, but it was too late—Elizabeth and Freddy had heard everything. Sampson looked past Norbridge and saw the two of them.

"Oh!" he said, his face full of an even deeper alarm. "I didn't know anyone was here."

Norbridge whipped around. "Freddy, I need you to go back to your room." He pointed to Elizabeth. "And, my dear, please remain here until one of us returns." He patted the base of his neck, the spot where her necklace lay. "Door locked."

Freddy gave Elizabeth a small salute, and then he, Sampson, and Norbridge left the room. Elizabeth was alone once again.

It's not over at all, she thought. The ache in her head was returning, badly again. For fifteen minutes she paced the room, thinking through what Sampson's news meant and trying to keep her agitation contained. Her head was throbbing, and she began to feel overcome by fatigue, even as she kept returning to a terrifying thought: Gracella's body had been smuggled into Winterhouse. The pain in her temples was intense; and so she sat on the sofa, closed her eyes, and rubbed her head for several long minutes.

Another knock sounded on the door, only this time Elizabeth wasn't startled but, rather, awakened. She looked around, realizing she'd fallen asleep on the sofa.

"Coming!" she called. She looked at the clock: 6:18. She'd slept for over an hour.

"Sampson!" she said when she opened the door. He stood before her with a covered silver platter, his red uniform crisp and bright as always.

"Hello, Elizabeth!" Sampson said. "Greetings from your one and only dynamic dinner delivery dude!" He gave a huge grin, his buckteeth clipping his lower lip.

"What's going on?" she said. "What happened with the Thatchers?"

"Everything is fine," he said. "May I come in? I'll explain it all."

Minutes later the two of them were sitting at the table in Norbridge's kitchen, a plate of baked trout and rice and carrots sitting invitingly before Elizabeth, though her appetite was suppressed by her bafflement.

"It was all a bunch of confusion," Sampson said. "Turns out they did have stuff sent, but it was months ago, and for some reason it just arrived now."

Something in this sounded suspicious. "Really?" Elizabeth said. "They forgot about it? What about the crate?"

"Like I said, it was just miscommunication. Then I got sort of carried away." He looked to her dinner plate. "Norbridge wanted you to have something to eat, though, so here I am!"

It all sounded very strange to Elizabeth, but she decided not to ask too many questions yet. "Well, at least I'm feeling better." She wanted to leave Norbridge's room and see for herself what was going on. "I'm pretty sure I'm feeling up to going to the party."

Sampson shook his head. "Orders from the boss. You're staying put tonight."

There was definitely something going on, Elizabeth thought, but she decided for now she would go along with whatever plan Sampson had. He sat across the table, watching her eat, and talking the whole time, first about how much everyone was hoping she was fully recovered and then about how nice Grace Hall looked for the New Year's Eve party.

"I'm fine, you know," Elizabeth said after a time. "I appreciate you staying here with me while I eat, but I don't want to keep you from your work."

"Oh, no, it's okay!" Sampson said. He patted his jacket at the chest and then along the sides, and then he pulled out a folded-up corner of a newspaper. "Hey, I know you're good at these things," he said, unfolding the paper to reveal a crossword puzzle he'd apparently torn out. "I got stuck on a few of these words and was wondering if you could help me."

Elizabeth's perplexity deepened; it was clear Sampson had no intention of leaving. "Are you sure you don't have to get back to work?" she said.

"Positive. If you don't want to do the puzzle, maybe we can play cards? Or Monopoly?"

"Sampson, did Norbridge tell you to stay here and keep an eye on me?"

Sampson set his teeth on his lower lip again, but this time he looked confused. "Uh, well, I was sent here to bring you dinner." He grinned, like a student settling on the right answer after being questioned by his teacher in front of the class.

"That's why you *came*," Elizabeth said, "but were you also told to *stay*?"

Sampson scrunched his face, struggling to find the right words. "Kind of," he said slowly.

"What's going on, Sampson?"

He adjusted the small hat on his head and began licking his lips furiously. "Okay, okay, listen, Elizabeth, if I tell you, you have to *promise* me you won't tell Norbridge or Jackson or anyone, okay?"

"I promise! But what's going on?"

Sampson leaned back and gave out a heavy sigh. "Oh, brother. I know I shouldn't tell you this. Okay, listen: Someone attacked Freddy."

"What! When did this happen? Tell me!" Without realizing it, Elizabeth grabbed Sampson by the wrist.

"A little over an hour ago," Sampson said. "Someone found him in the hallway."

"Who?"

"One of the guests! He was out cold, and it looked like he had been beat up."

Elizabeth felt sick. She let go of Sampson's wrist and put both hands to her face, wanting to hold back her tears and confusion—this news felt devastating.

She looked up. "How is he now? You saw him?"

Sampson shook his head. "They took him to the infirmary. That's all I know."

"Why would anyone do that? Why would anyone want to hurt Freddy?"

Sampson looked away.

"Is there something else?" Elizabeth said. "What? You know something."

"Whoever it was . . . they took . . ." Sampson began. An awful feeling descended on Elizabeth—she knew exactly what Sampson was going to say. He looked to her. "His key to the workshop was missing."

"I've been trying to warn Norbridge," Elizabeth said. "All of it. I knew this would happen." A picture formed in her mind: Someone had surely entered the workshop, broken into the summer door there, and entered the secret passageway.

Sampson stood. He was so agitated and worried suddenly that now, after doing his best to act calm and easy over the previous hour, he appeared able to let his guard down. "That's all I know, Elizabeth. I'm sorry. It's just a very bad situation out there right now, and Norbridge asked me to come here and keep you company."

"Like a jailer," she said glumly.

"Well, gosh, you don't have to put it like that. I'm just supposed to stay with you until Norbridge returns. More like a bodyguard."

Elizabeth nodded. She didn't want Sampson to get in any trouble, but the fact was she had to get out of Norbridge's apartment and see what was going on, had to help Freddy if she could. And then it struck her that what she really needed to do was stop whoever had broken into the secret passageways and make sure they didn't find whatever it was that was hidden underneath Winterhouse. There was no way she could ask Norbridge for "permission" to do this, and there was no way—if he had the slightest idea she intended to enter the passageways—he would agree to let her go inside. But now, right at this very moment, someone—or maybe more than one person—was inside the passageways and looking to find a charm that, if Elizabeth's deductions were correct, would bring Gracella more power than The Book ever would have. If she could get inside the passageways and somehow find the object, maybe she could get back into Norbridge's room before anyone else found anything and before anyone even knew she was gone. There was a maze of passages beneath Winterhouse; and she had no idea how she herself might find the charm, but she could only hope anyone else down there might be lost wandering.

"I understand, Sampson," Elizabeth said. She ran a finger along the edge of the tray on the table. "Still, I can't believe what happened, and I just hope Freddy is all right," she said, putting a hand to her forehead. "My head is killing me again. Maybe I should go lie down for a while, and you can just hang out here."

"That's probably about the best way we can handle it for now," he said, sitting back down at the table. "If you want to rest, go ahead. I'll just wait here."

"I think I will," she said, standing. As nonchalantly as she could, she removed the flashlight from where she'd left it on a shelf, and then she took her notebook from the sofa. "I'm super tired."

Sampson gave her a thumbs-up. "Get some rest."

She smiled at him, then retreated into Norbridge's room with a quick "I will," tossing in a yawn for good measure. She closed the door and silently locked it behind her. And then, after she'd listened at the door for five minutes to make sure Sampson wasn't going to check on her, and after she was certain he would assume she was asleep, Elizabeth put on her sweater, lifted the painting of Norbridge, Maria, and her mother away from the wall, pressed the door open silently, and clicked on her flashlight to look within. She lowered the painting behind her and stepped inside and felt the chill air filling her lungs, the strange quiet all around.

She was alone in the secret passageway.

CHAPTER 31

JOURNEY THROUGH A MAZE

ENTRY

Elizabeth opened her notebook and shined the flashlight on the eight lines she'd written before tucking the pad into her sweater pocket. She had no idea where to go now that she was inside the passageway, and she didn't know what she was looking for. All she had were the eight lines—and she didn't know what they meant.

She held the light up and looked ahead. From somewhere came a low hum, like the sound you'd hear if your sleep was disturbed by the noise of a truck idling or an airplane passing far overhead. It was the same sound she'd heard each time she'd pressed her ear to one of the four doors. As she recited the eight lines to herself, Elizabeth began to walk; when she had moved forward thirty feet, there was a fork in the passageway. She listened. The humming was louder to her left, and so she turned that direction and continued—though before she did, she made a mark on the wall with her pen so she could retrace her steps.

If I just follow that sound, she thought, *maybe I'll find what I'm looking for.*

She was glad to be able to focus on the humming noise, because otherwise she knew that the many things lurking behind this distraction would take over: She was alone inside a maze of corridors, looking for she didn't know what, and trying to avoid running into anyone else. She wondered if maybe she should have left a note in Norbridge's room; she wondered if the batteries in the flashlight would hold out; she wondered if it would get even colder the deeper she went, because she was already very cold and her frosty breath came like heavy steam from her mouth and nose. She tried not to think about Freddy, either, and hoped he was being taken care of and was not injured badly. Most of all she tried not to let the fear inside herself take over, even though she thought that at any moment she might turn a corner and see Elana or Selena or—worst of all—Gracella Winters staring at her from the gloom of a long passageway.

"They can't scare me," Elizabeth said, recalling the words that had sustained her through so many of the troubles last year. "They can't scare me."

After two more turns—and after making marks on the wall at each—she stopped and listened. The humming noise had grown louder. She shined the beam of her flashlight along the wall beside her, and then ran her hand over it—it was smooth and white, plaster that hadn't crumbled or spotted over the many years. She pulled her sweater closer to her, although it didn't feel like the temperature had changed. There was something she was trying to remember from one of her classes at school about how maybe, because she was now deep underground, the air wouldn't get any colder than it already was. She listened, turned her head left and right; the humming noise to the left was slightly louder, and she resumed walking in that direction.

When she made the next turn to the left, the plaster walls of the passageway stopped abruptly, and Elizabeth stepped into a rock-sided chamber.

I'm in the mine, she thought. She aimed the flashlight at her feet—dirt and gravel covered the ground, and she kicked at a pebble and heard it echo eerily upon the walls. The air smelled musty, tinged with something metallic. The humming noise was louder; everything around her grew darker, loomed over her more ominously.

"I will not be afraid," she said, and as she stood she thought she heard a voice from far off. She listened, tense with concentration. But after hearing nothing more despite standing for at least a minute, she felt sure it had all just been her imagination, and she continued onward through the tunnel of the mine.

At the next turn, as she listened to determine which direction to walk, she stopped and considered a chilling thought: If a person didn't know exactly which route to travel, it would be a simple matter to get lost in here for-ever among the scores of passageways. She shuddered to think of what it would be like to wander lost in the mine, alone in the cold and the dark.

The humming sound grew; Elizabeth shook off her gloomy thoughts and considered: *If it's true that I'm the only one who can hear the humming, then maybe anyone else would just get lost down here in all the tunnels.* She contin-ued onward, and because the ink of her pen didn't show up on the dark walls, she made a small pile of pebbles at each corner to mark her way.

The charm seems such a common thing, she thought. *In form as simple as a ring.* The words of the rhyme had been echoing in her head since she'd stepped through the door-way. *What could those lines mean?* she thought. *Is the charm a ring, or does it just look like a ring?*

Its might is all but hidden till / It sees itself in glass you fill. The lines she'd discovered on the first three doors had been strange enough, but she'd believed that when she found the final door, the poem would become clear. This hadn't proved true, and as she walked and held the flash-light before her, she kept thinking of the rhyme and tried to make sense of it.

Then alters to an object strong / Its power used for right or wrong.

Does that mean the charm turns into something else? Elizabeth thought.

The holder, heeding silent voice / Alone must make the fate-ful choice.

And then the person who has it has to decide what to do with it? she thought. Maybe, she considered, once she found the charm—whatever it was—everything would become clear. Now, though, with the buzzing in her ears and the gloomy walls of the mine all around, disturbing thoughts came to her: What if, despite how oddly Mrs. Vesper—or, rather, Selena Hiems—had expressed herself in the café a few days before, there was some merit to her words? What if the charm, the power of the charm, was something that ought to be not only discovered but used? What if it ought to be controlled, even possessed—and by Elizabeth herself?

She was the heir to Winterhouse, most likely the only one who had the ability—the right—to find the charm, and so what would be wrong in keeping it for herself to use for her own ends? Maybe Selena, despite her evil ways, was correct: Power was something to cultivate. How often had she felt powerless at Winterhouse when she was certain she was on the path of something important? How often had Norbridge tried to lead her away from pursuing a trail of clues, not just this year but the year before, too? He might mean well, but the fact was he so often became overly cautious, even disregarding—and this bothered Elizabeth. It made her feel that even though she had escaped her aunt and uncle, she was still only a girl who didn't have much to contribute to the adult world, couldn't be taken seriously because she was so inexperienced. Even in the library, where she'd been eager to learn and contribute, she felt inept half the time, and Leona had kept sending her to the office and out of the way, where she couldn't mess anything up. Maybe the charm was what Elizabeth needed. It would be just the thing to finally confer upon her the assurance that she was capable and accomplished.

"I want it," she whispered. "I want it for myself."

Like a clanging bell interrupting her sleep, Norbridge's words suddenly sounded in her ears: *We have to keep the faith. Hold it up in any light.*

Elizabeth shook her head, could hardly believe she'd thought to keep the charm for herself. In that momentary shock, the flashlight fell from her hand. It clattered on the ground with a tinny echo, the light blinked out, and Elizabeth found herself in a blackness deep and absolute. An instant panic ran through her, a confusion made worse by the intense darkness. She took a deep breath, calmed her nerves, and took stock of herself: *I will not be afraid,* she thought.

Elizabeth reached out a hand to get her bearings against the wall, and then she knelt and scrabbled around until she felt the flashlight by her feet. She pressed the switch with her thumb, and to her infinite relief, the light came on. The humming noise was louder than ever, like the sound of an endless breeze pushing through a canyon, steady and fierce. Elizabeth stood and scanned all around with the light, shining it behind her and then along the passageway ahead.

I must be close, she thought.

She continued, following the humming noise, scanning with her flashlight all the while. And then she stopped.

Something was in the passageway before her, a silhouetted shape that looked like a person standing motionless in the blackness.

CHAPTER 32

THE SECRET OF WINTERHOUSE

HOURS

Elizabeth drew closer. There, before her, was something human in form and as tall as her, covered by a thin sheet flecked with streaks of dust. The noise grew louder.

She came to a stop a few steps away and examined it. Until she removed the sheet, the mystery of what it was would remain. She kept her light on it, uncertain what to do.

Words sounded in her head above the endless humming: *Why don't you take a look?*

Elizabeth let out a cry of surprise and fright. Gracella's voice had whispered to her, and she felt a shock of fear ignite her skin. She turned and looked in all directions.

"Where are you!" Elizabeth called. The humming

ceased. She felt frantic and was sure something awful was about to happen. "Gracella, I know you're here somewhere!"

Her voice echoed eerily upon the walls, trotted away down the chambers in both directions, and then died in the darkness. Elizabeth's breath fogged around her in thick clouds, and she kept turning to look left and right, waiting. She was sure at any moment Gracella would charge at her, that a bolt of light would come flying in her direction. She stood listening and considered that she'd been foolish to have yelled, that by calling to Gracella she might have done the one thing that would reveal her location.

She swept her light all around once again, listened for a sound, and then turned to the sheet-covered thing beside her. The pendant around her neck felt warm. She put a hand to where it lay and pressed it to her skin. The humming noise arced up into a high drone as it resumed, so loud suddenly that it was almost deafening.

Elizabeth took a corner of the thin sheet and lifted it up and away as simply as removing a silk scarf from the back of a chair. There, unveiled now, stood a sculpture made of ice. It was a girl in an ornate evening dress, the expression on her face inscrutable and calm, looking for all the world like someone who had perhaps moved to a balcony during an evening ball to take in a moment of silence and night air. The girl's eyes seemed fixed on something in the distance, and strangest of all, her arms were lifted to hold, just before her, what appeared to be a small mirror, itself made of ice. She was posed in some stance where she looked to be signaling to someone or reflecting something unseen. And then it struck Elizabeth: The figure looked like her mother.

Elizabeth was stunned by the sculpture; she found it so unexpected and also so beautiful, and the fact that it seemed to be her mother was startling. She nearly forgot she was alone in a dark mine far beneath Winterhouse. The beam from her flashlight fell upon the mirror, creating a yellow-white splash of light. Elizabeth looked at her own reflection in it, a deeply polished plane of ice that captured her image almost as faithfully as the mirror in her room. She studied her face and then ran her eyes across the length of the sculpture. With a glance behind her, she shined the flashlight all around to make sure no one was approaching, and then she circled the sculpture to take in every fold and angle of the dress and the long waves of hair. She cast the light over every part of the figure, looked her up and down, and looked at her own self reflected in the mirror once again; then she stood completely still and tried to consider what to do next.

Where is the charm? she thought. *This can't be it.*

The humming noise grew louder; the pendant's warmth increased slightly, and Elizabeth placed her hand upon her sweater above it once again. She stared into the mirror, and the sound grew louder still. The first lines of the poem came to her: *The charm seems such a common thing / In form as simple as a ring.*

She slid the pendant from her neck and examined it in

the pale light; she studied the indigo disk with the word "Faith" etched into it. The most obvious thing about it—its roundness—struck her anew: *The same shape as a ring,* she thought. And then she looked into the mirror and saw herself reflected, only now she was rimmed in a crimson light and the image of the pendant was glowing deep red. *Its might is all but hidden till/It sees itself in glass you fill.*

For a split second her mind was flooded with the thought that she was looking into the glass of the mirror. And then her mind went blank. All Elizabeth felt was an intense sensation of excitement and strength surging through her. It was like *the feeling* she was so familiar with by now, but it was more powerful by magnitudes, as though something at the core of her had opened up and expanded and was pulsing outward in all directions. The sculpture and the walls around her were bright and starkly outlined, buzzing with an electric brightness.

The humming noise had accelerated to a high, charging, insistent noise that, rather than distracting from the surging of her body and the blinding light all around, added to it. Everything—what she felt, what she saw, what she heard—became a thousand times more alive than she'd ever known. She clenched her hand around the pendant, pressed her eyes closed as she lowered her head to it, pushed her fist to her forehead, and stood, vibrating with the most intense emotion of her life.

Elizabeth didn't know how long she remained that way, but after a time something ebbed slightly and she lowered her hand. She opened it to stare at the pendant and then her reflection in the mirror. The words of the charm came to her, the first clear thought she'd had since that moment she'd stared into the mirror: *Then alters to an object strong/Its power used for right or wrong.* It all made sense. The charm had been around her neck the entire time, for years, ever since her mother had left it with her. Elizabeth had only needed to have the pendant reflected in this strange mirror for it to finally become the thing it was meant to be: an object of power, hers and hers alone. She had figured out the secret of the second object. She had uncovered the riddle of the rhyme on the plaques and made her way through the maze of the secret passageway— and now the power was hers.

"Well done, Elizabeth."

She turned from where she stood beside the ice sculpture. There, not twenty steps away—silver-haired, eyes burning crimson, and wearing the same black cape she'd had on the last time Elizabeth had seen her in the Winterhouse library—stood Gracella Winters, enveloped in a thin red light. Selena Hiems—still in appearance like the aged Mrs. Vesper—stood beside her, the two of them looking to Elizabeth with uncanny leers on their faces, while Elana loomed behind.

"The charm," Gracella said. "It is yours."

CHAPTER 33

A DECISION MADE

DOMAINS

Elizabeth stared at them in a daze. All she wanted to do was keep the pendant pressed within the palm of her hand, wanted to maintain that feeling she had experienced, wanted to keep it hers forever. She held the necklace, felt the power racing through her. And then, for a fraction of a second, an image of Freddy, lying in pain on the ground, came to her. She shook her head and gripped the pendant more tightly. Selena and Gracella continued to stare with a weird frenzy in their eyes; Elana, though, appeared perplexed—scared, even.

"Elizabeth," Selena said, "now that you know how it feels, join us."

"The power is yours," Gracella said. "All yours."

"It's magnificent," Selena said, her eyes bright with hunger. "Tell her, Elana!"

"Yes," Elana said slowly, stepping forward to join the others. "Yes . . . magnificent."

"The four of us," Gracella said. "Forever. Think of that, Elizabeth."

Elizabeth only barely heard their words. She stared at the three of them but felt everything was passing in a dream. She wanted to move but also wanted to stay in place; she wanted to speak but also wanted to remain silently holding the pendant. The flashlight in her hand lit a circle around her; beyond that, all was black aside from the ghostly red glow around Gracella herself. The rock chamber was quiet. Elizabeth studied the three before her.

The words of the rhyme filled Elizabeth: *The holder, heeding silent voice / Alone must make the fateful choice.* An indistinct image of Norbridge arose in her mind. Perhaps he was in his apartment, looking for her, worried about her. It faded.

"I have to choose," Elizabeth said weakly.

"There's no choice," Gracella said, and she took a step forward. "There's only the power. You have it now. Share it with me, share it with us." She took another step toward Elizabeth. "Join with me. You have the power of the charm now, and I need you. I need your power."

"Don't come any closer!" Elizabeth said, and Gracella halted. She looked stricken suddenly, a touch weakened, but she stood glaring at Elizabeth. Selena, appearing older than before, stared with fearful eyes. Elana, all in white, was breathing so heavily her chest heaved. The three of them seemed scared—they were waiting for her to make some decision.

"What do you want from me?" Elizabeth said, holding her clenched fist before her.

"You have immense power now that you've brought the necklace to life," Gracella said. "If you share that magic with us, it will . . . sustain us. It will help us in ways you would have to witness to understand." She gestured wildly. "Just look at the sculpture. It's you! Riley Granger surely left it here. He knew you would appear one day to claim what was yours. Now let me help you, let me guide you. It's what you want."

Elizabeth looked at the three of them warily. She allowed her mind to clear as she summoned *the feeling* from deep inside her. Only now, with the pendant in her hand, it was more intense than ever. The walls of the mine began to shake as Elizabeth focused on them; several fist-size chunks of rock broke free and crashed to the ground before the three women.

"I told you, don't come any closer!" Elizabeth yelled.

Selena put out a hand to steady herself, and Elana turned to her with worry in her eyes.

"What's wrong with her?" Elizabeth said, looking to Selena. "What's happening?"

Gracella didn't move her gaze from Elizabeth. "She is faltering. It's all ending for her. Unless you help her, help all of us. If you share what you have gained, she can be restored."

"My aunt . . ." Elana said to Elizabeth, her eyes pleading. She stepped forward.

"Please, dear," Selena said weakly, stepping toward Elizabeth.

Elizabeth closed her eyes; she felt she couldn't keep them open, and somewhere in the darkness, she thought she heard Leona speaking, though she couldn't make out the words.

Elizabeth opened her eyes and the vision fled. "How are you even alive?" she said to Gracella. One part of her felt that Gracella was somehow making sense, that now that she had awakened the charm and felt its power, Gracella's words connected to the feeling she had experienced. Maybe Gracella could help her, maybe she had been mistaken about her all along.

Gracella took another step forward, stealthily, as if walking upon a floor she wanted to keep from creaking. "Join us," she said.

"How are you alive?" Elizabeth yelled. "Tell me!"

Gracella stood still. "My daughter gave part of herself to me. My dear Selena . . . sacrificed some of her own power to sustain me."

"You took years of her life," Elizabeth shouted, "and you killed Marcus, too." She took in a breath and focused again on the walls of the mine. A rumbling sound arose, and a huge chunk of rock broke off and slammed to pieces in front of the three women. Elizabeth tightened her grip on the pendant and thought of the strange poem once more: *The holder, heeding silent voice/Alone must make the fateful choice.* She squeezed the pendant, and a fleeting, unaccountable notion came to her that it didn't really matter that Gracella had killed Marcus. With a shake of her head, she wondered how that awful thought had entered her mind.

"There are some necessary sacrifices to be made along the way," Gracella said.

"Please, Elizabeth," Elana said, clasping her hands before her. She stumbled forward another two steps. "Please, help me . . ."

Gracella turned sharply to Elana. "Be quiet!" she yelled, and in that moment Elizabeth finally understood that Elana had joined the other two unwillingly; probably all along she had been reluctant to advance the schemes of Selena and Gracella.

Selena moved a step closer. The three women were only a few feet before her, Elizabeth realized. Selena looked to Elana with woeful eyes and appeared about to say something but was too weak to form words.

"Choose us," Gracella said, "choose what you're feeling right now. Simple, so easy."

Elizabeth's head began to pound; the pain had returned worse than ever. There was a choice to make, a decision, but she couldn't figure out what it was or how to solve it. Suddenly her vision clouded with images of Norbridge and Freddy and Leona, and the pendant in her hand grew cold. She saw Jackson and Sampson; an image of her aunt and uncle flitted before her, and then the paintings from the gallery of her mother and her grandmother seemed to hover indistinctly within her gaze. She saw all of them as she stood clutching the necklace.

Gracella let out a gasp, heaved forward violently before standing erect again and arranging her cape about her. She breathed heavily.

"Keep your mind on the power!" she yelled, and she snapped her eyes closed and raised both hands to the side of her head. She looked like someone trying to block out all sound and maintain a single thought. The strain pinched her face—her lips were tight, and her jaw was clenched. Her hands began to vibrate beside her head, and her body shook.

"Mother!" Selena cried out. She looked terrified, ambushed by pain and confusion, and she reached a hand in Gracella's direction; but Gracella simply stood, oblivious to all around her. "Mother, please!" Selena cried. "Stop!" She staggered in place.

Elizabeth looked at Elana, who appeared not to know where she was. Her face was dull, like someone who'd been drugged. She looked sluggish, and her black hair drooped around her face; all the life had gone out of it. Her arms dangled at her sides. She seemed asleep standing up, the cries of Selena and the weird stance of Gracella not registering with her at all.

The pendant was a dull lump in Elizabeth's hand, and she uncurled her fingers from around it. Gracella opened her eyes and shot her hands outward, and a tremendous blast of red light exploded from her. Elizabeth turned away—and when she looked again, she saw something that didn't make sense: Selena was a crumpled shape on the ground, a trickle of blood at her mouth; where Elana had stood was now an old woman, dressed in the same white clothes Elana had worn but with an aged face and white hair. Gracella stood between them, the look on her face cruel and severe.

"Do you see how much they care for me?" Gracella said slowly. "How much they are willing to sacrifice for me?"

Elizabeth held the pendant loosely; it was cold and lifeless.

"You killed your own daughter?" she said in a whisper. "To keep yourself alive?"

Gracella lowered her eyes into a cold glare. "They give willingly, which is what you should do. Join me and let me use your power, and you and I can't be stopped."

"I thought it was all four of us," Elizabeth said.

Elana begin to move, held up her hands to stare at them; an expression of horrified disbelief took over her face. "No!" she wailed, a terrible noise that echoed miserably off the rock walls. "No!" She extended her hands to Gracella. "Look what you've done to me!"

"Shut up!" Gracella screamed, turning to her. "You were useless anyway!" She took a step toward Elizabeth. "Do you see what you've made me do? All because of your selfishness!"

Elizabeth shook her head and was about to speak, but all she could think was that in Gracella's words and the sound of her voice and the look on her face—all of it was everything she never wanted from anyone, the anger and fighting and accusations and screaming.

"I didn't do any of it," Elizabeth said. "You caused it. Because you want this thing!" She held up the pendant. "You're willing to hurt people to get it, just to have more power."

"You have no idea what's at stake," Gracella said. "Choose the power! Say it, feel it in your mind, in your heart!"

Gracella's words echoed in Elizabeth's ears. It had been awesome to possess the secret of the necklace during those minutes after she'd held it to the mirror; the thought of having that sensation again, of going deeper with it in some way that Gracella was suggesting, was nearly overpowering. A small thought of Norbridge and Freddy and Leona and all the rest came to her again, and it restrained her from clamping her fingers around the pendant and making some simple and instant assent in her mind that would secure the power of the necklace for herself.

"Choose it!" Gracella screamed. Her face looked horrible, a mask of rage and hatred.

Elizabeth opened her hand and looked at the pendant glistening on her palm. "I choose . . ." she said.

Gracella's eyes widened as she waited for Elizabeth's words.

"I choose not to use this for evil." Elizabeth turned her hand over and let the necklace drop to the ground. It clanked with a dull echo. "I choose the good side." She looked at it on the ground; it was smaller and duller than she'd ever seen, a disk of marble strung on a listless chain. She looked up to focus on Gracella but was immediately distracted. A shrill sound—like ice popping on a frozen pond—arose, but from where, Elizabeth couldn't tell. And then suddenly the sculpture beside her burst from some fierce explosion within it, and a thousand shards of ice rained on the dirt floor. Elizabeth twisted away, and then all went silent.

The crimson light that had filled the passageway was gone. There was no sound anywhere. Elizabeth lifted her flashlight and shined it before her. There, on the ground, lay Gracella, withered and crumpled in her black clothes, completely motionless. Selena lay where she'd been, the awful slick of blood still at her lips. And Elana—or, rather, the old woman she had become—stood with her arms out and her face an eerie mask of incomprehension, her eyes barely open.

"What happened?" Elana said feebly. Her voice was an old woman's, unsteady and low.

Elizabeth shined her light on the necklace on the ground. It looked like a dull and tiny thing now, simply a piece of jewelry. "I don't know," Elizabeth said. She turned her flashlight back to Gracella. "I don't know."

The sound of voices came from the far turn of the passageway.

"Elizabeth!" someone called, and the sound vibrated upon the walls. "Elizabeth!"

A light was shining from far down the chamber, a dull reflection of yellow.

"I'm here!" Elizabeth called. "I'm here!"

A burst of light filled the passageway, and then everything was bright and there was noise and confusion everywhere as Norbridge, Jackson, Sampson, and five others entered the corridor.

"Norbridge!" Elizabeth said, throwing herself into his arms. "Norbridge!"

She began to sob uncontrollably, barely hearing him say to the others, "Take care of all of this! Get some more help down here if you need it, but let's take care of everything here!"

He curled his head close to hers and whispered, "It's all right, Elizabeth. It's all right."

CHAPTER 34

A FINAL VIEW

ALIVE

At mid-morning two days after New Year's, a group of a dozen guests—including Egil P. Fowles, Mr. and Mrs. Wellington, and Mr. and Mrs. Rajput—stood on the platform around the broad white disk in the camera obscura room. Elizabeth, Norbridge, and Leona were there, too; and everyone stood looking to Freddy, visible only by the light of the small bulb in the control panel beside him. The rest of the room was dark, and the disk of the screen seemed to hover in black silhouette before the group as they awaited what Freddy would reveal.

"So when I let the light in through the box up there," Freddy said, gazing toward the ceiling, upward along the rope he was holding, "the image will display right here on this round screen. We're lucky it's a clear day, because if not, we wouldn't be able to see anything."

"I understand the cloudy weather will be returning tomorrow," Mr. Rajput said glumly. "And then no one will be able to see anything here at all."

"Shh!" said his wife. "Let him continue."

"It's okay," Freddy said. "Any questions before I show it to you?"

"Is it truly the case," Mr. Wellington said, "that this is the first public viewing offered here in decades?"

"I can confirm that," Norbridge said. "We had, unfortunately, allowed this attraction to fall into disrepair and ended up closing this room."

"I saw this apparatus myself over forty years ago," Egil P. Fowles said, "and I am certain each of you will find it exhilarating, sublime, and transporting. In short, a wonder. Do you know Aristotle was aware of the workings of the camera obscura well over two thousand years ago?"

"Ever the instructor, Professor Fowles!" Norbridge said to him. "For now, however, let me go on record as stating I am exceedingly proud of Mr. Freddy Knox here for returning this camera obscura to a working state." In the pale light, Norbridge looked to Freddy, and the small group began to applaud.

"Thank you," Freddy said, beaming. He flexed his biceps. "Camera. Ace arm."

"Freddy?" Norbridge said, extending a hand toward Freddy in invitation. "Please proceed."

"Okay, Mr. Falls," Freddy said. He gave a tug on the

rope he was holding, and once again that vibrant burst of light and color Elizabeth recalled from several days before blossomed on the white disk. Everyone on the platform gasped in delight. Before them, in brilliant hues of gray and white and blue was Lake Luna and the mountains beyond.

"Astonishing!" Mr. Rajput said, with more excitement than Elizabeth had ever heard in his voice.

"That is beautiful, Freddy," Leona said.

"Extraordinary!" Mr. Wellington said, and they all stood admiring the image and gesturing to this and that on the screen. A jay flew by, and everyone marveled to see it glide along, as though it was a miracle that what they were looking at was really and truly a view of the world just outside the hotel's walls at that very moment.

Elizabeth caught Freddy's glance and shared a smile with him. The bruising around his eye had subsided; it was now only a purple-green splotch that looked a fraction as bad as it had three days before when she'd visited him in the infirmary. She gave him a thumbs-up, and he laughed with delight.

The group took in the view on the disk for several minutes, and then Freddy adjusted the box to offer another direction and then another. He zoomed in and out, to show an approaching bus in close-up or to take in the vista of the valleys far to the east. It seemed that no one wanted the demonstration to end, that everyone would have been content to have Freddy continue with his demonstration for hours. But after a good thirty minutes, Norbridge made a few final-sounding comments, the people on the platform began offering congratulations and thank-yous to Freddy, and then only Freddy, Elizabeth, Norbridge, Leona, and Egil P. Fowles remained.

Freddy switched on the lights, and the room was bathed in bright yellow once again.

"Well, that was an enormous success," Leona said. "Bravo to you, young man."

"I concur wholeheartedly," Egil P. Fowles said, adjusting his glasses with both hands. "Stupendous. It's a shame you're unable to attend Havenworth Academy. We'd love to have your questing, practical intelligence as a presence at our school."

"Elizabeth will be there!" Freddy said.

"And we are ecstatic about that," Professor Fowles said, looking to her. "Monday. Classes resume."

Even with everything that had happened over the past several days, Elizabeth's attention had been turning to the excitement of starting at a new school. "I can't wait," she said. Not only was she looking forward to meeting new people and starting at what she felt would be a wonderful school, but she was also ready to step into a new routine. After the unsettling events surrounding the pendant and Gracella and the passageways, Elizabeth was eager for the normality of the classroom.

"We have a new student teacher this semester, as well," Egil Fowles said. "Norbridge, you'll find this of interest. He's at the college over near Bruma, and he'll be doing his training with us. Hyrum Crowley is his name. Damien's grandson."

Elizabeth felt a strange thrill run through her at this name. "The writer?" she said.

"The very one," Egil Fowles said. "Seems like a bright young man."

Leona shook her head lightly. "Well, his grandfather was certainly interesting."

"I've read every one of his books," Norbridge said loudly. "Every one! The man was a weaver of words, a sorcerer of sentences, a professor of paragraphs!"

"You liked his books?" Freddy said.

"Loved them!" Norbridge looked to Elizabeth. "You, too, yes?"

"They're very good," she said. She couldn't say why, but the thought that the great writer's grandson would be at Havenworth Academy made her even more eager to start at the school. "Kind of on the strange side, but good."

"Aren't we all?" Egil P. Fowles said, which made everyone laugh. "But I must depart now." He checked his watch. "My wife will be expecting me shortly. Kudos to you, sir," he said, shaking hands with Freddy. "Elizabeth, we'll see you bright and early on Monday. Norbridge and Leona, *au revoir*, *adiós*, and *Gesundheit*." With a general salute, he walked down the ramp and out the door.

"Good man, poor chess player," Norbridge said, gazing downward.

"Who's going to give the demonstrations once Freddy

leaves?" Elizabeth said, and even as the words left her mouth, she regretted saying them. She turned to Freddy. "Gosh, I don't want to think about you being gone."

"Maybe I'll come at Easter," Freddy said. "Unless, of course, my parents change their minds. Again." For the first time that morning, his smile disappeared.

"I'll drop them a note," Norbridge said. "Perhaps I can encourage them to join us for Easter."

Freddy stood tying the long pulley rope to a railing beside the control box; he looked dejected. "Just as long as I can come back to Winterhouse. If they don't come, it's no big deal."

"I hope they do come," Elizabeth said. "It's nice to have your family around." She gave Norbridge a smile; but even as she did, she found herself thinking of Elana, who was still resting in the infirmary and suffering, it seemed, from a sort of shock. Elizabeth had only glimpsed her from the doorway, once, the day before, and Elana looked as old and undone as a ninety-year-old woman in a nursing home. Elizabeth couldn't help but feel sorry for her—even after learning that she and Selena and the Powters had never left the hotel but had hidden, along with Gracella, in the Thatchers' room before making their assault on Winterhouse three nights before.

"What do you think is going to happen to Elana?" she said.

Norbridge shook his head. "No idea at this point. Her parents and brother are long gone, so I don't know. For now, she'll stay here."

"I feel awful about what's happened to her," Elizabeth said. "I think she was just doing what the people in her family told her to do, but I don't think she liked it. A few times it even seemed like she wanted to warn me about what was happening. She didn't deserve this."

"I'm of the same mind," Leona said. "Just awful, that family. The whole lot of them. Awful."

"I wouldn't mind if Rodney turned old," Freddy said. He'd explained to Elizabeth that it had been Rodney himself who had attacked him, surprising him from behind and then hitting him, stealing the key, and leaving him unconscious in the hallway. "Or at least maybe, like, forty or fifty."

"Be charitable, Mr. Knox," Leona said. "Be charitable."

"What sort of people would 'loan' their own daughter to Selena and Gracella, even if they were all related?" Norbridge said, shaking his head sadly. "Hard to understand. If there's any way to track them down, I'll look into it. I wouldn't be surprised if they decide to cook up some new scheme to get back at us."

He looked to Elizabeth. "I agree with you, too, that Elana's not to blame for any of this. If there's anything I can do to help her somehow, I'll try my best."

"Maybe I can visit her when she's feeling better," Elizabeth said.

Norbridge said nothing, but he nodded slowly—and warmly—to her.

"What happened to Selena?" Elizabeth said.

Norbridge inclined his head to Elizabeth and gazed

downward. "Six feet out of the way in the Havenworth Cemetery. Really and truly. Not that I want you to verify that with any future visits, but still. I witnessed her burial myself."

"And you're sure Gracella is no threat?" Freddy said. "Totally, completely, for sure?"

This was a strange part of the story to Elizabeth, something Norbridge had explained and that, although she accepted it, remained ominous. After everything had been secured in that part of the passageway far below Winterhouse where Elizabeth had found the ice sculpture, and after Elizabeth had left with Norbridge and Elana had been carried back to the hotel and Selena's body had been removed, Gracella remained where she lay. The five men who'd joined Norbridge and Jackson and Sampson, despite every effort, had been unable to lift her body. Even when they brought several others down to assist, Gracella's lifeless form resisted all attempts to budge it. In fact, all of her—not only her body but her clothing as well—was as hard as rock, as though the moment she'd expired she had transformed into stone. Lying on the ground, she seemed more a statue than a person who had once been alive. In consultation with Norbridge, everyone conceded there was nothing to do but leave her in place. And so he'd had a concrete wall built around her—leaving her entombed— and then had both ends of the passageway filled with rocks and secured with mortar. If, on the one chance in a million Gracella somehow was not truly dead, she would be unable to escape from the chamber she'd find herself in should she awaken.

"Let me put it this way," Norbridge said. "We've done everything we can to protect ourselves from her. That's all we can do. Remain vigilant."

Even at the mention of Gracella's name, Elizabeth found herself back deep below Winterhouse and staring into those cold eyes as the sorceress spoke to her. The incident was too immediate, too frightening. She'd been over it several times in conversation with Norbridge, but it was all almost as alarming still as it had been when it happened. The one thing she hadn't mentioned to Norbridge— the one thing she kept turning over in her own mind—was the recurring feeling of temptation she had felt throughout the entire search in the passageways and the moments when Gracella had confronted her.

"But you never answered her question," Leona said, and Elizabeth, although confused by what Leona was saying, was glad to not have to dwell too long on thoughts of Gracella.

Norbridge turned to her with a look of annoyance he was working hard to maintain. "And just what question is that, Miss Springer?"

"Who will provide demonstrations after that sad day when Freddy departs the hotel?"

Norbridge looked surprised. "I hadn't given it any thought."

"Why doesn't Elizabeth do it?" Freddy said.

Elizabeth felt instantly uncertain. "Wait a minute. I don't know about all this stuff. And I'll be in school, too."

"She has a point," Leona said. "And then there is her budding career as my assistant—"

"On the weekends!" Freddy said. "Like just a couple of times every Saturday and Sunday!" He looked to Elizabeth. "What do you think?"

"Maybe you can show her the ropes, so to speak, and she can make up her mind," Norbridge said.

Freddy held his hands up and looked to Elizabeth. "Yeah? What do you think?"

"I guess I could try," she said.

"You'll be running this hotel before long," Leona said with a laugh.

Elizabeth laughed with Leona and thought again of how she'd felt when she'd first heard those words from Kiona. There was something both exhilarating and scary about this prospect, about considering a destiny she wouldn't have even guessed might be hers two weeks earlier.

"I just barely started living here at Winterhouse," she said. "I don't really think I'm going to run things."

Norbridge looked to Leona. "And I'm not going anywhere anytime soon." He paused, turned serious. "But someone will need to run this place someday."

"What was that you once told me about Winterhouse?" Elizabeth said. "About it being more than just a hotel?"

"It is," Norbridge said. "Here at Winterhouse there is

a . . . it's like a . . ." He looked to Leona. "You're better at this than I am. Can you explain?"

"We're one of nine," Leona said flatly.

"What?" Elizabeth wasn't sure she'd heard her correctly.

Leona nodded. "That's right. One of nine. I know this may sound like mumbo jumbo, but there are nine places in the world where the spirit of goodness resides and where it must be protected. Winterhouse is one of these places."

"Are you kidding?" Freddy said. "That sounds—"

"Crazy," Norbridge said. "Flabbergasting, even. Gobstopping, as the French say."

"The British," Leona said. "But he's right. I wouldn't believe it if someone told me."

Elizabeth shook her head and then pressed her hands to her temples. "I don't think I can take it all in right now."

Leona shrugged. "That's the whole story already. And I agree. Let's just enjoy the day."

"Well, now, Leona," Norbridge said, "there's a bit more to the story, but that's good enough for now." He held out a hand to her. "Shall we go? Leave these two here with this contraption?"

Leona nodded gracefully, took Norbridge's hand, and with a dual wave, they headed down the walkway.

"Oh, and Elizabeth," Norbridge said casually, "please meet me in the lobby at four this afternoon."

"Are we going somewhere?" she said.

Norbridge continued walking, and without looking

back he said, "Yes. Your new room is ready, and I want to help you move in."

His last words were muffled as the door closed behind him and Leona. Elizabeth stood shaking her head with pleasure. "I guess I really am staying here."

"Lucky, lucky," Freddy said.

"I agree."

Freddy tugged one of the ropes. "You don't have to learn this if you don't want to."

Elizabeth looked at the disk, then gazed up to the ceiling. "I guess if I'm going to live here, I might as well know as much about everything as possible. Show me where I start."

Freddy scratched his cheek, looked at the control panel, and then squinted at Elizabeth. "You know what would really help us concentrate right now?"

Elizabeth shook her head.

"A swim in the pool and then a bunch of Flurschen." He pointed to the door. "Come on."

It was right as they were closing the door behind them that Elizabeth thought she felt, for a moment, a rumbling from far beneath her. It was just a hint of a tremor, but she was certain she felt something.

Freddy looked at her. "You okay?"

"Did you feel that?" she said. "Like something shook a little?"

"I didn't." He shrugged.

She stood listening, waiting to hear more.

One of the women who cleaned the rooms at Winter-house turned a corner with her cart of supplies and began pushing it down the corridor as the floor rumbled. Freddy looked to it as the woman rounded another corner and disappeared. "That's probably what you felt. Her cart."

She was about to agree when a man, maybe forty years old, approached from the near hallway and said, "Do either of you know, is the library on the first or second floor?"

"You're in luck," Freddy said, "because this is the assistant librarian here." He turned to Elizabeth, and the man smiled pleasantly.

"It's on the second floor," Elizabeth said. "If you take

the elevator down, right when you get off you'll see a sign pointing the way. You can't miss it."

"Wonderful!" the man said. "I've heard it's quite large."

"Yes, it's enormous," Elizabeth said.

"I'm looking for something with stories from King Arthur," the man said. "Do they have much in that area?"

"Absolutely," Elizabeth said. "Second level of the library in section O-16."

The man's eyes went wide. "You really do know that library, don't you?" he said. And with a dip of his head he said, "Thank you," and then departed.

Freddy turned to Elizabeth. He pulled his head back with exaggerated appreciation. "Look at you!" he said. "That was impressive!"

"Hey, what can I say?" Elizabeth said.

"I'm gonna be sorry to leave here tomorrow," Freddy said, "but maybe I'll be back in a few months."

"I hope so, Freddy. That would be the best."

"You'll take care of the camera obscura for me?" he said.

"Absolutely."

Freddy looked in the direction the man had departed. "You really love the library, don't you?"

"I love this whole place," Elizabeth said.

"So do I. And I can't believe everything that happened here again this year. I gotta hand it to you, Elizabeth. You really saved the day. Norbridge and all of them have got to be really happy you're here."

Elizabeth was full of too many emotions to consider

everything Freddy was saying. New Year's Eve had come and gone, the strange events of the necklace and the secret passageways had ended, and now her friend—her best friend—was about to leave the next day and she would be starting at a new school. So much had happened; so much was beginning.

"I'm happy I'm here," she said.

Freddy flashed her a double thumbs-up.

All she wanted to do was go swimming and talk with Freddy and roam the halls of Winterhouse and sit in the huge dining hall for dinner and soak up all the magic of the day ahead. She'd earned it, she wanted it—and she belonged.

"Besides," Elizabeth said, "Winterhouse is my home."

END OF BOOK 2

ACKNOWLEDGMENTS

Thank you to: Rena Rossner for her committed, steady guidance; Christy Ottaviano for her insightful and devoted collaboration; Chloe Bristol for creating illustrations with such charm and beauty; and Jessica Anderson, Lauren Festa, and Brittany Pearlman for their unfailing professionalism. Above all, thank you to Jacob, Olivia, and Natalie for the care and optimism they bring to all their undertakings; and to Rosalind, for the joyfulness she shares with everyone and the untiring support and inspiration she provides me.

BEN GUTERSON is the author of *Winterhouse*, which was an Indie Next List Pick. He was a high school and middle school teacher in New Mexico and Colorado for a decade before working at Microsoft as a program manager. Ben lives near Seattle in the foothills of the Cascade Mountains.

BENGUTERSON.COM